The Poe Puzzler

A Raven's Apprentice Mystery

Neil MacNeill

Neil MacNeill

Also by Neil MacNeill
Exit Row
A Stillness in the Pines

First Edition
© 2025 Neil MacNeill

Published by
Munn Avenue Press
300 Main Street, Ste 21
Madison, NJ 07940
MunnAvenuePress.com

This is a work of fiction. Names, characters, businesses, places, events, locales and incidents are either the product of the author's imagination or used in a fictitious manner. Any resemblance to actual persons, living or dead, or actual events is purely coincidental.

Library of Congress Control Number: 2025914956
Hardcover ISBN: 978-1-960299-89-5
Paperback ISBN: 978-1-960299-88-8

Printed in the United States of America
Cover Design: CarKnack LLC

Neil MacNeill

To Marcy, who reintroduced Ocean City to me

Neil MacNeill

Somers
Point
Great Egg
Harbor Bay
North
End
9
Marmora
Ocean City, NJ
Corson's Inlet

Neil MacNeill

"The greatest mystery of all is not how we live,
but how we die."
– Nathaniel Hawthorne, *The Minister's Black Veil*

"There is a mystery in all things,
and the mystery is greater than the thing itself."
– Herman Melville, *Bartleby, the Scrivener*

"What would C. Auguste Dupin do?"
– Nathaniel Melville Poe

Neil MacNeill

Chapter One
Don't Call Me Nathaniel

Call me Nathan. Not Nate, and definitely not Nathaniel. What were my parents thinking? At least they didn't name me Edgar. That's what happens, I guess, when you have a famous last name and your folks are obsessed with classic American literature.

When I was around 12, I tried to go by Melville—my middle name—but too many kids called me Melly. You wouldn't know it to look at me now, but I was a pretty chubby kid. So "Melly" plus chubby ... well, it didn't take me long to realize I was better off where I'd started. Still, you can imagine the childhood taunts: "Hey, Poe, where's your raven?" and "Yo, Poe, how's that telltale heart of yours?" In high school, it got uglier: "Hey, Poe, how's that cocaine habit of yours?" and "So, Poe, you gonna marry your 13-year-old cousin?"

These many decades later, I've come to accept my given name. More than that, I've made the most of it. Some would say I've capitalized on it with "Small Mysteries," my private investigations agency. Of course, I'm not really a P.I., and it's not really an agency. But

I'm getting off track, aren't I?

Let me begin again, for the record. You're talking to Nathaniel Poe, year-round resident of Ocean City, New Jersey. But please, call me Nathan.

I feel pretty awkward talking to a reporter while I'm in this hospital bed, my right leg suspended sky-high in this sling and my flimsy gown showing more of me than I want to reveal. Okay, let me get past that. I'm sure you want to hear the whole "human interest" story of what happened to me yesterday evening, and how I ended up buried up to my neck in the sand as the incoming tide brought the Atlantic Ocean closer.

It all started about two weeks ago when I found a folded sheet of paper stuffed into my mailbox.

My house is on the North End of Ocean City. The "quiet end" is what I like to call it. Even in the summer, the North End is far enough removed from all the beachgoers and tourists for me to keep my sanity ... and my privacy. You know the stats, right? Ocean City's population grows tenfold in the summer.

I'm lucky I can afford a place at the Jersey Shore. It's certainly not from my teacher's pension. Most of the down payment came from my wife's life insurance. She would have loved it here ... but fate had other plans.

I live alone now, and I like it that way. Don't get the wrong idea. I do have a few close friends and two nosy neighbors to keep me company. But once the summer months roll by, almost everyone leaves, and Ocean City is a different place. Some neighborhoods look like ghost towns, and the weather can get pretty nasty, but the solitude and dramatic storms suit me fine.

It was a late October day like any other when the first message appeared—the puzzle question, the game. I was standing on my front porch, going through the mail, and in among the flyers and credit-card offers, I found a folded sheet of paper. All it said on the front was, "To Mr. Poe"—no stamp or postmark. Whoever stuffed it into my mailbox presumably did it after the mail was delivered. I know Dave, the mailman, pretty well, and he would have told me if anyone had the nerve to use my mailbox for anything other than official U.S. mail! At first I figured it was a neighborhood action group trying to get like-minded citizens to oppose something the city council was doing. You know, the usual "people need to take action" message.

You can imagine my surprise when I unfolded it and read the typed message. "Answer this if you can: Where did Edgar Allan Poe die? Reply to P.O. Box 667, Ocean City, NJ."

Asking me, a retired English teacher and possible distant relative, if I knew where Edgar Allan Poe had died—really? I wasn't sure if I should laugh or be insulted. Every kid learned that detail about Poe in high school. I certainly taught more than a few lessons about Poe's life and his mysterious death.

I almost tossed out the note with all the junk mail, but a little voice in the back of my head told me not to. Someone was having fun with me—or so I thought at the time—and even though it was the most obvious of Poe questions, I decided to play along. What could be the harm?

I scribbled the answer on the same sheet of paper—"Baltimore"—stuffed it in an envelope, addressed it to the P.O. box and placed a stamp on it. Since I'd planned to drive downtown later that day, I figured I'd stick it in a postbox and see what happened next.

Then I got on with my life. But over the next couple of days, I did go through my mail more carefully to see if there were any other puzzles.

It was later that week when I noticed something stuck under the welcome mat by my front door. I figured it was a leaf, or some flotsam blown by the autumn wind, until I realized it was another note, this one on brown paper. "The puzzler strikes again!" I thought. It actually thrilled me—something to ease the boredom of fall in South Jersey.

Again, it was addressed to Mr. Poe, but this time, the question was more esoteric—something most people wouldn't know. Written inside, it said, "Why did Poe hate Griswold?"

"Aha!" I said to myself. "Now things are getting more interesting." Rufus Griswold was Poe's nemesis. They had a nasty feud that lasted many years and certainly damaged both their reputations. Without diving into one of my many reference books on Poe, I couldn't recall exactly who started the feud—either Poe published some damning critique of one of Griswold's works, or vice versa—but I did recall there was at least one lawsuit. And, of course, Griswold got the last laugh by writing Poe's biography after poor Edgar's untimely death, demonizing Poe as an indolent drug addict.

As I stood on my porch, mulling over this latest puzzle, something was bugging me, something about the dark theme of these first two questions ... beyond the connection to Poe, that is. But it didn't rise to the surface of my consciousness. At least not then.

Lost in thought, I didn't hear Mrs. Gyulalyi come up behind me. "What you have there?" she asked.

Mrs. G is amazingly stealthy for a large Hungarian woman. For all the heft she carries around, she always seems to appear out of nowhere, sneaking up on cat paws to look over my shoulder. It's unnerving how this 70-year-old woman can find the least opportune moments to nose into my affairs. I shouldn't complain. She is a good neighbor. Just nosy.

"It's a sort of puzzle someone is sending me. This is the second one. Some anonymous person is testing my knowledge of Edgar Allan Poe with these questions—kind of ridiculous, considering my background, not to mention my lineage."

Mrs. G frowned and said nothing for an awkward moment, then demanded, "You give it to me," and reached out her hand.

She has all sorts of strange Hungarian customs, and I had no idea what she was going to do. But it was Mrs. G, and I was pretty sure she wouldn't damage the note.

When I handed it to her, instead of grabbing it, she put a palm on either side of the folded paper, pressed her hands together and brought them up to her face, as if in prayer. She closed her eyes and took a deep breath.

"Rossz ember!"

She was always mumbling something in her native tongue. While I didn't understand all the phrases, I could usually sort out what she meant. And this didn't sound good.

"This is bad man," she told me. "Bad man!" She lowered her hands, returning the note to me. And then she did something I'd never seen her do before—she wiped her hands together and then flicked out her wrists, as if she were trying to cast out something odious. This strange Hungarian juju was beyond me, but her gesture was obvious. She wanted nothing to do with the note.

She stared at me, a blank look on her face as if nothing at all unusual had just happened. "Storm's coming," she said. With that, she turned and walked back to her house.

At first I thought her comment held some deeper meaning, some intimations about my mystery note. But then I felt the ocean breeze picking up and saw dark clouds churning above the rooftops across the way. So, it was just the weather. Still, Mrs. G's strange reaction to the note and the fast-approaching storm delivered a none-too-subtle psychic punch.

"Ah, bunk." I refused to go down that path. Time to adjourn to my ersatz agency to better inspect the note and consider the possibilities.

Chapter Two
Small Mysteries

The illustrious world headquarters for "Small Mysteries" is a guest bedroom at the back of my bungalow.

All said, I couldn't have asked for a better setup. You know how these old shore houses are—rambling layouts with uneven floors and some peculiar add-ons over the years. Since my house backs onto an alley, "Small Mysteries" has its own entrance, five steps up, that sets it apart from the rest of the house. It also gives my clients some privacy by not coming in the front door. I'm absolutely sure, however, that Mrs. G is aware of all the comings and goings. Nothing gets by her.

Besides the typical aluminum storm door, my office door is pretty unusual for a shore house. It's old and solid wood, unlike the usual Home Depot or Lowe's doors. It has three narrow, arched windows at the top and raised panels at the bottom in the shape of an X. I love the look of it. It might be made of cherry or oak or some other hardwood, but it's been painted so many times in a dark brown color that it's hard to say. It fits the office and it fits me.

I'd describe the overall atmosphere of my office as "cozy." Its two small windows are fitted with heavy burgundy drapes, and I've got a couple of high-backed Victorian chairs for visitors. A few years ago, I found an old oak desk and a library chair at a thrift shop in Somers Point. The desk weighs a ton—my friend, Berni, and a couple of her weight-lifting buddies muscled it into the room. When I'm gone from this earth, it will more than likely remain in the house.

Of course, I have bookcases. They're filled with novels and literary reference books and histories of all sorts. To give the place some atmosphere, I've decorated it with Poe memorabilia: a framed letter from Poe to "Muddy," his mother-in-law (I paid way too much for that at a Philadelphia auction), a movie poster from Vincent Price's "The Pit and the Pendulum," and a large, 19th century map of Richmond, Virginia, Poe's sometimes home. Near the ceiling, on my highest bookcase, sits a bronze sculpture of a raven. I keep reminding myself to paint it black one day. I thought about trying to find a "pallid bust of Pallas," but I doubt anyone would get the reference.

This inner sanctum of mine is also the warmest room in the house, so it's a favorite haunt for Lenore, my cat and constant companion. No, she's not a black cat. That would be too much of a cliché. Her fur is mostly white except for a little brown and black "beret" on her head. It makes her more interesting than if she were all white … no offense to all-white cats everywhere!

Lenore is a wonderful lap cat, soft and fluffy, but she also has multiple personalities. She goes a little wild at night, playing with her cat toys and running around the house like a manic kitten. Until I got Lenore, I'd always thought white cats were pretty ordinary. Not her. She's friendly to most people, sometimes too much so. When she senses someone is not a "cat person," she'll rub up against them even more. I honestly think Lenore can be a bit spiteful.

Anyhow, I was at my desk that October afternoon, Lenore on my lap, and the "mystery note" laid out on my blotter. I did my best to channel my inner C. Auguste Dupin, Poe's famous fictional detective. Three central questions came to mind: How, why, and who?

The "how" of it was kind of creepy when I thought about it. Someone had walked up on my porch, opened the mailbox by my front door and stuffed the note inside. For the second note, they'd come right up to my door again, this time sliding the note under my welcome mat. It takes a bit of nerve to invade someone else's privacy, even in that small way. And I was shocked that Mrs. G hadn't seen them do it. I needed to question her about that.

Now *why* would someone do this? It could be a practical joke. If so, the puzzler had to be someone who knew me—that also goes to the "who" part—and they'd decided to have some fun with this Poe guessing game. But was it fun? At least it was so far. And what if it wasn't a joke? This needed more ratiocination, as Dupin would say.

The daylight was fading, or maybe it was just the storm that darkened the room. I turned on my desk lamp. I can't solve a mystery in the dark.

So, back to *who* would do this. I was sure it wasn't Mrs. G or my friend Berni. That would be completely out of character for both of them. The sender could be one of my former clients, but that also didn't seem to fit. Most of them are older women who've misplaced some keepsake or heard a strange noise that can't be explained. So, it had to be someone else, maybe someone from my past who was trying to reconnect. If so, it was an odd way of doing it.

There are so many people in my past. I've taught thousands of students and interacted with dozens of co-workers during my teaching career. But not one of them came to mind as the kind of person who would play this game.

Lost in all this cogitation, I hadn't even noticed the plinking of rain on the windows or the gusts of wind rattling the panes. I was in my zone, where ambient sound didn't enter. So I was more than a little startled when someone banged open the storm door and drummed on the door from the alley.

Lenore leapt from my lap in a panic—she's such a scaredy cat sometimes—and I sprang to my feet to see who was there.

Chapter Three
A Nice Cup of Tea

"Berni! You look a fright." Even in the cool autumn weather, Berni is always out on a bike, either one from her extensive collection or a bike she was fixing up for a client.

That afternoon, she was standing on my back steps, wet to the skin through her spandex outfit.

"That storm came on kind of fast," she said, shaking her head to one side like she'd just been for a swim. "I thought I could out-race it, but then I saw your lights on and decided to take a break." Lenore, tail high, scampered up to say hello and rub against Berni's legs. Once she realized her fur was getting wet, however, she let out a mmrip and scooted away. "You really should fix that storm door," Berni said. "It felt like it was locked and then it sprang open."

"Oh, it's on my to-do list," I said.

She rubbed her hands over her bare arms, and I realized what a poor host I was being. "Come in, come in. Let me get you a towel."

Berni brought in the salt air. Even with the rain

teeming down, the ocean made its presence known. The scent of wet sand and beached seaweed is always on the breeze at the shore; you just notice it more sometimes. I grabbed a bath towel from the hall closet and tossed it to her. She caught it like a pro, of course, and began wiping herself down.

The rain-soaked Lycra outfit left very little mystery to Berni's physique. She's fit, very fit. Not that I don't admire her shape, but she and I are just friends, nothing more. And as she often reminds me when I look at her wistfully, she's not wired that way. Not to mention she's 20 years my junior.

"Take off your helmet and those awkward bike shoes, and let me make you a nice cup of tea."

She pulled off her shoes, unclipped her helmet, and rubbed the towel over her head. Her short blonde hair, flattened by the helmet and the rain, now stood up in spikes—kind of cute on her. "Anything hot would be great," she said.

"I found this little shop in P'ville that carries Golden Darjeeling. It's the perfect tea for a rainy afternoon."

"You know me. One tea's like another, as long as it's not that frou-frou herbal stuff."

She followed me down the hall to my tiny kitchen and sat on a stool by the counter. "So what's doing, Nathan? You deep into one of your 'small mysteries'?"

"If you really want to know, yes. And my client is myself."

She gave me a quizzical look, so I showed her the note and told her all about the Poe Puzzler. She was silent for a moment. The old cast-iron radiators clicked and clanked, working to keep the chill away. I let her mull things over. When I'm too invested in all the details, Berni can often cut to the chase.

Finally, she held out a hand and said, "So, where's the first note?"

"Um, I mailed the first one back."

She rolled her eyes. "And you call yourself a P.I.?"

That kind of stung, but she was right. I should have at least copied it. So much for holding onto evidence. But at that point, I still felt like the whole thing was some kind of game.

"Okay, so this is all you have to go on." She took a closer look at the brown-paper note. "How are you going to reply?"

It was rare that Berni asked me about literature or the lives of famous writers, so I dove in. "Poe and Griswold were writers and also critics, so you can imagine how they reacted when one of them wrote a negative review of the other's work. I think they first met in 1841, and ..."

"Stop!" Berni raised both hands, palms out. "I don't want an English lesson, you lit nerd. Just tell me how you're going to get back to this puzzler of yours."

I'm sure my face turned red. And I should have known better. I tried to bring the conversation back. "That? Oh, I'll reply to the same P.O. Box he—I assume it's a 'he'—wrote on the first note. Box 667."

Berni's eyes twinkled, and I could tell she was about to yank my chain. "At least it's not Box 666."

I groaned. "No. I doubt this is about some kind of Devil worship."

She got up from her stool and stretched, but kept her eyes averted. "You never know, Nathan, my friend. Beware."

I couldn't tell if she was serious or not. Probably not, knowing Berni. Still ...

"I should get back before dark," she said. "The storm sounds like it's passed."

As we walked down the hall to the back door, I rummaged through the closet for an old dish towel. "Here, wipe down your seat. It can't be comfortable riding a wet bike."

"Done it before," she said. "Will certainly do it again. But thanks."

When I opened the back door, a fresh breeze greeted us. As quickly as the rain had come, the sky was mostly clear now, with just a few fast-moving clouds. The only evidence of the storm was a few small puddles in the alley. The setting sun cast long shadows, making even mundane items like fence posts and trash cans look distorted, almost sinister.

There were plenty of portents being thrown at me, but I had yet to really notice them.

Chapter Four
Fresh Chop Suey

The third note appeared the next day.

My Saturday morning routine is to drive downtown and park my old Saab on Asbury, as close to Ward's Pastry as I can get. If I arrive before they're sold out, I'll buy a "chop suey" pastry and a small coffee, then find a nearby bench where I can sit in the sun and savor my treats.

I'm sure you've been to Ward's, right? It's a gastronomical landmark downtown, with the best cookies, pastries, and donuts. Chop suey is my favorite. Imagine a kind of hot cross bun but lighter and sweeter. Blended into the batter are little chunks of candied fruit like you might find in a you-know-what. No, do not go there! Any association with Christmas fruitcakes is right off. A chop suey is soft and sweet with little taste delights of fruit and nuts in every bite. And it's covered in creamy white icing. Some people like to put butter on them, but that's gilding the lily in my eyes.

After soaking up some vitamin D and sugar that morning, I dropped my answer to the Griswold question in a mailbox near City Hall. And this time, I did remember to send a photocopy, not the original.

As I drove home, I felt the promise of a new day. What a change from last night's storm! The sky was mostly clear and azure blue, with high, feathery clouds heralding fine weather ahead. I considered lowering the top on my convertible, but the air had just enough autumn chill to make me reconsider.

Once I got home, I parked at the curb—no shortage of spots in October. That's when I noticed something red in the boxwood shrubs by my front steps. My Poe Puzzler made it obvious—it stood out like a rip-tide warning flag on the beach.

I reached into the boxwood and plucked it out. Instead of a folded piece of paper, this time it was an envelope. Where can you even get a red envelope, except at Christmas? I was about to tear it open right there, but an inner voice told me to be more cautious. And wouldn't you know it? That's when Mrs. G appeared by my side.

She likes to go out for breakfast with her lady friends on Saturdays, so I shouldn't have been surprised. Still, she crept up on me like a ninja, giving me a start.

Once I'd gathered my wits, I tried to explain what was going on. "Another puzzle. This time in a red envelope. What do you think?"

"Hmph."

I waited for more, then remembered what I wanted to ask. "Did you see anyone hide this envelope in the shrub this morning? Did you notice any strangers lurking around the neighborhood?"

"Nem." I knew enough of her native tongue to understand that word. It's funny how upset she got with me when I told her it reminded me of the Russian "nyet." That'll teach me not to mix up ethnicities with anyone from "the old country."

I'm sure she saw the expectant look on my face, so she added, "Bad sign," her jaw tight, her eyebrows lowered. She crossed herself and mumbled under her breath. Maybe it was a prayer or some old-world spell to ward off evil—she intertwines religion and folklore with ease.

Our conversation, such as it was, came to a halt when a white Lexus SUV pulled up and her friend honked the horn. In an instant, she spun around and got into the car. As they drove away, I heard the cackling of old lady laughter. I guess my "bad sign" didn't bother her all that much.

With Mrs. G's blessing or protective spell on my side, it was time to get to work on this new puzzle. As I climbed the steps and unlocked my front door, I carried the red envelope by a single corner, pinched between thumb and forefinger. I'm not sure if I was thinking about fingerprints or something equally absurd, but I definitely wanted to treat this third missive better than I had the other two. I vowed to take my time, and be as meticulous and thorough as a self-described P.I. should.

Sunlight streamed through my office windows, brightening my mood. Maybe my Puzzler was going to come clean with this third note, and let me in on the joke.

No such luck.

I stared at the envelope, placed squarely in the center of my desk. It had the familiar address typed on the front:

"To Mr. Poe." Other than its blood-red color, it seemed innocuous enough.

Rather than rip it open, I retrieved my antique letter opener from the top drawer. My wife had bought it for me in a small shop in Verona when we were there many years ago. Some Poe scholars believe the fictional setting for "The Masque of the Red Death" was Verona, but others disagree. Still, it was a good excuse to visit the town and explore the old castle.

My memento from Italy was sharp enough to slice open the envelope with little effort. Inside, matching red stationery held a single sentence: "Find your next Poe question at 7 p.m. tonight where Waverly and Seaspray meet."

What a letdown. Not only was my mystery man's identity still a secret, but there wasn't even a Poe question in the envelope.

Waverly Boulevard and East Seaspray Road come to a point near a popular surfing beach, not too far from my home. It was almost within walking distance, but not in my condition. As much as I'd tried to follow through with aqua therapy and daily exercises after the accident, I couldn't walk too far without pain shooting up and down my right leg.

My head was spinning as I tried to get a handle on the whole situation. Just what was my Puzzler up to? Did he have some sinister motive for asking me to go to a secluded intersection after sundown? He hadn't even waited for my answer to his second question, the one about Griswold and Poe. The logic of all this escaped me.

Lenore jumped into my lap, kneaded my thighs for a

moment, then circled around and fell fast asleep, her soft purrs a soothing lullaby. Even with her gentle coaxing, though, I couldn't get comfortable.

Enough with all these mental exercises! In Poe's stories, Detective Dupin is a man of action as well as intellect. He didn't solve mysteries by sitting at his desk. Time to follow his lead and get off my rump to do some proper investigating.

I eased Lenore from my lap and transferred her to the seat cushion. She issued a small complaint, but then went right back to sleep. If only I could relax as easily.

It didn't take long to drive to the designated spot. The neighborhood at Waverly and Seaspray is very high-end, with newer, multi-story homes, many with privacy walls to keep out prying eyes. The houses there wouldn't look out of place in the Hamptons! Even the grass along the sidewalk was perfect—the uniform green sod looked like it had been trimmed with a laser. Parking my old Saab on the street probably lowered the property values. This time of year, however, most of the residents had gone to warmer climes.

I eased to the curb on Seaspray, about a half block from the intersection, trying to take in the big picture. It looked ordinary enough on this autumn morning. The two streets met at a ninety-degree angle where a wide sandy path was cut into the dunes to access the beach. A split-rail fence on either side delineated the path and helped protect the vegetation from foot traffic. If my mystery man wanted to spy my movements this evening from the mounds of sand and scrub grass, it would be easy enough to hide there. That's if he showed up at all. I got out of my car to take a closer look.

As I started up the path, I noticed one of those free libraries on the left side—you know, the little glass-fronted kiosks with a "take one, leave one" sign. I glanced inside, but there was nothing unusual about it, just a few dated best-sellers and some self-help books. It was an odd spot for a free library, though, since this beach was only for surfers, not sunbathers who would be more likely to grab something to read on the beach.

The bushes grew larger on the other side of the path, but just beyond the fence and almost hidden in the greenery, I glimpsed a homemade memorial with an array of seashells surrounding a small wooden cross. When I spotted the name on the cross, I had to steady myself against a fence post.

The past came rushing at me. I'm sure there are plenty of women named Anna in Ocean City, women who have died. But seeing my wife's name on that memorial left me reeling.

I haven't told you about the accident, have I? It will be 5 years come December. Anna had just received a year-end bonus, and we'd gone out to a fancy restaurant to celebrate. We drove in her Miata. As we ate, the weather turned nasty, with sleet blowing on the wind. I was going to take the wheel on the way home, but Anna insisted I'd had too much wine. I think about that decision a lot ...

A drunk in a pickup truck ran a red light on the White

Horse Pike. He hit the car on my side. The impact sent the Miata spinning on the icy road. It smashed into a pole on Anna's side. They told me her death was almost instantaneous. Maybe they said that ... maybe that was just to make me feel better. I'm just fortunate I blacked out before I had to watch her die.

Hunched over on that sandy pathway, my breath ragged and my vision blurred, I knew I needed help. Someone to talk to. I staggered back to my car and eased my way to Berni's shop.

Chapter Five
Berni, I Need You!

Berni's Bike Shop is on the south side of the island. She doesn't sell new bikes, but does a pretty good business in used bikes and repairs, especially in summer. In the off-season, she finds discarded bikes and fixes them up for resale.

You wouldn't know it to look inside, but her shop is pretty well organized. At least that's what Berni tells me. It's crammed full of tires and wheels hanging from the ceiling, bike frames lined up in a kaleidoscope of colors, and shelves on every available wall with bins for small parts and hardware. The smell of rubber and 3-in-1 oil brought back childhood memories of racing slot cars in my parent's basement.

When I arrived at the open garage door, electronic dance music was booming from oversized speakers. Wearing an old gray coverall and a bandana on her head, Berni was poised to attack a rusted bike frame with an electric grinder. Her safety goggles made her seem so professional, so intent.

"Berni!" I yelled to be heard over the music. At first,

she didn't hear me. I tried again, louder. "Berni, I need you!" That got her attention.

She set down the grinder, pulled off her goggles, and killed the music. Wiping her hands on an oily rag, she eased around all the detritus on the floor to join me. "Nice to know I'm needed." She smiled, but when she took a good look at me, her expression changed. "You look like you just lost your best friend."

"I did," I replied. "Almost five years ago."

Berni's a good listener. I can always turn to her when my emotions ... my nightmares ... get the better of me.

Once she realized the state I was in, she grabbed my arm and led me up the stairs to her apartment. "I don't have any special tea or anything like that," she said as we climbed to the second floor, "but I can offer you an energy drink and a granola bar."

"Water will be fine."

Her apartment is a one-bedroom unit with a modern, efficient layout. I took a chair at the kitchenette table and tried to calm my mind and my breathing, knowing I needed to lay everything out for Berni in a clear and rational manner.

But once we were both settled, she dove right into the hardest part. "So, I know this is something to do with Anna. What was the trigger this time?"

As blunt as her question was, I wasn't offended. Her expression was so open, her demeanor so calm. I felt I could tell her almost anything, and she'd accept it at face value, without judgment.

"Where to start?" Fragments of the day rewound like a movie in my mind: The memorial to Anna, the free library, the sandy path at the intersection of two roads, the note on my desk, talking with Mrs. G, the red envelope in the boxwood ... the note!

"I need to talk about the third note first."

"Third? Didn't you just reply to the second?"

"That's the thing. The puzzler isn't waiting for my responses."

Berni pushed back her chair and stood up, pacing back and forth in the tiny room. "Alright, let's put a pin in that for now. Give me a blow-by-blow—everything that happened this morning from the moment you got up."

She let me talk without interrupting. When I paused, Berni let the silence drag on until I became uncomfortable. That forced me to keep talking. Of course, the last part was toughest. I couldn't explain everything I went through when I saw that homemade memorial ... to Anna ... but Berni understood. This wasn't the first time she'd helped me confront my inner demons.

"So ..." She sat back down. "So, this is not heading in a very good direction, Nathan, my friend." She reached across the table and laid her hands on mine. "I have to say it ... your Poe Puzzler is setting you up for a confrontation."

Maybe I'm naïve or I have too rosy a view of my fellow man, but I still couldn't imagine anyone having that big a grudge against me. "Who would do this? Who have I pissed off so much that they'd go to all this trouble to confront me in this odd way?"

"Pretty hard to see anything positive about this puzzler now," she said.

"Well, what do we do? If it's as bad as you say, should I contact the police?"

She stared out the window, as if looking for inspiration in the clouds. "I wouldn't do anything official yet. You really don't have much to go on." A sly smile appeared on her face. "Getting in touch with Patrolman Bob, on the other hand, might be the way to go."

"I really don't think he likes that sobriquet," I said.

"There you go again using those twenty-five-cent words!" She got up and rolled her neck, then crossed her arms to grab both shoulders, doing some sort of isometric stretch to get the kinks out. "But Bob? Heck, everybody calls him Patrolman Bob. There are a lot worse things you could call a cop. Besides, he's one of the good guys. And he understands the law isn't all black and white—there's plenty of gray area in between."

I nodded, trying to figure out how to explain all this to Bob without sounding like one of Small Mysteries' paranoid clients. "Okay. I'm pretty sure he gets off work at 5:30, and the note said to go to Waverly and Seaspray at 7:00."

That's when the idea struck me. I raised a pointed finger to the ceiling for emphasis. "Let's get a jump on this guy by showing up early."

"Now you're thinking like a P.I.!" Berni beamed at me.

And so we laid our plans.

Chapter Six
The Interpretation of Dreams

I sent a brief text to Bob—I wasn't sure if he could take a personal call while on duty—and drove back home feeling energized. I still had a hole in my life, I couldn't get past that, but plotting our next move with my mysterious Puzzler gave me something to look forward to. And I was pretty confident Bob would play along.

No sooner had I walked through my front door than Mrs. G crept up behind me like a silent shadow. She didn't bother with any niceties before confronting me.

"You have bad dreams." She held a well-worn book against her ample bosom.

"Um, I don't remember most of my dreams."

"You say! Bad signs. Bad man chasing you."

She brought the book up to eye level so I could see the cover.

"Zoltan Dream Book. Now we see what all this means."

I tried to suppress a laugh. This was a new one, even for Mrs. G. I might as well consult a fortune-telling machine at an amusement park.

"You laugh at me!?" I could see the steam rising in her—never a good thing.

Lenore was usually eager to rub against Mrs. G's legs and get a quick pet behind the ears. But this time, she stuck her head around the corner from the hallway and hesitated.

"No, no, Mrs. G. It's just the idea that this dream book will tell me anything useful about my Poe Puzzler ... well, it's kind of ludicrous."

She stomped a foot on the floor. That sent Lenore high-tailing for safety. Mrs. G raised the book in one hand like a preacher at a revival and gave me a hard stare. "Zoltan knows! Zoltan book tells you warnings. Zoltan book save you from much trouble."

I was cornered. I had to play along, just to keep the peace. "Okay, tell me, then. Tell me what Zoltan's book says."

She sat at my kitchen table without hesitation, so I figured I'd better join her. She mumbled in Hungarian as she flipped through the pages. Pausing at a particular passage, she looked up at me again. "You dream of bears chasing you?"

I forced myself to keep a straight face. "No, no bears."

"Maybe wolves instead?"

"Really, Mrs. G, no wild animals chasing me."

"Hmph." More page-turning. "You dream you hide from angry father under table?" Now that was more interesting. Questionable grammar aside, it was almost Freudian. "I don't know. Maybe. Really, I just don't remember my dreams."

She closed the book and grabbed my arm. "You dream of Anna?"

I stared at her, not responding, trying to tamp down my emotions—again. It was one thing for Berni to ask me about the accident, about Anna, but no one else had that right. Not even Mrs. G.

She didn't wait for an answer. "You think on this. We talk later." With that, she spun on her heels and left.

I let out a breath, glad I hadn't lashed out at her. Knowing Mrs. G, however, she wouldn't let sleeping dogs ... or bears or wolves, for that matter ... lie.

Chapter Seven
The Great Trash Bin Mystery

When you reach a certain age, a mid-afternoon nap is a well-earned indulgence. In the summer, I stretch out on a loveseat on the front porch. Once the weather turns, the old green chair in the living room serves just as well. Its upholstery is a bit tattered—some from age and use, some from Lenore using it as a scratching post—but it's incredibly conducive to napping.

Lenore always joins me. She can be just about anywhere in the house, but if she hears me settle into that green chair—maybe I do groan just a bit as I sit down—she comes running and jumps onto my lap. The two of us are in dreamland before you can say "Roderick Usher."

On that Saturday afternoon, deep in R.E.M. sleep, the trilling of my cell phone jarred me awake. I might have dreamt about a bear; I can't remember. Trying not to disturb my slumbering kitty, I reached into my pants pocket to grab the phone and uttered an incoherent hello.

"Is that you, Nathan? You sound different. Are you

okay?"

It was Mrs. Murphy, an all-too-frequent client of Small Mysteries. She could be difficult to deal with—everything was a crisis to her—but she paid me well, and often plied me with Irish soda bread. All in all, it was a pretty good trade-off.

"Oh, Mrs. Murphy. Yes, it's me. I'm fine. You just..."

She launched into a tirade before I could continue.

"Well, it's happened again. I know you must think I'm crazy, but I swear to Saint Brigid it's true. Who would do such a thing to me? I mean, we all try to do our part for the environment, and for Ocean City for that matter, to limit our household waste. I'm sure you do, too. And, of course, I recycle, but this has nothing to do with that. No, heaven help me, it's the trash again, Nathan. Someone is putting their trash in my bins. I won't stand for it. I just won't."

About a month earlier, Mrs. Murphy had tried to convince me that someone had switched her trash bins for older ones that were almost identical but much more scratched and beat up. Although I was quite certain this hadn't happened, I did my level best to investigate, and of course, I found no evidence of this dastardly deed. She wasn't mollified. Still, I got a delicious Bakewell tart out of that job.

Once my brain cleared and I could get in a word edgewise, I tried to reassure her. "I understand how you feel, Mrs. Murphy."

"Well, I certainly hope you do, Nathan. We've been neighbors for more than a few years now, and I've relied on you to take care of any number of vexing problems for me, so I most certainly hope you do understand." She took a breath, which usually meant she was winding up to deliver her request. "Now, Nathan, I know it's Saturday afternoon ... not that you keep banker's hours or anything ... but could you please come over so I can show you this disgraceful behavior by some ... some miscreant in our neighborhood?"

Sticking garbage in someone else's trash cans wouldn't qualify a person as a miscreant in my book, but as I've said, Mrs. Murphy was a repeat client of Small Mysteries, and other than waiting for "Patrolman Bob" to get off work, I didn't have much on my plate ... although I did look forward to another Irish treat once I'd investigated her new mystery.

I stifled a yawn, covering the phone so she wouldn't be insulted by such rudeness. "Okay, I'll be over in about 15 minutes."

"That sounds wonderful, Nathan! I'll put the kettle on."

Resigned to cutting my nap short, I tapped Lenore twice on her back—our signal that it was time to get up. She jumped down, flopped over on her side, stretching out her paws until I could see between her toes, and gave me a mournful look. "I know, Lenoreo." Yes, I do have some unusual nicknames for her. "Duty calls."

I padded to the bathroom to splash water on my face and find a more presentable shirt. Time to don my professional persona and think like C. Auguste Dupin!

It's not unusual for seasonal renters to put their trash in the wrong bins, especially people in multi-unit dwellings. While Ocean City has pretty strict rules about labeling trash bins and lids, and exactly where to place everything on collection day, I could understand how out-of-towners might get confused.

But Mrs. Murphy lives in an old single-family home, just down the block from me, and there were darned few renters in town in October. What's more, garbage collection only occurred once a week this time of year, on Mondays. So, on a Saturday afternoon, almost all garbage bins would be pretty full ... even Mrs. Murphy's. All that made her complaint seem odd. Of course, almost all of Small Mysteries' jobs were pretty odd.

Before I walked over to her house, I grabbed my P.I. kit from the trunk of my Saab. When I arrived, she was waiting at the front door, one hand on her hip, no doubt checking her watch to see if I had kept to my "15-minute" promise.

Only about 5-foot-4, she had the straightest posture I've ever seen in an older woman. Her plain, high-waisted dress—green, of course—looked like it had just been ironed, and her dark auburn hair was tied back in a tight bun. She reminded me of some teachers I'd known over the years. They ran their classes with military precision – every desk and chair geometrically aligned, cabinet drawers clearly labeled, and books arranged in alphabetical order on every shelf.

She led me to the back alley where her trash bins were neatly lined up against the garage door. With a flourish like an Atlantic City magician, she whisked off the lid to one of her two bins. Sure enough, it was filled to the brim with white plastic trash bags. I know she expected some reaction from me—probably outrage—but I just didn't get it. And my silence set her off.

"These are not my bags," she insisted in shrill tones. "I use gray recyclable plastic bags. Not only that, but I do not generate this amount of garbage." She pulled the lid off her second bin. It, too, was full to overflowing. The more I thought about it, her biggest concern was that she'd get a reputation for being wasteful.

With a sigh, I realized there was no getting around it—it was time to dive into her garbage. Such is the glamorous life of a small-time **P.I.**

"Why don't you go back inside, Mrs. Murphy, and let me take a closer look at this?" I needed time to think without her second-guessing my every move.

"Very well, Nathan. You do your job. I'll go check on the tea." A smile appeared on her face, the first one I'd seen since arriving. "And I'll have some homemade scones with Irish butter waiting for you when you're done."

Now, there's an incentive!

The compact **P.I.** kit I keep in the trunk of my Saab has everything I need for most investigations. It's got a Gerber multi-tool with a 3-inch knife blade, a tactical flashlight, a small but powerful pair of binoculars, an eyeglass-repair kit, tweezers, a kitchen spatula, disposable masks and gloves, several sandwich-size plastic bags, wooden chopsticks, and yes, a large, traditional magnifying glass. It all fits into a segmented canvas messenger bag that I'd bought at the Library of Congress gift shop.

None of that did me any good.

I donned the mask and gloves, and pulled one of the offending white plastic garbage bags out of Mrs. Murphy's bin. Then I looked around to find a spot for my forensic research, a place where I could comfortably sit other than on the concrete slab of her driveway. I recalled that when we'd walked between the houses to get to the back alley, I'd almost tripped over a large metal hose pot on the side of her house. Leave it to Mrs. Murphy to be so fastidious with an ordinary garden hose! The hose pot was the perfect size for a makeshift stool. I knew she wouldn't have approved, so I made a mental note to "put it back exactly the way you found it," a perennial comment of hers.

I disconnected the coiled hose and pulled it from the pot, then flipped it over on the driveway. Once I'd found a somewhat comfortable position—legs spread eagle with the garbage bag between—I got to work. Even after this minimal exertion, however, my glasses had completely fogged. Off came the mask. I was used to cleaning Lenore's litter pans, so how odoriferous could the garbage be?

Next, I tried to untie the knot in the bag, but I couldn't get a grip on the plastic ties. Off came the disposable gloves. If I were a longshoreman, some seriously blue language would have ensued. But as a former teacher, I'd learned to hold my tongue.

With renewed dexterity sans gloves, I was able to untie the knot without ripping the bag. I spread it open to look inside. A wave of pungent food odor wafted up to me. I turned my head and exhaled. At least it wasn't summer!

After a few moments of mouth-breathing, I retrieved the chopsticks from my bag. I was ready to play a game of Operation, extracting the pertinent contents from the rest of the garbage with medical precision. But I didn't need to use the chopsticks, either. Near the top of the pile of detritus, I spotted a torn envelope. The addressee was clear – Mr. and Mrs. Jacob Weiszman, a retired couple who lived three doors down.

Well, that cleared up one mystery, but I opened up several more bags. It was highly unlikely that the Weiszmans were surreptitiously putting their trash bags in other people's bins. Totally out of character. But it did appear that someone was playing musical chairs with trash. I know I should have talked to Jacob and Marjory, but I was afraid the conversation might reinforce their perception of me as a snoop. Long story, but I really didn't want to bother them.

So, now came the hard part—convincing Mrs. Murphy that there wasn't a garbage conspiracy in town.

Chapter Eight
Scones and Suspects

Ask any two people to describe a scone and you're liable to find broad disagreement.

First, there's the nebulous origin story: English, Irish, or Scottish? Supposedly, the word "scone" first appeared in a Scottish poem from 1513. Mrs. Murphy might counter that the Irish knew how to make scones earlier than that. They just didn't write poems about them.

Then there's the question of what to put on a scone—clotted cream or butter? There's a big disagreement between the Brits and the Irish … as if they needed anything more to disagree about. Don't even start with the polyglot of fruits, spices, and flavors in American scones. And who decided to make them triangular instead of traditionally round?

Tell an Englishman about the wonders of pumpkin spice scones and they'd laugh and say, "That's never a scone!" Of course, the first thing they'd tell you is that you're pronouncing it wrong—"scone" rhymes with "don" in the UK.

None of that mattered, as Mrs. Murphy's fresh-from-the-oven scones titillated my taste buds. Flaky and moist, slathered in creamy Irish butter and with a side dish of raspberries, this delectable treat made me forget all about trash-bin mysteries. I'd missed lunch, and it was too early for traditional afternoon tea, but my stomach didn't care. Mrs. Murphy's scones were what C. Auguste Dupin would call un petit bijou, transporting me to a very happy place.

When I reached for my third scone, however, she brought me back to reality. "Do you think Jacob is getting senile?"

It took me a beat to follow. "You mean you think Mr. Weiszman put his garbage in your trash bin ... because he didn't realize it wasn't his?"

"Well ..." She put her hands on her hips and gave me one of her hard stares. "Surely you know that famous rationale for finding answers to complicated mysteries. What's it called? Uggam's Raisin?"

Malapropisms are pretty common among my clientele, so I'm a seasoned pro at suppressing laughter. "Oh, yes," I replied, working hard to keep the tone of my voice even. "Occam's razor—the simplest solution is most often the best." Now I had to throw cold water on Mrs. Murphy's reasoning, without appearing to, you know, throw cold water on it.

"That's a good point. But we don't really have multiple possible solutions. At least not yet..." I trailed off and let the silence linger, knowing Mrs. Murphy would soon fill it.

Instead, and in a none-too-subtle move, she slid the basket of scones out of my reach. I guess I wasn't going to get another until I'd worked out The Great Trash Bin Mystery. With a resigned sigh, I laid out what we actually knew about this case. "Let's deal with some facts first."

"Do you want a paper and pencil? That always helps me sort things out." She started to rise from her chair, but I waved my arms to stop her.

"No, there's no need for that yet." Still, I paused to organize my mental whiteboard before continuing.

"Number 1: The Weiszman's trash is in your bin."

"Number 2: As far as we know, this is the first time it has happened."

"What about switching my trash bins last month? Doesn't that count?"

Mrs. Murphy still wouldn't accept the fact that she was mistaken about that "mystery"—her trash bins had not been switched; hers just got a bit beat up by the garbage collectors. "Now you know we sorted that out already, Mrs. Murphy."

"Harrumph!"

That was about as much consent as I'd get from her. I tried to regain control of my thoughts and continue laying out the facts of this mystery. But articulating the next point took a bit more cogitation. "Number 3: In most cases here in Ocean City, residents and renters are the only people who handle their trash bins."

A broad smile appeared on Mrs. Murphy's face, and I got ready for a gotcha moment. "You're forgetting something, Mr. P.I."

Here it comes.

"The Bin Busters! You know, those nice young men who move our trash bins out to the curb in the early morning hours before the garbage trucks roll in?"

She had me there. I'd always dealt with my own trash bins, not least because I often disposed of shredded client files. I tried to regain hold of the narrative. "So, other than you, and possibly Jacob Weissman, who may or may not be senile, the 'nice young men' from Bin Busters are ... probably ... the only people who have interacted with your garbage."

"Bingo!" she said, but her elation at one-upping me faded quickly. "Those nice young men," she said, shaking her head. "They're so clean-cut and wholesome. I can't imagine any of them doing something so .... underhanded ... like putting the Weiszman's garbage in my bin."

When's the last time you heard someone described as clean-cut and wholesome? On old reruns of Ozzie & Harriet? I smiled and made an affirmative noise. No reason to burst her bubble when it came to "nice young men" these days.

"So, if you don't think Jacob Weiszman is senile," she said, "and I'm sure those young men couldn't have done this, where does that leave us? Who's our prime suspect?"

"It's early days, Mrs. M. We don't have a pattern of activity yet; just a single event." She started to object, but I raised a palm to stop her. "Please. Let's take this one step at a time." She looked crestfallen.

"It's Saturday afternoon. Trash collection is on Monday morning. How about this? Starting Tuesday, I'll periodically examine your trash bins, looking inside them for anything out of the ordinary. That will narrow the possibilities ... not to mention it may help us determine whether this was just a singular event."

She didn't seem at all satisfied, but she also didn't offer a rebuttal.

"So, now that we have a plan, could I have another scone, please?"

Chapter Nine
Art and Protests

Back at home, I tried to get The Great Trash Bin Mystery out of my mind so I could concentrate on our plan of attack for the Poe Puzzler that evening. Berni had already set up a group text with Patrolman Bob and me, laying out our scheme. She'd grab a Manco & Manco pizza, pick up Bob a little after 5:30 p.m. at the police station on Central, then swing by and get me. We'd be well-positioned at the corner of Waverly & Seaspray, a good hour before my 7:00 p.m. "appointment" with the Poe Puzzler.

That still gave me plenty of time to either sit and stew in my own juices or do something to take my mind off all the drama of the day. I decided on the latter and rummaged through the clothes hamper to retrieve my painter's smock. When I uncovered the easel in the corner of my living room—the room with the best light for painting—I took a critical look at my work in progress.

Living in Ocean City, you'd think I'd paint the usual beach scenes, seascapes and other bright and cheery places. There are way too many of those in all the local rental homes and gift shops. So, I leaned toward darker themes, and I was relatively pleased with my latest effort.

Picture a deserted pier on a winter's night. Waves crash against the pilings. A full moon peeks out from behind dark clouds. A lone figure stands at the end of the pier, gazing into the distance, his long coat whipping in the wind. That's what I was trying to capture, all in hues of blue, green, and gray.

I always start with perspective lines, in this case running from the bottom of the canvas to about two-thirds of the way up – to where I've placed the end of the pier. And I also like to set my images slightly akilter, never symmetrical. That would be too boring.

Friends have told me I'm a talented artist, but I know they're just being kind. I'm a studied artist, spending way too much time considering each brush stroke. Anna, on the other hand, she was a true artist ... so creative and natural. We'd often talked about getting in touch with a local gallery to exhibit her artwork, but it never went beyond idle conversation. It's one of the many regrets I have about our life together. Most of her oil paintings are stored in the attic, but three of them hang in my bedroom. I gaze at them when I need solace.

And so I stared at my own half-done painting, waiting for the muse to visit. All the basic elements were there—sea, sky, and pier. I'd add the moon and the figure of the man later. What should come next were contours, character, and a sense of movement. That's what makes a seascape come alive.

I squeezed a line of cobalt blue onto my palette

board, then placed a dab of cadmium lemon alongside it. Blending the two with my palette knife gave me a deep shade of aquamarine. With a wide, flat brush, I added subtle swirls to the flat-blue sea.

I paused to consider the effect and almost wiped it clean until I forced myself to accept that I could always paint over it. Unlike life, oil paintings give you second chances.

All of my ruminations were rudely interrupted by a ruckus outside—a rumbling exhaust and people shouting. Lenore's ears perked up, and she sprang from her resting place on the green chair. I carefully set down my brush and palette, and rushed to the front door.

A ragtag line of people was marching up my street, led by an old farm tractor pulling a trailer. What made this curious, of course, is that there are no farms on the island. The farmer must have trundled over the 9th Street bridge, to the annoyance of locals and tourists alike. More curious still was a man in a whale costume standing in the trailer, shouting into a bullhorn: "Save our shore! Save our shore!" Behind him, a line of protesters, mostly kids on foot or riding bikes, followed along as if he were the Pied Piper.

There'd been several protests over the past few days—people linking arms on the beach or parading down the boardwalk—but this approach was new, and I hoped not a sign of things to come. I had no interest in taking sides on this issue. I simply didn't know enough about offshore wind farms and their impact on the environment to make an informed decision. And considering what was going on in my life, I had no time to find out more.

The kids chanted along with the costumed whale. Some held handmade signs spelling out similar sentiments: "Protect Our Coast!" or "Stop the Wind Farms!" It wasn't at all clear how disturbing the peace and quiet of an autumn afternoon in Ocean City would have any impact on this proposed project. And as the last of the group proceeded up the street, I had a mental image of Mrs. Murphy rushing out of her house, waving a rolling pin at the protesters. That made me smile.

I was about to return to my artwork when a young girl, surely no more than five or six years old, ran up my steps and held out a green flyer. She was certainly brave to approach a stranger. Of course, I bent down, took the flyer, and thanked her. She blushed and ran down the steps to join her mother at the end of the line of protesters.

The charm of that little interplay faded when a thought struck me – that's how the Poe Puzzler could have delivered his messages. Kids had been stuffing flyers into our mailboxes for the past week. How could I have missed that clue? While this gave me a plausible answer to the "how" of my mystery, I still had no idea as to the "why" or "who."

Needless to say, the muse had now flown. I was in no mood for painting. A thin line of clouds was blowing in from the shore, and the afternoon light was fading. My time would be better spent planning for the what-ifs that might occur that evening.

Chapter Ten
The Appointment

Berni was right on time. As soon as she pulled up in her old pickup truck, Bob swung open the passenger door and stepped out, balancing a pizza box in one hand. "You slide into the middle, Nathan," he said. "I want to have an easy exit … if it comes to that." I was hoping to see Bob in uniform—that might carry some weight if we had to confront my Puzzler—but he was in his "civvies."

"One second." I unlocked the trunk of my Saab and rummaged through the P.I. kit. The only thing I figured I'd need was my pair of binoculars.

Few modern vehicles have a wide bench seat like an old Chevy pickup. We fit just fine, even with the binoculars dangling from my neck and the pizza box warming my knees. Bob was the heaviest of us three, but he wasn't wearing any of his bulky police gear – he was off duty, after all. He and I had plenty of elbow room, and Berni was able to steer without banging into me.

It was a short ride. She eased to the curb on Seaspray, in about the same place I'd parked earlier that day. It was not quite 6:00 p.m., but the daylight was seeping out of the sky. No moon, either, so we'd have to keep a keen eye out. I raised the binoculars to my eyes and scanned the area. We had an ideal vantage point, but there wasn't much to see. No pedestrians or dog-walkers were out on that October evening. All the nearby houses were dark. The view through the windshield was like a theater tableau. Now we had to wait for the actors to take the stage. I'm not good at waiting, and I realized I hadn't had anything substantial to eat in some time – pastry and scones aside, of course.

Still, I tried hard not to be the first to dig into the pizza. Berni had picked it up, after all, and I'm sure Bob was hungry after a day of police work. I didn't want to be rude.

I've tried some of the other pizza joints on the boardwalk. Manco & Manco is still my favorite. I'll often sit at the counter and watch them make it. They don't seem to have any special ingredients or cooking secrets, but oh my, it is pizza perfection – a thin, but not too thin crust, mildly spicy sauce with just a touch of sweetness, and a perfect tang to the cheese. No need to add any toppings; a plain tomato pie from M&M is my Number One.

So there we sat, with aromas of tomato sauce, melted cheese and pizza crust filling the passenger compartment. Resist! I thought. But my growling stomach gave me away.

"Is that you, Nathan?" Bob called me out. "Go ahead, man, dig in."

Now that I had permission, I didn't hesitate. As I lifted the lid of the pizza box, my stomach called out again.

It was easy enough to separate a single slice, but a string of cheese just wouldn't let go. If I were at home, I'd twirl it around my index finger and lick it off. That wouldn't do when sharing. I pulled the slice higher, and it finally came free.

With a practiced grip, I forced the slice into a gentle curve—who needs utensils? The pizza was halfway to my mouth when I remembered my manners. "Pick you out a slice?" I asked Berni.

"Thanks, but I'll grab my own."

"Me, too," Bob chimed in.

A satisfied silence filled the truck, with just a softly muttered "mmmm" every now and then.

Both Berni and Bob were pizza-and-beer guys. I prefer a glass of red wine – Chianti or Merlot. Given our circumstances, we had to settle for water. Berni pulled a couple of small bottles from her door pocket and passed them to us. It would do.

After we'd each devoured a few slices, the windshield started to fog. "Better start her up and turn on the defroster," Bob said. "But dim the instrument lights. I don't want to be more obvious than we already are."

It was only 6:30, but I was growing impatient. "Do you think he's going to show up?"

Bob skooched sideways in his seat and gave me his policeman's stare. If I didn't know him better, his square jaw, close-cropped hair, and linebacker physique might intimidate me. But deep down, Bob was really a teddy bear. "Okay, so, Berni's filled me in on most of the details," he said, "but what, exactly, did the note state?"

It was good to see he was taking this seriously.

"It said I'd find my next Poe question at this intersection at 7 p.m."

"And you've already checked that little free library cabinet earlier today, right?"

I felt my face flush. I had looked through the glass door at the books inside the wooden cabinet, but I hadn't opened it up to examine inside. What kind of P.I. was I?

"Um, I glanced inside."

Bob didn't answer, but his silence spoke volumes.

"Now, let's not get ahead of ourselves." Berni was a pro at tamping down emotions. "Let's just wait and see if this guy shows."

"Yeah, okay," Bob muttered.

No more conversation at that point – the drone of the defroster was the only accompaniment to our thoughts.

I picked up the binoculars and scanned the area again, trying to see anything out of place. The widely spaced streetlamps flickered on and grew brighter, casting pools of light on the sidewalks. Where the two streets met, beach sand had spilled out onto the pavement. The little book kiosk was clearly illuminated, but there were plenty of dark shadows on the sidewalks between the lights. Shrubs and small trees in front of the upscale houses also offered easy hiding places.

"Over there!' Berni whispered. "On the left."

A lone figure in a hoodie appeared, walking down Waverly. He glanced in our direction but didn't change his pace. I focused the binoculars on him, but all I could make out was his gray sweatshirt.

"Get ready to go." I could feel Berni tense alongside

me. Bob put his hand on the door latch.

The guy walked up to the little free library and opened the cabinet door. He pulled something from his sweatshirt pocket and stuffed it inside. This was my Poe Puzzler, I was sure of it.

"Let's go!" Bob shouted and jerked the door open. Berni sprang out a split second later.

The guy in the hoodie turned our way. It didn't take him long to realize something was up. At the sight of Bob and then Berni barreling toward him, he dashed down the path to the beach.

Me? I shoved the pizza box onto the dashboard, but the straps of my binoculars got caught in the lid. I yanked it out and tried to get up, not realizing I still had my lap belt on. Halfway up, and I was pulled back down to the seat. I scrambled to undo the belt, but my fingers were slick with pizza grease. So, I was forced to be a spectator.

Our perpetrator had already disappeared into the darkness of the beach path, but Berni sprinted ahead of Bob and was gaining on the guy.

Then it all came undone.

It must have been the sand on the pavement or a curb hidden in the shadows. Bob went down hard. I watched him fall and roll onto his side, probably clutching an imaginary football to his gut.

Berni turned toward us and took it all in. She hesitated just a moment before stopping the chase. She ran back and knelt by Bob, checking to see if he was okay. I finally got my seatbelt unlatched and joined them.

The Poe Puzzler had slipped through our pizza-stained fingers.

Chapter Eleven
The Italian Connection

It was Patrolman Bob's turn in the green chair, his right leg propped up on a stool and an icepack on his ankle. Lenore curled up on his lap and fell asleep.

After our failed attempt to confront my Poe Puzzler, we'd reconvened at my place. But before I could show them the note I'd retrieved, we had to go through some "woulda, coulda, shoulda" venting.

Berni paced back and forth as best she could in my tiny living room. She seemed more upset than me. "I was gaining on the guy! If I hadn't turned back to check on Bob, I would have caught him. Maybe once I'd shown him my kickboxing moves, he'd think twice about harassing you."

Berni – my protector! Not your traditional roles, I know, but as I've said before, Berni is very fit.

Bob looked lost in his own thoughts, shaking his head and mumbling. "You didn't have to come back for me, Berni."

That didn't get past her. She stopped, hands on hips. "I couldn't leave you on the ground like that. I didn't know how badly you were hurt."

Bob shrugged. "Just a sprain ... probably."

I didn't voice my own regrets, but I had plenty. If I hadn't tangled myself in the binoculars' strap, pizza box, and seatbelt, I could have at least helped Bob while Berni chased the guy. No way could I have run after him, but Berni could have. We'd been so close.

Bob brought an end to my mental recriminations. "So, whatta we got?"

I almost whipped out the Puzzler's note right then, but waited for Berni to speak.

"Well ..." Berni drew out the word. "We kind of know what he looks like."

This was exciting news! "Did you see his face?"

"Well, no."

There went my hopes, dashed against the rocks of the First Street jetty.

"But we know he's definitely a guy, not a woman. We know about how tall he is and his general build. I'd say he's young because he ran pretty fast, even in the sand." She closed her eyes and scrunched up her face. "I'm pretty sure he has dark hair and a beard ... and glasses."

"That's something," Bob said. "Not that there aren't hundreds of young men with dark hair and beards in town ... even in the off-season."

I blew out a breath, anticipating my moment.

"What about the note?" Bob asked.

"I was wondering when you'd ask!"

As the culprit had escaped into the darkness of the beach and Berni had sprinted back to our stricken patrolman, I'd finally extricated myself. Once we were sure Bob could walk, Berni helped him limp back to the truck, and I investigated the Little Free Library. Sure enough, a bright red envelope addressed to me was right on top of the books. I'd stuffed it into my back pocket before getting back into the truck with them. And now that everyone else had had their say, it was time for the big reveal. I reached back and pulled it out.

Berni crossed her arms and glared at me. "So? Open it!"

"Just a moment." I dashed back to my office to retrieve my antique silver letter opener. Might as well do this in style. Nearby street lamps illuminated the room with soft light, enough for me to reach into the desk drawer and retrieve my Italian keepsake. I held it up to my eyes and ran my thumb along its sharpened edge—it gleamed.

With an unfounded sense of satisfaction, I returned to my friends, red envelope in one hand, Italian letter opener in the other. "Let's see what my mystery man is asking me now."

Berni smirked, but Bob was having none of it. "Cut the theatrics, Poe, and open it."

I placed the envelope in the middle of the coffee table and sat on the couch. Berni hovered over me. Lenore jumped down when Bob leaned forward for a better view. "Should I put on gloves?" I asked. "You know, fingerprints …"

"Enough with the CSI routine," Bob said. "Get on with it."

I tucked the letter opener under the flap and sliced open the envelope. My pulse was racing. I unfolded the note and read it to myself. "Huh. That's too easy."

Bob threw his hands up in frustration. "What's it say?"

I shrugged and read the note aloud. "Why did Prince Prospero have the gates to his abbey bolted and welded shut?"

Berni didn't get it. "That's about Poe? I mean, Edgar Allan Poe?"

"Prospero. That sounds Italian," Bob added.

"Well, you're both right," I said. "Prince Prospero was the main character in Poe's 'The Masque of the Red Death,' which was likely set in Verona, Italy – where I got this letter opener."

"So, this Italian prince welded shut his gates because …?" Berni was trying to reason it out.

It was obvious to me, but I guess not to them. "To keep out the Red Death, of course!"

Conversation stopped. Each one of us probably mulling over this new puzzle and its implications. For me, it was more of the same – my Puzzler was asking me questions that most people who'd read Poe would know. But from Berni and Bob's reaction, maybe not.

Bob broke the silence. "Look, there's a theme here."

"Of course there is—questions about Poe and his works," I said. I'll admit, I knew even then there was something more sinister going on, but I probably didn't want to admit it.

"No, you're not getting the point!" Bob's outburst startled Lenore, who jumped down and hid in the hallway. With obvious effort, Bob pulled himself up from the green chair and hobbled back and forth. My living room was getting pretty crowded with just three people in it. "Tell me the first question, the first 'puzzle,' as you call it."

"Where did Poe die?"

"And the second one?"

"Why did Poe hate Griswold?"

Bob nodded, a satisfied look on his face. "So, whatta we got? We got 'die,' 'hate' and 'death.'"

Berni's eyes went wide. "Wow, do you think that's it, Bob – a death threat?"

"I don't see any other way to look at it." He limped back to the green chair and eased himself down, letting out a grunt. He was obviously still hurting. "Maybe it's because I'm a cop, but that's the way I see it."

Berni kept shaking her head. "So, if that's the case, can we put out an all-points bulletin or something? Or at least alert the police about this guy?"

"Whoa!" Bob's face lit up. He was actually laughing at us. "There's no criminal act here. A guy is sending notes to Nathan. Maybe they're kinda odd, or maybe it's just a weird back and forth about Poe—Edgar Allan, that is." He let that sink in. "Yeah, I know, my gut says the guy is threatening you, but the law and my gut don't often agree. The most you could claim is harassment. Good luck with that."

My shoulders slumped. "So, we've got nothing … nothing new to go on … nothing we can do?"

Bob's silence told me he didn't disagree.

Berni was more positive. "Look at it this way – the guy probably thinks I can identify him. That should give him second thoughts. Besides, we scared him away."

I wanted to believe her, but in my heart I knew things don't often work out that neatly.

Chapter Twelve
Nevermore

Sunday dawned crisp and clear. It was one of those special autumn mornings when you felt the cool, sharp scent of the ocean on the breeze, but when you faced the sun, your whole body breathed in its warmth. I'm not a church-goer … not since Anna … but I do like to mark the sabbath by setting aside my worries to commune with nature. That's easy to do in Ocean City, especially if you walk along the beach in the morning while most people are still in bed.

Lenore always gets me up early. Even though I feed her at night, she's ready for breakfast by 6:00 a.m., if not earlier. And she lets me know it. She starts with a gentle reminder—jumping on the bed and walking up alongside me, sitting patiently, staring at me. If I keep my eyes shut, she waits to make her next move, placing a paw on my cheek. That usually pulls me out of my dreams. If not, Lenore becomes more aggressive, finding something on my nightstand to push off the edge. One morning, when I was groggy and really wanted to get more sleep, she knocked over my old clock radio. That got my attention. Oh, but I love my little feline companion.

After dishing out her breakfast and making myself a bowl of oatmeal with blueberries, crushed walnuts, and a sprinkling of brown sugar, I donned my fleece-lined jacket and Irish cap for my perambulation on the beach. I didn't get far.

Mrs. G stopped me before I could walk past her place. She was watering the beautiful hibiscus plants by her front door. Their red, white, and yellow flowers belied the coming winter. "You find bad man?" she demanded.

"Yes and no. I saw him. I'm pretty sure it was him. But he got away."

"Hmph!" It was hardly a word, but she made her disappointment clear.

Seeing her reminded me that I wanted to follow up on something. "When we talked yesterday, I'd asked if you'd seen any strangers around the neighborhood."

"So?" She wasn't going to make this easy.

"Well, you said you hadn't seen anyone."

No response.

"I mean, what about all those kids riding their bikes around town, handing out protest flyers about the ocean wind farm?"

"Just kids," she said. "Kids riding bikes. They say no windmills. Ha! Like that Spanish fellow, he rides against windmills."

It took me a moment. Of course, Cervantes … Don Quixote. There was more to Mrs. G than met the eye. Just because she spoke broken English didn't mean she wasn't well-read. But I had to get her back on track.

"Okay, but was one of them bigger, maybe wearing a gray hoodie?" I was reaching, and I knew it. "Did you see a big kid handing out protest flyers?"

"Big kids, little kids." She threw her hands up to emphasize the point. "Just kids."

I had to let it go. Mrs. G looked at the world through a different lens. But I could tell I'd left her in a positive frame of mind. As I walked away, I heard her humming the theme song from "Man of La Mancha." Sometimes I think getting a straight answer from Mrs. G is one of those impossible dreams!

The sun was still rising above the horizon when I climbed up the ramp to get over the dunes. I stopped at the top to gaze out at the primordial elements. It was like entering another world, leaving behind the pavement, parked cars, and houses. Even the seagulls seemed awed by the glorious morning. Their plaintive cries were more muted than usual. Where sea and sand met, tiny sandpipers swooped down to peck at the receding surf, and then, in concert, took to the wing again as the waves rolled in.

On that October morning, I had this elemental world mostly to myself. To the south, I saw the approaching headlights of a municipal tractor raking the sand, smoothing out any imperfections. When I looked northward, I caught the distant outline of a couple strolling hand-in-hand, and a lone figure walking a dog.

It was still too early for the usual joggers, strollers, and surfers.

I relished my solitude … just me, the earth, the sky, and the water. This was how I recharged my batteries, breathing in the salt air and living in the "now." After a few moments standing in the sunlight with my eyes shut, slowly tamping down all the mental worries that often bubble to the surface, I headed toward the water.

Once past the boundary of dunes with its short run of boards and split-rail fencing, there's a section of open sand that's tough for me to navigate. It's too soft and uneven, too easy for me to lose my balance. But closer to the ocean, everything firms up and I can get my footing. Even then, I can't walk far or fast, but what walking I do is the best kind of exercise, simply because it doesn't feel like exercise. And I enjoy it much more than my aqua-therapy sessions.

I usually walk as far north as the Great Egg Harbor Inlet before turning around. Further on, as the northern end of the island curves back toward the bay, the dunes are more irregular, with no clear path for walking. It's a natural funnel for the wind, which whips through the inlet and churns the water into whitecaps. Most Ocean City visitors or even residents never venture into this wilder part of the beach.

Lost in thought that morning, however, I walked past the mouth of the inlet before I realized where I was. But my subconscious knew all too well. I was heading toward the path that led over the dunes to Seaspray Road and Waverly Boulevard—our rendezvous point from last night.

The beach was rough. The city never grooms the sand that far north. Broken shells festooned the dunes, and the wind created geometric ridges in the sand, curling and curving like zebra stripes of white on white. I don't know what I expected to find—footprints from last night? Some evidence that the Poe Puzzler had left? It was certainly no place for me to relax. I forced myself to turn around and head back to my familiar Surf Road Beach.

The seeds of worry had taken root, though, and I started to replay the events of the previous night in my imagination.

If the guy in the hoodie really was my Poe Puzzler, and given the note I'd found in the Little Free Library, he had to be, had we scared him away … for good? Was he just some prankster, someone from my past whom I'd inadvertently offended? Did he actually mean me harm, as Patrolman Bob had suggested … or as I preferred to believe, was he seeking some milder retribution for a perceived insult?

I thought of Poe's The Cask of Amontillado. "The thousand injuries of Fortunato I had borne as I best could; but when he ventured upon insult, I vowed revenge." That sent a chill down my spine that no amount of sunshine could ease. "Bunk!" I said aloud. I've got an active imagination, but I'm also a rational man. Still, all this mental cogitation darkened my mood. I walked and worried, and eventually found myself back where I'd started.

Trying to vanquish my negative thoughts, I faced the dawning day one more time, taking deep breaths of salt-scented air and letting the rising sun warm my face. I don't practice meditation, but this certainly came close. Feeling more relaxed and "centered," I turned my back on the sun and sea to head home.

That's when I saw a glint of sunlight reflecting off a bottle at the top of the dunes. It was propped up in the sand, squarely in the middle of the path I'd taken not 20 minutes before. It certainly wasn't there earlier. Someone had littered my pristine beach, and I felt a silent rage directed at the anonymous lout who'd done it. Then paranoia hit me like a blow to my head. No, it can't be.

I clambered over the loose sand to reach the top of the dunes. As I got closer, I saw it more clearly—a wine bottle with red stains across its white label. A white label with a black crow on the front. Not a crow … a raven. No, it can't be!

Out of breath and more puzzled than ever, I stood over the offending thing. My vision clouded, but the name of the wine jumped out at me: "Nevermore." I tried to laugh, but it came out as a wheezing cough. The Poe Puzzler. My Poe Puzzler had been here. He'd followed me. He'd placed this bottle where he knew I'd find it. What kind of message was this?

I whipped my head from side to side, searching for a distant figure, someone watching me. Surely he'd want to see me discover this taunt. Was he inside one of the nearby houses on East Surf Road? Was he that guy I'd spotted earlier walking a dog? Was he driving the city's tractor, grooming the sand? That would give him a perfect opportunity to spy on me, to follow me here. No, no, I won't let this take hold of me.

There wasn't a single footprint in the sand at my feet, not even my own from earlier. Was my Puzzler that devious, that meticulous?

Get help. I reached into my pocket for my cell phone, then realized it wasn't there; I never take it to the beach for fear of dropping it in the surf.

I tried to think. What should I do? What would Berni or Bob do? Maybe there were fingerprints … fingerprints on the bottle? If my Poe Puzzler had placed it in the sand, he must have held it by the neck. I could pick it up by the base and leave his prints intact. I bent down, brushed away grains of sand clinging to the base of the bottle, and caught an odd coppery smell. It didn't register at first. Using my thumbs and forefingers as pincers, I grasped the bottom of the bottle. It was damp and slipped out of my hands. The red wine on the label was still wet … no, not wet, tacky … too tacky. I rubbed my fingers together. My God, it was blood!

The sound of the waves faded into the distance. My pulse pounded in my ears. I held my hands up to my eyes and saw the dark red stain on my fingers. Blood … fresh blood. It couldn't be human, could it?

I fell to my knees and thrust both hands into the sand, squeezing my fingers into fists, frantically trying to rub the blood off. But when I raised my hands to look, it was still there.

Home. I had to get back home. I scrambled down the steps and ran headlong toward the road and houses and civilization.

Chapter Thirteen
The Raven Has Flown

By the time Berni came over, I'd scrubbed my hands raw. No amount of hot water and soap seemed to rid my skin of the blood. Dark remnants hid in the creases—anyone could see it. I thought about using bleach, but knew that would be a mistake. Typical English teacher, I couldn't get Lady Macbeth out of my head. "Out, damn spot, out!" I might have been hysterical.

When I'd run back home, I'd struggled to get my house key out of my front pocket. I was sure I'd left some bloodstains on my pants. They immediately went into the washer, and I dropped my key into a pan of disinfectant. I couldn't bear the thought of the blood still on me, still with me.

I should have called Bob and gotten the police involved. But was finding a bloody bottle in the sand a crime? And if so, who was the victim? Yes, of course it was me. Maybe not in a legal sense, but it was obvious what was going on.

Berni would understand. She was always my go-to, my crutch. She'd help me.

The knocking at my office door brought me back to the present.

"Nathan!" Berni paused with one foot on the threshold. "Um, maybe you should put some pants on."

I looked down and realized I was still in my underwear.

"I mean, we're good friends, Nathan. Just not that kind of friend." She was doing her best to lighten the mood. It wasn't working.

"It was the blood, Berni, all the blood. I had to get the blood off me … off my clothes." Still standing at the back door, I rubbed my hands together, imagining every last spot of red clinging to me.

"Okay, yeah. Get dressed and let's talk this out." She eased past me. "I'll put the kettle on and we can have one of your 'nice' cups of tea."

"No!" I might have shouted. I don't remember clearly. "We've got to go back and get that bottle … the bottle with the blood on it." She froze in her tracks. "It's evidence, Berni. I need the evidence."

"Okay, we can do that." We stood staring at each other, waiting for one of us to move, to get going.

"It's like Poe's MS. Found in a Bottle."

Berni shook her head. "You're losing me, Nathan. MS?"

"It's short for manuscript. The story's about a manuscript found in a bottle floating in the sea. It was a warning … a warning to other sailors."

"Okay …"

"Don't you see, Berni? There's no manuscript, no message in the bottle, the bottle he left for me to find.

The bottle is the message."

She put a gentle hand on my shoulder. Even so, I might have flinched. "Get some pants and shoes on." She turned me from the doorway and directed my steps down the hallway. "You've got to chill, Nathan. Seriously." She let out a held breath. "Get dressed and we'll drive over and get that bottle for you."

Berni always seems prepared for anything. She parked her truck near the ramp to Surf Road Beach and pulled a pair of work gloves from under the driver's seat. But as she went to open the door, I stopped her.

"Do you have a box or container?"

She tilted her head, not following.

"We need to put the wine bottle in a box – so we don't contaminate it."

"I've got some grocery bags in back. I always carry a few. That should do." She stepped out of the truck, but I didn't move. Not at first, not until she leaned her head in the door and gave me a look. "You are coming, aren't you?"

"Yeah. Of course." I undid my seatbelt, opened the passenger-side door, and stumbled out. My movements seemed slow and awkward. Like I was in a dream.

Berni must have realized what I was going through. She came around to my side of the truck and held out her arms. "Boy, do you ever need a hug. Come on ..."

Of all our human senses, touch is so under-appreciated. A warm embrace ... a hug ... a hug from a friend has such power to heal. The simple touch of one body to another, melting away anguish and despair, and filling you with hope and reassurance.

"It's going to be okay," she whispered. After a moment, she released me, lifted her hands to my shoulders, and gave me a searching look. "Are you feeling better now, Nathan, my friend?"

"I think I am."

"Okay, let's go get that bloody bottle."

The sun was higher in the sky but obscured by a layer of clouds. In the hazy brightness, shadows were subdued, colors muted. Berni waved an arm toward the ramp, a smile lighting up her face. "Show me the way," she said.

I took the ramp—the long way up to the top of the platform. Berni took the steps that I usually avoided, two at a time, of course. She met me at the top of the barrier dune, but when I looked to where the boards ended in a sandy path to the ocean, I froze. "No, it can't be." Did I say it out loud?

"What is it?" Berni glanced down at the sand, then back at me. "Just show me where the bottle is."

I rubbed my eyes, willing myself to breathe, to think. "It was right here. In the sand by the end of the boards." I was mumbling, but Berni heard me.

"Are you sure, Nathan? Maybe it was further down the beach."

"No!" I lashed out at her, at the world. "No! It was here. In the sand. Right here. He put it exactly where I'd see it, where I'd practically trip over it." I got down on my knees and dug my hands into the sand, sifting it through my fingers. "There's got to be blood in the sand.

There was blood on the bottle. Some of it has to be in the sand."

Berni stood over me. I looked up and saw her scanning the beach. Didn't she believe me? She glanced down, and we locked eyes. "Nathan." Her voice cracked. She tried again. "Nathan, I don't see … "

I pulled myself up and grabbed her hands. "Don't you believe me? I'm not crazy. The bottle was here. He put it here in the sand. My Poe Puzzler."

She looked away. "I don't doubt that you …" Her voice trailed off.

I let go of her hands and fell to my knees again. "He's toying with me. That's what he's doing." It came out as a whisper. I knew I was talking to myself.

Berni knelt next to me. When she reached out to touch my shoulder, I shrugged her off. "Let's go back to your place and talk this out," she said. "Okay?"

"No, Berni, it's not okay." I felt my blood pressure rising. "Just go. Leave me alone."

"Nathan, please …"

"Go!" I screamed at her and saw her face redden. She got up and walked away without another word.

I don't know how long I knelt there, digging in the sand, trying to find any hint of red mixed in with the gray and white grains. There was no blood, I finally admitted. Was I going crazy? No, the bottle had been there, wet with blood. The Poe Puzzler was gaslighting me, trying to make me question my sanity. I couldn't let him win.

But I also couldn't deal with this alone.

Exhausted, I staggered back down the ramp. Berni was waiting for me, leaning against the hood of her truck with arms crossed. I wasn't sure what to do. Did she really think I'd imagined all of this?

"Come on, Nathan," she said. "I don't doubt you saw that bottle. This Poe Puzzler is screwing with your head. But we're not gonna solve anything by burrowing through the sand. Let's go back to your place and figure out our next steps, okay?"

I was still coming to grips with my anger and disappointment. Berni and I had only known each other for about four years, but we'd become close friends. I wouldn't let this come between us. Not when I needed her most.

She opened the passenger door, and I got in. I took my time putting on my seatbelt. When she leaned in to check on me, I saw the concern on her face. "We'll sort this out," she said. "Let's think about it calmly. Put on your Auguste Dupin hat so we can figure out what this SOB is up to."

It was the best thing she could've said to get me out of my funk.

Chapter Fourteen
What About Alice?

By the time we got back to my place, I was thinking more rationally. Berni was right—we had to come up with a solid plan to deal with the Poe Puzzler. But you can't do that on an empty stomach.

I put the kettle on and made a small pot of Scottish breakfast tea, a robust black tea that always revitalizes me. I put out two small plates and cups with saucers on my little kitchenette table. There were no fresh pastries in the house, so I got out a box of spiced wafers from the pantry.

While I was preparing our tea, Berni hunched over her phone, no doubt looking up something on Google. She's a wizard with that sort of thing, using her thumbs in ways that mine never worked. Once I poured the tea, she looked up at me. "I found something interesting," she said.

"Well, don't keep me in suspense."

"There is a wine called Nevermore. It's from the Pacific Northwest, a Pinot Noir from – get this—Gothic Vineyards. About $25 a bottle."

"Let me see. Do they show a picture of it?"

She handed me her phone, and sure enough, that was the bottle I'd seen. The label looked more parchment than white, but had the same drawing of a raven.

"I'm gonna do some legwork," she said. "Visit some liquor stores in Somers Point and Marmora to see if they stock it."

"Okay." I sprinkled a half-teaspoon of sugar into my cup. "Do you think the wine is rare enough that some clerk would remember who bought it?"

She raised her eyebrows. "Maybe. Maybe not. Unless the guy had to special order it." She paused. "Worth a try, though."

I smiled and reached across the table for her hand. "I'm sorry I lashed out at you. I thought ... I thought you didn't believe me."

She patted her other hand on mine. "It's okay, Nathan. This is all pretty crazy."

We crunched on our spiced wafers and sipped our tea. I felt the tension flow from me. It was a relief to be back in Berni's good graces. I savored the sharp taste of cinnamon on top of the sweet molasses flavor of the small cookies. They even have a hint of cloves. It's a shame they're only available in the fall.

"I've been wondering if we should talk to Patrolman Bob again," Berni said.

It didn't take much thought for me to rule that out. "I don't see the point. We don't have the bottle, so there's nothing but my word about what happened."

"Hmm."

Our cups clinked against the saucers as we drank our tea. Berni seemed deep in thought. Then she broke the silence. "You know, this has to be someone who really doesn't like you."

I had to laugh. "That's obvious. And that's what makes it so hard to figure out. I'm sure I've made enemies over the years. Everyone makes enemies, whether or not they realize it, but who could have it in for me like this? Who could hold such a grudge?"

I stirred my tea and watched the liquid swirl around in the cup, a mesmerizing little maelstrom. It seemed like a reflection of my own emotional whirlpool, spiraling me down, taking control. Like Poe's "Descent into the Maelstrom." Most readers ... certainly most of my high-school students ... thought it was a simple Gothic tale about overcoming a terrifying force of nature. There's so much more to Poe's story, though—the tenacity of the human spirit, the delicate line between perception and reality.

Berni jarred me from my musings. "Maybe it's someone from your high school. Someone you really upset."

"But I've been retired for over four years. Why now?"

She stared at her teacup. A shadow flitted across her face, and she glanced up at me, but then looked down again.

"What?" I asked.

She spoke in the softest voice. "Maybe it's someone much closer to home."

"Who? I don't have many living relatives, and

certainly none that would do this to me."

"Sorry to bring it up, Nathan." She gazed directly into my eyes. "But could it be Alice?"

I froze, the teacup halfway to my mouth. "Alice? Now? After five years?"

"She's the only person I can think of who really hates you."

I have to tell you about my sister-in-law, Alice. She's younger than Anna … than Anna was. Alice is beautiful, wealthy, self-assured, and self-righteous. She always knows what's best for you, and she never hesitates to let you know it.

Alice never approved of me. She went as far as telling her sister she was marrying beneath her station. I haven't spoken to Alice in years. Not since the funeral.

Because of the damage to my leg, I was in the hospital for several days after the accident. Alice flew in from California and made all the funeral arrangements. She never asked what I wanted. Never asked what Anna would have wanted. During the service, she never once looked at me. Then she flew home.

It was days later when I got a large UPS package. I put it on the dining room table and cut it open. Inside was a heavy plastic bag. A horrible odor seeped out when I untied it. I forced the bag open and saw all of Anna's clothes, the clothes she was wearing when she died. Reddish brown bloodstains were everywhere, on her dress, her bra, her shoes. I ran to the bathroom and threw up.

I didn't connect the dots at first. All I could think was, who would do this? The return address was unreadable. Did the funeral home think I wanted her bloodstained clothes? After I'd composed myself, I tied the bag shut again and was about to take it down to the trash. That's when I saw a handwritten note in the box.

It was from Alice, even though she hadn't signed it. All it said was, "It should've been you."

"I don't want to go there, Berni. It's been 5 years."

She nodded but averted her eyes. "I know your Poe Puzzler is a guy, but Alice could have put him up to it."

"Damn it, Berni! Why did you have to bring her up?"

She got up from the table and stood over her chair, gripping the back of it. Her knuckles were white with tension. "Nathan, you don't like to talk about all this, about Anna ... there, I've said her name ... and about Alice. But you've got to face your demons someday. Maybe now is a good time to start."

Berni went off to question liquor store clerks, and I was left to think about Alice. Of all the people on earth, she was the last one I wanted to talk to. On the other hand, Berni was right—Alice was the only person I could think of who really hated me. It was hard to imagine that Alice was behind the Poe Puzzler, though. She knows more about shorting stock and leveraged buy-outs than literature. She probably couldn't quote a single line from Poe's works, even "The Raven." Still, I had to eliminate her as a suspect.

I pulled out my phone to check my contacts. With any luck, I had deleted her information years ago, and could use that as an excuse not to call. But when I scrolled to the W's, there she was—Alice Woolton, San Jose, California.

There was nothing left to do but call. It was early in California, but not too early. As one of my fellow teachers used to say, "God hates a coward!" I screwed up my courage and touched the number. It rang and rang, and I almost hung up, but then she answered. Not with a "Hello," of course. That would have been too polite.

Her voice was sharp. "Why are you calling me?"

"Alice. It's Nathan."

"I know that. What do you want?"

"I've been ..." I should have sorted out what to say beforehand, but if I'd thought about it too much, I never would have called. "I've been getting these strange notes, odd sort of questions about Edgar Allan Poe from someone."

"What's that have to do with me?"

"I just wanted to make sure it wasn't you." Silence on the other end of the line. "That you weren't sending me these messages."

"Nathaniel, I don't want to have anything to do with you. I thought I'd made that clear. I never should have answered this call. I don't want you in my life." She paused only long enough to get a breath. "Don't call me again."

The line went dead. My hand was shaking when I put down the phone. At least, I thought, I'd put an end to the Alice theory.

Chapter Fifteen
A Vague Profile

Exhausted from the emotional toll of the morning, I sank into the green chair, anticipating a refreshing nap. Lenore immediately jumped on my lap, softly kneaded my thighs for a moment, and then settled into a white, fluffy ball. Clearing my mind, I drifted deeper into unconsciousness ... until the phone rang. It was Berni, and she sounded excited.

"Hey Nathan, I've got some interesting news." I took a moment to reply. "Were you napping? Oh, sorry, but you'll want to hear this."

"Um, what did you find out?"

She took a breath before rattling off her progress. "So, I went to a bunch of liquor stores in Somers Point, you know, by the old circle on Route 9. None of them carried Nevermore Pinot Noir, and I couldn't find anyone to talk to besides checkout clerks. So, I drove down to Marmora."

She paused. Was she looking for acknowledgment? "Okay," I said, stifling a yawn.

"And I struck gold there. You know that big liquor

store in Marmora, right across the 34th Street Bridge?"

Again, she waited for me. I heard a loud whooshing noise over the phone. "I'm with you, Berni. What did you find out there?"

"Sorry. I don't have Bluetooth in this old truck." The rumble of tires on pavement was louder than her voice.

"I talked to the manager ... surprised he was there on a Sunday ... and he remembered special ordering the wine."

"That's amazing! So, what did the guy look like?"

"Oh, he was older, looked like a smoker. You know, he had that kind of wheezing breath when he talked..."

"Berni! We're not communicating. Not the manager. The Puzzler—was it the Poe Puzzler who ordered the wine?"

"Ha! Yeah, my bad. Hold on a minute. I've got to make this turn."

I hoped she wasn't juggling her phone in one hand while steering with the other, but that's what it sounded like.

After a moment, she continued. "So, he described the guy as kind of young."

"Surely he checked his ID, right? How young?"

She laughed. "I asked him about that. All I got was 'he was legal.' But get this—he said he had a closely cropped beard, dark hair, and glasses. That sounds just like the guy I chased last night."

As I began to process all this, I smiled. We'd connected with the Poe Puzzler pretty easily just by following the trail of the wine bottle. But now what? "Did he say anything else about the guy? Did he pay by credit card or cash?"

"That's the reason the manager remembered the guy. Before he'd agree to order the wine, he demanded a deposit. The guy paid in cash. Who does that?"

"And did he give you any better description?"

"All he'd say was he looked like every other young guy who comes in the store. Not much help there."

Still groggy from my truncated nap, I tried to get the wheels turning. "So, maybe he paid in cash because he didn't want a purchase record with his name on it. Or maybe he has bad credit and can't use a card."

"Yup, either one could fit."

My mind was getting into gear now, leading me to logical conclusions. "This may be a stretch, but he might live on the south end of the island, close to the bridge, or maybe even in Marmora."

Berni didn't respond right away. All I heard was wind and road noise.

"And Berni..." I waited to be sure she could hear me.

"What is it, Nathan?"

"I called Alice." The sound of truck tires on pavement and wind whistling through an open window filled the silence. "Did you hear me?"

It took her a moment to respond. "Yeah. I'm letting that sink in."

"I doubt it's her, Berni. It just doesn't fit."

"Okay, if you say so." Another jumble of noises from her pickup told me she was still on the line. I waited for her to say something more.

"Listen, I've got to get some work done at the shop," she said. "Are you okay ... you know, by yourself?"

"Of course, Berni. Come on! I'm not that needy."

"Got it. Catch up with you sometime tomorrow."

We said our goodbyes, and now my mind was whirling with the possibilities. Time to pull out the big easel and write down my thinking. I gave Lenore a couple of gentle pats. She got the signal and jumped down, rolled onto her back on the living room floor, and gave me her sad kitty look. "Yes, I know, Lenor-e-o, not enough nap time. Maybe later."

I would love to buy a big whiteboard, like a real P.I., but it seems an extravagance, and it probably wouldn't fit in my little house. I pulled out my largest artist's easel from the hall closet, attached a big sketch pad, and set it up in my office. Putting my thinking down on paper, I reasoned, might help me profile my Puzzler.

I drew a line at the top and wrote "Poe Puzzler Profile"—a nice bit of alliteration. But when I jotted down his attributes, it was a pretty meager list: "Young man, less than 30. Dark hair and short beard. Glasses. Maybe lives on South End or Marmora." I stopped and waved the marker in the air, waiting for something more to come to me. Finally, I added, "Knows or has researched E.A. Poe. Some connection with me."

That was it. Auguste Dupin would be in tears!

I set this "ratiocination" aside and decided I'd be better off working on my presentation for the library next month. The activities director had asked me to give a talk about Poe's connection to Arthur Conan Doyle and Agatha Christie. I could probably do it off the top of my head, but I knew I had to be better prepared.

The name of the talk came to me right away—"The

Perceptive Detective in Literature: Poe, Doyle and Christie." That had a nice ring to it. Now I needed to find some specific references, even passages in their novels, to show how Dupin was the archetype for Sherlock Holmes and Inspector Poirot.

It gets dark early this time of year, and the morning clouds had turned to gray with rain on the wind. The hours flew by as I immersed myself in research, combing through Sherlock Holmes and Agatha Christie mysteries for some specific references. I looked up from my desk and realized it was late afternoon ... and I was hungry. A nice cup of tea would take the edge off, so I felt my way down the hall in the gloaming and turned on the stove-top light. That's when I felt the presence.

You know how you get a prickly feeling in the back of your neck when someone is looking at you? Of course, we don't have eyes in the back of our heads, but I can usually tell when I'm being stared at. And at that point, I knew it. Before I turned around, I reached into a kitchen drawer and pulled out a carving knife. If the Poe Puzzler was at my door, I was going to be ready.

When I eased my neck around, I saw a dark silhouette at my front door. I froze, waiting. Would he say something? Would he try to open the door or even break it down?

"I know you there," Mrs. G bellowed. "Open up. This heavy."

I bent over and let out a breath. At least I was mindful enough to put the carving knife back in the drawer before I opened the door. Mrs. G was carrying a large casserole dish, and it instantly filled my tiny kitchen with the scent of paprika and garlic. My stomach growled.

Chicken paprikash—one of my favorite dishes of hers. What a treat!

"You eat," she said. "Hungarian comfort food. Not too spicy."

When I asked her to join me, she declined. "I already eat. Your turn." I placed a trivet on the kitchen table, and she set the casserole down, turned to leave, but then hesitated. "I see you and Berni go back and forth this morning. You find Bad Man?"

"No. He left me a message ... of a sort. A bloody message."

She shook her head, but didn't comment. As she opened the door to leave, she had one more thing to say. "You remember dreams tonight. Then we talk."

Mrs. G and her dreams! I'd be lucky to sleep through the night, but at that point, rest was the last thing on my mind. I readied myself for a feast.

Such a special dish deserved more than a glass of water. A recently opened bottle of California Chardonnay in the refrigerator would go nicely. After the incident on the beach, there was no way I was going to have red wine.

I pulled out one of my better china dishes and good silverware, not my usual thrift store stuff. With a hot pad in hand, I lifted the lid of the casserole and let my olfactory senses anticipate what my tastebuds were about to experience—onions sauteed in garlic and butter ... or maybe even in lard ... tomatoes, fresh cream, and lots of paprika.

Mrs. G makes a big deal of getting "only good

Hungarian paprika" that's not only more aromatic than the usual store-bought stuff but also has a richer red color. In addition to tender cuts of chicken, her Hungarian dish had little fat dumplings. I made the mistake of calling them German spaetzle once. Never again! I got a big lecture about how these were Hungarian nokedli. I know better than to argue, but really, they're just shorter, stubbier spaetzle.

I dug in, and all my anticipation paid off. Yes, I was hungry, but Mrs. G's chicken paprikash was the perfect dish for a rainy autumn evening. After the first mouthful, however, I realized it was very hot—spicy hot. A gulp of cold Chardonnay helped, but I needed something to take the heat down. I scrounged in my fridge and found an old container of sour cream. After the smell test confirmed it was still good—my nose is a far better judge than sell-by dates—I mixed it into the casserole. That made all the difference. At least heartburn wouldn't keep me up tonight.

I've tried to get the secret recipe from Mrs. G, but all she would ever tell me was "good chicken, good paprika—from Hungary. No peppers."

As I devoured my dinner, all the trauma of the morning was almost forgotten. Almost.

Chapter Sixteen
Trash Bin Ballet

A promise is a promise, especially to Mrs. Murphy. So I was up before sunrise to stake out her garbage. I had to rule out the "wholesome young men" from Bin Busters, as well as the remote possibility that Mr. Weiszman was surreptitiously transferring his trash to Mrs. Murphy's bins. Such is the life of a "Small Mysteries" P.I.

Lenore was more than happy to eat her breakfast early. She did her usual figure-eight through my legs as I opened the can. Cats may be creatures of habit, but when it comes to food, any time is good.

One look outside in the pre-dawn light revealed a gray day ahead—overcast with light drizzle, as forecast. I steeped a strong pot of tea for my Thermos. Nothing special this morning, just pure, unadulterated PG Tips black tea. And since I'd be sitting in my car for some time during this stakeout, I grabbed some of my spiced wafer cookies and put them in a paper bag. They really are addictive.

My usual habit on garbage-collection days is to wheel my trash bins to the curb the night before. Although the town fathers frown on that practice, I hadn't received a summons yet. But this unenforced rule gives Bin Busters a decent business model. These high-school kids ride their bikes up and down the streets, pausing only to move trash bins from back alleys, where the trucks don't fit, to the curbs before the garbage trucks roll in. Many of the older residents in town certainly appreciate the convenience.

Although Mrs. Murphy lives just down the block, I needed a comfortable place to observe the coming action, so I hopped into my old Saab to move it a little closer. Just like me, however, my trusty conveyance doesn't enjoy waking up early. And she let me know it when I turned the key.

That rrr-rrr-rrr sound went on too long before her engine coughed to life. I'd probably need to schedule service before winter set in, but that thought flowed into and out of my mind like water through a sieve. There were more important things to deal with at that moment.

I maneuvered closer to Mrs. Murphy's house and found an ideal vantage point. The street was quiet except for the cheep-chirrup of house sparrows darting through the trees. There was enough moisture in the air to fog the windows, so I kept the engine running and the defroster on. Now, it was down to staring out the windshield, waiting for the Bin Busters to appear.

A movement in the shrubs up ahead caught my eye. Our resident rabbits were waking up to the day. Three of the cute little guys ventured out, their noses twitching as they tested the morning air for danger. One by one, they scampered onto the wet grass next to the sidewalks, no doubt searching for any morsels of food the gulls hadn't scavenged.

I was so captivated by the antics of the rabbits that I almost missed the approaching cyclist. Pedaling fast in the misty morning, he appeared like a phantom—gray hoodie pulled tight over his head, a glimpse of a face as he sped by. A young man's face. A young man with dark hair and a slight beard, and glasses.

I almost dropped my Thermos as I scrambled to open the car door and get a better look. Could this be my Poe Puzzler? His appearance certainly matched Berni's description from the other night.

As I stepped onto the pavement, two more cyclists came into view. To my eyes, they could be triplets—gray hoodies hiding young bearded faces. They came to a stop on either side of the street, paying as little notice of me as to the rabbits. After laying down their bikes on the sidewalks, they disappeared behind the houses and reappeared a moment later, pushing trash bins to the curbs.

Of course! The Bin Busters in action.

Their movements were so choreographed, their timing so synchronized, I was reminded of the scene in A Wrinkle in Time where identical children came out of identical houses to bounce balls in perfect time with each other. Back behind the next houses on the block they ran and returned with trash bins to place at the curb. Once three or four residences had been served, onto their bikes they climbed and pedaled down the block to repeat their trash-bin ballet over and over.

I wouldn't describe them as wholesome young men,

but they were admirably industrious and efficient. No wonder Mrs. Murphy was so enamored of them.

My sense of wonder faded once the hard truth set in. Any one of these Bin Busters could be my Poe Puzzler. Maybe they were too young ... or maybe not. Had I reached the age where all young men looked alike?

With shoulders slumped, I climbed back into my tired old Saab and stared out the rain-dappled windshield. Everything I'd seen made me realize how hard it was going to be to identify my new nemesis. And nothing I'd seen had helped me solve Mrs. Murphy's trash bin mystery.

Then an intriguing thought occurred to me – what if there was some strange domino effect going on with her trash? What if each house's trash bins on our block held someone else's garbage? I almost dismissed it as paranoia, but then decided to check out my own bins.

Rather than do an awkward K-turn, I put the Saab in gear and drove around the block so I could pull to the curb in front of my house. I'd search my trash bins and maybe a few others between my house and Mrs. Murphy's to see how widespread this phenomenon was. But my timing was off.

As I came back around the block and turned onto my street, a large municipal garbage truck blocked my progress. I almost flagged down the driver and told him what I wanted to do, but I could easily imagine the push-back I'd get. And I really didn't want to add to my reputation as the town eccentric.

My plans were thwarted. I inched ahead impatiently as the garbage truck huffed and chugged from house to house, from trash bin to trash bin. There was nothing I could do about it. They'd empty the bins into their truck, and Mrs. Murphy and I would start the week with our bins as empty as my hopes of solving any mysteries—hers or mine.

Chapter Seventeen
Edison's Method

Back at home, I busied myself with mundane chores—doing the laundry and washing the dishes—hoping a new path forward would surface in my consciousness. But as I rinsed, dried, and put away the china and silverware, my mind was a blank.

I'd heard a story once about how Thomas Edison came up with new ideas. He would sit in a comfortable chair, his arms draped loosely on either side, with a pie pan in each hand. Then he'd close his eyes and visualize the recalcitrant issue. Basically, he'd go into a trance. If he dropped the pans, he knew he'd gone too deeply into slumber, and he'd start over. But if he remained in that semi-conscious state of meditation, a clever solution would often come to him. It sounded like malarkey to me, but in my current state of hopelessness, it was worth a try.

I'd attended a mindfulness seminar at the library last year, so I knew the basic steps to meditation. If I were going to try the Edison Method, though, I needed to substitute something for the pie pans. No doubt Mrs.

Murphy owned all manner of pie pans, but I could only imagine her questions if I asked to borrow a couple—that was a non-starter. I looked around for a suitable pie-pan proxy. Lenore's cat toys didn't seem appropriate. It had to be something with more heft. I searched my kitchen cabinets until I found the appropriate objects—two saucepan lids.

My comfy chair of choice was the green "napping" chair in the living room, so I sat down with the lids in each hand and went through the steps of clearing my mind and counting backwards to reach a meditative state. It took a while for my "monkey brain" to settle down and stop jumping from one thought to another. Finally, I zeroed in on the sound of my mantel clock. Its soft tick-tock lent a soothing rhythm to my breathing, and I felt my consciousness ebbing.

Everything was going fine until the sudden arrival of an eight-pound cat on my lap. I let out a cry but kept my eyes closed. Lenore gave me a plaintive mrrip, looking for some affection. She'd just have to settle down without my customary petting. I tried again. Ten...nine...eight, going deeper. Deeper and deeper. The sounds of the washer and dryer faded into the distance, and a mental image of the Poe Puzzler began to form in my mind.

With each slowly drawn-out breath, the image became clearer. I saw him standing in the dark in the middle of my street. In one hand, he clasped a bunch of envelopes. In the other, a book. He had his gray hoodie pulled up over his head, so his face wasn't visible. I could tell he was looking at me, though, because I saw light reflected in his dark-rimmed glasses.

I moved my mental image closer, my perspective zooming forward as if I were walking out my front door and onto my porch. As my mind's eye brought me nearer, he turned his head, further obscuring his face. But I saw his hands better now. The envelopes in his left hand were different colors—white, brown, and red. His right hand held not one book, but several thin volumes.

That intrigued me more. I tried to focus on the titles of the books, but they were covered in clear plastic. All I could make out were some block letters and numbers on the base of their spines.

Library books!

The clatter of metal lids hitting the floor brought me out of my meditation, and an instant later, I felt a sharp pain in my thighs. As my eyes sprang open, I saw Lenore leap from my lap and dash down the hallway, bristling tail held high. I rubbed my hands against my thighs to ease the pain and closed my eyes again to recall what I'd envisioned.

Of course! If my Poe Puzzler wanted to taunt me with questions about Edgar Allan Poe, he'd need to do his homework. He could go to Sun Rose Words & Music on Asbury and buy some books about Poe, but that didn't seem to fit. I thought he'd more likely get the information for the riddles without the "baggage" of owning books. He might also search online. But if he really wanted to dive into the subject, he'd want to page through some books. And what better place to do that than at our local library? Maybe it was a long shot, but this could be a lead to discovering his identity.

Time to see if my friend Nicole, the assistant

librarian, would help me out.

"Now, Nathan, you know I can't do that. I can't reveal any of our patrons' borrowing information." Nickie and I were nestled in a quiet corner at the far end of the stacks in the Ocean City Public Library. We sat at a small table out of earshot of anyone else. I'd hoped she might bend the rules for me, but I guess librarians aren't known for being rule-benders.

"At the federal level, we have ECPA and FERPA restrictions," she continued, "not to mention New Jersey privacy laws and our own library policies." She tucked a lock of auburn hair behind an ear. Every time I saw Nicole, she had a different hair color.

She must have noticed my distraction, so I tried to bring the conversation back to layperson's terms. "Um, help me out with your acronyms, please, Nickie."

She clucked her tongue. "ECPA is the Electronic Communications Privacy Act, and FERPA, which may not apply in this case, stands for the Family Educational Rights and Privacy Act. These are federal laws, Nathan!"

I raised my palms in surrender. "Okay. Understood." Before I pressed further, I waited a moment for her to settle down. "Maybe there's a way around my request that doesn't break any laws ..."

She raised an eyebrow, but allowed me to continue without citing any more legal statutes.

"What if I asked you how many books you have in the catalog by and about Edgar Allan Poe?"

She shrugged. "I mean, you could find that out for yourself in our online catalog. Keep in mind, however, that many of our patrons request inter-library loans, so you'd have to consider the entire county-wide catalog. And a patron might just get their reference material from our shelves and have a good old-fashioned note-taking session in the library."

"That's fine, but let's assume for now he borrowed the books," I said. "So, let me take it one step further. Would you be able to tell me how many of these Poe books have been signed out or downloaded in the past few months?"

She pursed her lips, and I noticed her lipstick color was a pleasant complement to her hair. Nickie had been one of the best students in my English lit class more than fifteen years ago, and after I'd moved to town and found her working at the library, we'd gone from student/teacher to equal colleagues who shared a love of books. But I was getting distracted. "I guess what I'm asking is if you could work with me on this ... help me do the research?"

She shook her head, but I caught a slight smile at the corners of her mouth. Was "research" a librarian's secret password?

"I'd have to get permission from Jackie, our director." I could see the wheels turning in her brain. "If I helped you during my off hours ..."

I was pretty confident she'd sort it out. "Could you look into it, please? I've got my aqua therapy session in a few minutes, so I could stop by afterwards ... or maybe tomorrow?"

"Tomorrow is better." She sighed, but there was a definite sparkle in her eyes. "You owe me, Nathan. You know that, don't you?"

I smiled back at her. "You always were one of my favorite students, Nickie."

"That was a long time ago." She looked down, as if embarrassed for some reason. "It's taken me years to get used to calling you Nathan and not Mr. Poe. And, besides, as I recall, you had quite a few favorites."

"Only the best and the brightest!"

While this library research could be a dead-end, it just might lead me closer to the identity of my Poe Puzzler. Either way, it felt good to be following up on a lead ... even one from my imagination.

Chapter Eighteen
Group Therapy

The smell of chlorine was almost more than I could take. So was Brad, our therapy taskmaster.

"Okay, now backwards! A count of thirty. Let's go!" The cavernous pool room echoed his commands. No one could be a slacker on Brad's watch. As I'd learned in my first session, he would call you out. I've had a few tough therapists in the years since the accident. Some were more subtle, others more aggressive. They'd all helped me to one degree or another.

Aqua therapy was new to me, however, and I was just getting used to the routine. My doctor had recommended it, and since the Ocean City Community Center now housed a modern, well-maintained pool in addition to the library, the fates seemed to point me in that direction.

Long yellow ropes held up by floats ran the length of the pool, separating the lanes for the high-school swim club. Our aqua therapy class only used a small portion at the shallow end. For the comfort of non-swimmers, we never went beyond chest-deep.

About a dozen of us shared the pool that afternoon, and Brad paired us off, two per swim lane, as we came out of the locker rooms. I was joined by a 40-something woman who introduced herself as Tammy—no last name.

We were a motley bunch. Except for a young woman of high-school age, probably recovering from some sports injury, Tammy and I were the youngest ones there. I suppose most of the older folks were dealing with arthritis or balance issues.

Tammy was tall and graceful. She didn't seem to have any trouble getting into the water or doing the exercises, so I wondered what had brought her to aqua therapy. Then I saw the black wrist braces. I guessed she was there to deal with an issue with her arms. Of course, it would have been impolite to ask. Her modest black swimsuit had white and tan stripes running from shoulders to hips. They accentuated her height and complemented her complexion.

"Okay, now turn to your right—90 degrees—let's do some side-stepping." Brad continued to push us. "One and a breath, two and a breath. Count with me! If you need support, hold on to one of the ropes." We made our way in a strange conga line from the shallow end.

"So, I think I know who you are," Tammy said between breaths. Our hands almost touched as we grabbed the nylon rope to keep steady.

"Really? I'm sorry, but I don't recall ..."

"Now, back again!" Brad yelled to the group. We reversed direction and side-stepped back the way we'd come. My eyes were tearing up from all the chlorine in the water. We came to an awkward stop as my arm reached the tile coping at the shallow end.

"Good job, everyone!" Brad applauded. He took his job much too seriously. "Okay, that was a good workout. Let's take a few minutes to catch our breath. Good job!"

Tammy turned to face me as I pushed my back against the pool wall, glad for a momentary reprieve from the exercises. "Oh, other than our session last week, I don't think we've ever met in person," she said. "But you're Mr. Poe, the English teacher, aren't you?" It was then that I noticed the gold flecks in her dark eyes. They seemed to flash a warning.

"Yes. Retired now, but that's me." It wasn't unusual for me to come across former students or their parents in town, even though I'd taught in Linwood and not at Ocean City High. "Did your children go to Mainland Regional?"

Tammy's face darkened. "Not children. One son. But, yes, you were his English teacher there, I'm sure of it now."

Something about her tone put me on guard, so I tried to phrase my next words carefully. "I don't think I caught your last name ... or rather, what's your son's name?"

"Eli. Elijah Davis."

I flipped through my mental Rolodex but could not associate the name with any of my students. "When did he graduate?"

She glared at me. "He didn't. And I remember your name because he often told me how unfairly you'd treated him."

I felt my face redden. No appropriate response came

to me.

"You'll have to excuse me," she said as she ducked under the rope and waded to the pool ladder.

Brad started his rah-rah routine again. All I heard was a buzzing in my ears as I watched Tammy storm off to the women's locker room. Brad glanced her way but didn't react to her sudden departure.

I went through the motions for the rest of the session, feeling numb. Brad scolded me for not keeping up. I didn't care.

Tammy's words hurt. No matter how jaded teachers get, we all hold a golden kernel of hope deep inside that keeps us going. It's the hope that someday and in some way, we'll have made a positive impact on our students' lives. Teaching, according to some people, is a calling. Most teachers I know would pooh-pooh that term. I think it's more that we share an optimistic view of changing the world for the better, one student at a time.

For Eli Davis—and I still could not place him—I'd evidently failed.

Once I was home, I thought about going back to the library to look at the high school yearbooks. But if Eli hadn't graduated, he might not be in any of them. Juniors always get short shrift in yearbooks. So, I just sat at my office desk and Googled him: "Elijah Davis Linwood NJ." After a few dead ends, I found a posting— an old obituary from a local funeral home. He was 17 years old when he died, the summer between his junior and senior years.

The article didn't mention the cause of death, and that made me think it was drug-related or maybe suicide. My God, had I contributed to this?

I did the math in my head. He must have been in one of my last classes at Mainland Regional. Those months after losing Anna were a dead spot in my memory. I'd taken a short bereavement leave in January, but then finished the school term before taking early retirement. If Eli was in my class at that time ... well, God only knows how I'd treated him ... or anyone else that term.

A troubled student. A young man who thought I mistreated him. Why couldn't I remember him?

I closed my eyes and tried to picture my junior-year English classes, reaching into my memory. My mind's eye went row by row from the front of the classroom to the back. I remembered the bright kids, the ones who seemed to actually care about learning and their futures—Jacob, Ali, Taylor—they stood out. And there was that young woman in the back row who always had a chip on her shoulder. Chloe? I think that was her name...

I opened my eyes and stared at the obituary photo again. The memory hit me like a jolt of electricity. Elijah. A sullen kid who never finished his assignments. He'd nod off in class, and when I'd call on him, he'd just mumble in reply. Elijah Davis.

Did I ever ask if he needed help? Did I go to the guidance office and try to find out more about him, and why he acted that way ... to see if he needed counseling? No. I'd failed him. And now he was dead, from who knows what cause.

I let out a laugh that was more of a grunt. Had Eli not died, he would have been a perfect suspect for my Poe Puzzler.

Chapter Nineteen
Tea and Sympathy

The rest of the afternoon passed slowly. I putzed about the house, doing mundane chores, but found myself stopping in my tracks, staring off into nowhere. Rationally, I told myself, I didn't cause Eli's death. Had I contributed to it? Perhaps.

Tammy's anger was justified. But why had she waited four years to confront me? Was that the sole reason she'd joined the aqua therapy group? I could ask Brad, but he'd no doubt tell me it was personal information that he could not share. That was the state of things today, wasn't it? In trying to protect everyone's privacy, we were often kept from helping the people who needed it most.

Whatever apology I might give Tammy, it would probably mean little to her. Especially after all these years. It would only help me deal with my guilt. I had to do something. I couldn't deal with this ... this shame ... without some act of contrition. Maybe I could order one of those "in memory" plaques that are affixed to the benches on the boardwalk. That didn't seem right, though, especially since I didn't think Eli was from Ocean City.

My cell phone rang, bringing an end to my self-flagellation. I took a deep breath before answering. The caller ID told me it was Mrs. Murphy.

"I've been waiting patiently for your call," she said without introduction.

I drew a blank, then realized she was talking about her trash bins.

"I saw you out there this morning, you know. Sitting in your car while those nice young men brought our trash bins out to the curb. What were you hoping to accomplish?"

My morning stake-out seemed like a distant memory now. And so trivial. But Mrs. Murphy was a good client and a friend ... in her own unique way. "Yes, Mrs. Murphy. I was hoping to make some connection, to come up with some explanation for your ... you know, trash bin issue."

"Well, did you or didn't you?"

Time for another deep breath. I wasn't in any mental state to get into this. "Um, not really, at least not yet."

Silence on the line. Was her temper building, or was she giving me some space? I took the lead. "Look, I've got some issues to deal with today. I'll get back to you tomorrow. Promise!"

"Well, I certainly hope you can sort out your issues. Would you like to come over for some afternoon tea?"

The tea was tempting, but not with Mrs. Murphy. I had to put her off. "I appreciate that. I really do. No, I need to work through some things on my own. Is that okay?"

"Of course, Nathan." Her tone was more conciliatory now. "I'm sorry to bother you with my insignificant problems."

I hadn't pegged her as passive-aggressive, but this was getting close. Let it go, I told myself. "Thanks, Mrs. Murphy. I'll stop by tomorrow."

"Now, you take care of yourself, Nathan."

I almost laughed at that. "Right. Well, bye for now."

No sooner had I disconnected and put the phone down than it rang again. Please, save me! But it wasn't Mrs. Murphy calling back. It was Berni.

"Hey, Nathan. I was going to get some takeout, and I thought, why not share? Are you up for Chinese?"

"Yeah. Sure." Berni was always quick to read my moods, and I guess this time it was obvious.

"Whoa, you sound down. Did something happen?"

"In a manner of speaking." How could I explain over the phone? I forced a more positive response. "Chinese sounds good, Berni, but bring it over here, please. I'll set the table and make some tea."

"You got it. Moo Shu pork and Happy Family okay with you?"

God, the irony – happy family. "Yeah, that's fine. And thanks, Berni."

I pulled out a small wooden box containing my favorite oolong tea. It's a perfect complement to Chinese food. Too many takeout places give you bland, pre-packaged tea bags. I know the owner of a good Chinese restaurant in Somers Point, and I've talked him into selling me some of his best oolong—loose leaves, coarsely cut, and dried to perfection. It's a particularly flavorful oolong with a subtle flowery aroma and a darker than usual color, and it doesn't have the bitterness of green tea.

I set the table for two and tried to figure out how to explain the day's events to Berni.

White teacups with white saucers, a scattering of white takeout boxes, and white dishes strewn with rice, duck sauce, and tiny veggies—Berni and I had made a mess of my little kitchen table. She'd probably eaten twice as much as I had; I simply couldn't build up an appetite. Besides, I was doing all the talking.

She'd nodded and made affirmative noises to let me know she was taking it in ... along with all the beef, shrimp, baby corn, and water chestnuts in the Happy Family. I had a hard time even looking at that dish after I'd made the mental connection to Elijah Davis's very unhappy mother.

I stopped talking and waited to see how Berni would react. She didn't say anything for a while, so I grabbed one of the Chinese pancakes, spread some plum sauce on it, and rolled it up to chew on.

She swallowed a mouthful of food, took a sip of tea, and looked me in the eye. "So tell me this," she said. "In the high school where you taught, how many classes would a junior-level kid have?"

I raised my eyebrows, not sure where she was going with this. "I don't know, six or seven. Maybe more."

"So, Eli Davis probably had classes in algebra, history, some science like biology, and maybe a foreign language, Spanish or something, right? Not to mention Phys Ed."

"Sure. That would be a normal course load." My thinking was a bit foggy at that moment, so I didn't make the connection that Berni found so obvious. Then the lightbulb went off. "You're saying other teachers should've acted when they noticed what Elijah was going through, right?"

"Exactly, Sherlock! Or should I say Dupin?" She took another bite of the Happy Family, somehow managing to smile and chew at the same time. "I'm not trying to say you didn't mess up."

"Thanks, Berni. I really needed to hear that ... and watch your double-negatives."

She spoke with a mouth full of veggies. As thin as Berni is, she can eat like a trucker. "Every high school student comes in regular contact with a dozen or more teachers and counselors, not to mention close friends ... people who could've or should've helped this kid out. You don't have to take this weight on."

I wasn't buying it. "I know what you're trying to do, Berni, and I appreciate it. But that doesn't help me right now. I failed this kid when he needed me. His mother made that clear. And I can't excuse that."

She scrunched up her face and slowly shook her head back and forth like she was fighting to keep from saying something. Then it came out. "No! You can excuse that. You're feeling vulnerable right now, and this is a shock to you. I get that, Nathan. But here's the thing. You don't even know how this kid died. He could've been hit by a car. He could've been involved with a gang and gotten into some trouble. Maybe he overdosed. Any number of things could've brought about his death."

She paused, waiting for me to reply. Rationally, I knew she was right. Emotionally, I wasn't there.

"His death was tragic, Nathan. Any kid who dies is tragic. But it's not all on you to set the karmic wheels on track again."

"There's another part of this. Something that just occurred to me."

She blew a lock of hair away from her cheek and gave me a sad look. "What else, Nathan?"

"I know Eli isn't my Poe Puzzler ... couldn't be, since he died four years ago." I took a moment to gather my thoughts. "But if he'd lived, he could have been. He could've held a grudge about how I'd treated him."

"That's pretty wild reasoning, Nathan."

"Don't you see? How many other students did I treat badly that last semester at Mainland Regional? How many other kids' lives went downhill after graduation, with one bad turn after another, and all of it starting with a teacher who didn't give a damn or worse? I could've planted a lot of bad seeds."

Berni didn't reply. I'm not sure she could have said anything to ease my guilt. There was certainly guilt enough to spread among all of his teachers and friends and maybe even his parents. The way I saw it, we were all complicit. What I knew for sure is that I'd let down Elijah Davis. And it was a short leap of logic to realize I'd more than likely let down dozens of other students that last term.

I wiped my hands on my napkin and stood up, taking my dinner plate with me. "Those last few months teaching, well, I wasn't myself. I wasn't the best teacher. And it's tough with teenage boys. They're going through so much emotionally." I slid my plate into the sink and ran the hot water. The gushing sound from the faucet was soothing, like white noise.

Berni joined me with her dirty dish. "You wash, I'll dry," she said.

The mechanical motions of this mundane chore helped me allay my thoughts of death and guilt. I was working out a solution, not for Elijah Davis's mother, but more for me.

Once we'd cleared the table, put away the leftovers, and cleaned up our mess, Berni stood beside me again. She reached out and put a hand on my shoulder. "So, how are you going to deal with this? Are you going to contact Mrs. Davis ... if that's her name?"

I let out a ragged breath. "I don't know. That might not do any good." I placed my hand over hers. "This may be over the top, but I was thinking of setting up a small scholarship in Elijah Davis's name."

Her eyes went wide. It's not hard to read Berni's body language. I knew she'd try to talk me out of this idea. I didn't give her the chance. "Probably just a couple hundred dollars for the student who shows the most improvement in English," I said. "It would be anonymous. Tammy Davis wouldn't have to know it came from me."

Berni looked down, not meeting my eyes. She lifted

her hand from my shoulder and walked toward the door. "This is really half-baked," she said. "Not to mention the school would need her permission to use her son's name in this scholarship."

That set me back. "Maybe I haven't thought this through," I mumbled.

Berni rolled her neck, and I heard a soft crunching sound. "Well, here's the thing, Nathan, my friend. You'll likely see her again at your next aqua therapy session. Offer to buy her a cup of coffee and talk about Eli. Apologize and explain what you were going through at the time."

She must have seen the sour look on my face. I guess my body language was as obvious as hers.

"I know." She smirked. "Make it tea, not coffee."

That got a chuckle out of me.

She grabbed her jacket from the back of the chair and got ready to leave, then turned to face me at the door. "I hate to raise this now, but I have to."

"What is it?"

She looked at the floor, then brought her eyes up to mine, a wry smile at the corners of her lips. "Your Poe Puzzler's been quiet today. No notes. No bloody bottles on the beach. That doesn't fit the pattern."

"Yeah, that is odd."

When Berni left, I found myself at sixes and sevens. I thought about going back to my oil painting or working on my library presentation, but I wouldn't be able to focus. My mind was filled with a manic jumble of "what if" and "how come" and "why didn't I..."

The scholarship idea seemed less and less appropriate, and Berni's last comment suddenly took center stage—the Poe Puzzler had gone quiet. Up to that point, his riddles and taunts had been increasing in frequency. What could this silence mean?

I knew better than to think he was done with me. Placing that bottle in my path and then removing it not 30 minutes later was a nasty, premeditated deed, not least because it made me doubt my own sanity. After pulling that off, there was no way he was going to stop. If anything, he'd be emboldened.

So why was he waiting? And what would he do next?

These questions would play havoc with my sleep, but I was exhausted, so I made an early night of it and headed off to bed.

Chapter Twenty
Deflated

I awoke the next morning with a start. I rarely remember my dreams, but this one was vivid. My first conscious thought was to wonder what Mrs. G and her dream book would make of my nightmare. Was there anything in that thick volume of hers that could translate my strange imagery into something useful? Maybe it was all Freudian ... or even simpler than that.

In the dream, I was back at school, teaching a lesson on Classic American Literature. As students filed into my classroom, they placed their homework assignments on the corner of my desk. I pulled the top one from the stack and started to review it. But as I reached out my hand, I saw with horror that it wasn't a hand at all—it was a monster's paw. My students didn't seem to notice; it was all completely routine to them. After I'd read a few lines from a student's paper, I extended my claws and raked the paper to shreds. I flung it aside, grabbed the next paper, and did the same with it, ripping it apart. The scene repeated, over and over—no drama, no reaction from my students, just my willful destruction of their work.

It was obvious what my subconscious was trying to say. I had been a monster, not the good teacher I'd thought I was. That wasn't true, not really, not for most of my teaching career. But the last term after Anna's death, well, I'm not sure who I was.

Dreams are fine for creative inspiration. Ask any writer. But I don't consider them as anything more than your mind at play while you're sleeping. Maybe that's because I don't remember very many, or because my brain works more rationally ... usually.

I forced these musings to the back of my mind, got up, and got ready to visit Mrs. Murphy. I'd promised I'd be over first thing to talk to her about the Trash Bin Mystery and what I'd seen of the Bin Busters. After feeding Lenore—that always comes first—I took a shower and donned my jeans and the first clean shirt I pulled from my closet.

Mrs. Murphy always appreciated proper etiquette, so some sort of food offering was in order. It would be an insult to bring her store-bought scones. That was her domain, and I daren't tread there. Fortunately, there's a nearby cafe, Positively 4th Street, that makes exceptional muffins.

While I was still rattled by my curious nightmare, the cobwebs of sleep had been swept away, and my rational mind started to take control. I could even put aside my appetite for muffins.

The more I thought about the events of yesterday, the less sense they made. Something was off about the whole Elijah Davis scenario. It was like trying to force a jigsaw puzzle piece where it wouldn't fit. Why did Tammy Davis wait four years to confront me? Was it just a coincidence that she was in my aqua therapy class ... or premeditated?

I decided to contact Brad, my therapy coach, and ask him about her. Of course, I couldn't just come out and say, "Hey Brad, is Tammy legit? Does she really have something wrong with her?" I noodled that one for a moment, then crafted an email using a hypothetical.

"Just a quick question for you, Brad. Do you need a doctor's referral or a prescription to join our aqua therapy group? I had a prescription, but is it required? Let me know, please."

I hit "send," and was about to close my laptop when I saw an email from Berni. It was brief, just telling me she had an interesting idea, and we'd talk later. That piqued my curiosity, but I had other priorities.

The day was bright and cloudless. As soon as I stepped off the porch, however, I shivered in the salt-tinged ocean breeze. Back inside for a jacket.

My second attempt at facing the morning ended even worse. When I unlocked my Saab and sat in the driver's seat, something felt wrong. My car was sitting at an odd angle, the hood on the passenger side tilted down. I got out, walked around to the car, and spotted the reason— the right front tire was completely flat. How had I missed it getting into the car? And how was I supposed to drive to Positively 4th Street and get those blueberry muffins now?

I stood there, calculating how long it would take to change the tire versus how displeased Mrs. Murphy would be at my tardiness. That's when I noticed something red stuffed between the spokes of the front wheel. So, he's at it again.

The wheels on my Saab have 10 spokes, unlike the usual five on most models. That makes them harder to clean ... not that I wash my car very often. In this case, it meant retrieving the note from between the wheel and the brakes would not be easy, especially without tearing the paper.

I was about to squeeze my fingers into the tiny space between the spokes when a thought struck me. If my Poe Puzzler had slashed the tire, I could call Patrolman Bob and make a formal complaint. Simply deflating the tire, on the other hand, would probably be considered a prank or nuisance, nothing worth bothering the police about.

I felt all around the tire's tread and sidewall, even reaching under the car, for evidence of willful damage, but came up empty. Now that my hands were covered in road grime, brake dust, and greasy schmutz, it was easier to have a devil-may-care approach to pulling the note out. All I needed was patience—something that was in short supply.

Some mild cursing and scraped fingers ensued before I held the folded red note in my filthy hands. My right leg was aching from crouching down, and since I was no longer concerned about cleanliness, I sat on the curb, wet with morning dew, and opened the crumpled note. After the bloody bottle incident, I didn't know what to expect. But it seemed my Poe Puzzler was back to his earlier, more literary form.

The message was direct: "For you: 'I remained without motion. And why? I could not summon the courage to move. I dared not make the effort which was to satisfy me of my fate.'"

There was no call to action—no P.O. box or other instructions. This was purely a test of my knowledge of Poe's works, matching wits with my Puzzler. Of course, I knew it was from "The Premature Burial." Even a novice could have figured that out. The Puzzler's message continued the dark themes of his earlier notes. That's easy with Poe—dark themes are prominent in almost all his works.

There was also some wry humor here, though. The flat tire ... forcing my car to "remain without motion." Perhaps, just perhaps, my Moriarty enjoyed a dry joke. Or was I ascribing far too pleasant an attribute to my nemesis?

Lost in thought, I failed at first to notice the dark shadow appearing on the fender above me. As I looked up, a chill ran down my spine. No, this can't be. Then I heard my neighbor's unmistakable voice behind me. "Bad man, again?" I closed my eyes and let out a ragged breath.

"Yes, Mrs. G. I would say it's definitely the 'bad man' again."

With a grunt, I got up from the curb, stuffed the rumpled note into my jacket pocket, and brushed my palms together in a futile attempt to clean them. Mrs. G stepped back. "You look like mess," she said.

Rather than respond, I shook my head.

A slow smile spread across her face, and she spoke in a sing-song voice. "I bet you dream last night ..."

I closed my eyes and contemplated the long conversation that would ensue. "Yes, yes, you got me on that one, Mrs. G. I had a bad dream."

"Aha!" She stomped a foot on the sidewalk, obviously pleased with herself. "You tell me!"

I rubbed a hand across my face, unaware that I was quickly becoming unpresentable, especially for meeting with Mrs. Murphy.

Mrs. G tilted her head to one side and pointed at me. "You really look like mess now." I started to reach up a hand to wipe my face again until I realized it would only spread the dirt around. Patience ...

"Here's the thing, Mrs. G. I'm late for an appointment."

She raised an eyebrow in disbelief.

"Um, it's with Mrs. Murphy."

"Oh. Her." The two ladies were cordial to each other, but didn't see eye to eye.

"I told her I'd come over first thing, and then I forgot my jacket, and then the flat tire, and now..." I took a good look at my dirty hands. "And now, I'm a mess. As you said."

She folded her arms across her ample bosom, waiting for me to continue tying myself into knots.

"I'll come see you this afternoon. I promise."

She gave me a hard stare, like she was looking into my soul for signs of subterfuge. "Okay. You promise."

With that, she turned on her heels and walked back to her front porch. But it didn't end there. With one hand on her doorknob, she turned to stare at me again. "You promise!" she shouted.

Back inside I went, pulling off my jacket, jeans, and shirt. The jacket was still presentable, so I brushed it off and draped it over a kitchen chair, then undressed and put my jeans and shirt into the washer. I scrubbed my hands and face in the bathroom, donned another pair of jeans and a clean shirt, and almost walked out the door when I remembered I needed some sort of breakfast treat for Mrs. Murphy. I thought about calling her, but I didn't want to hear her retributions. Actions would be better than words.

All I had in the house were my reliable spiced wafers, which paled in comparison to the blueberry muffins I'd been anticipating. They would have to do, but I needed to dress them up so Mrs. Murphy wouldn't look askance at them. Pulling a chair close to the refrigerator, I climbed up, good leg first, and rummaged around in an upper cabinet until I found what I was looking for—a Lenox china candy dish with gilded edges. It must have been a gift from someone or a thrift-shop buy.

I arranged a handful of spiced wafers on the dish and draped it in plastic wrap, then stood back to examine my handiwork. It still wasn't right. A search through my collection of wrapping paper in the hall closet came up with some green tissue paper. Wrapping the whole affair like a present might make Mrs. Murphy more likely to forgive my tardiness.

With my mostly clean jacket back on—it was still

chilly out—and the tissue-wrapped Lenox dish in hand, I greeted the morning for the third time. I tried very hard not to look at my Saab's flat tire as I walked down the block to explain all the reasons for being late to my Number One client.

Mrs. Murphy was waiting on her front porch. Not a good sign. "Some of us have a different definition of 'first thing,'" she said, hands on her hips.

"I'm sorry, but you wouldn't believe what I've gone through this morning." We locked eyes, and I waited for some sign of sympathy. "I got a flat tire, and then I got all dirty trying to sort that out, and then … well, I never got to Positively 4th Street for blueberry muffins." I decided not to mention the Puzzler's latest note. No need to get into that discussion. The silence between us dragged, but a subtle shift in her expression told me she was softening up.

"I'm sorry you had a difficult time of it this morning, Nathan, I really am." She glanced down at what I was carrying. "But it looks like you brought me a peace offering." The green tissue paper ended up being my best move that morning. "Well, let's not stand here putting manners on each other. Come inside." She opened the door and stood aside for me to enter. "Mind you, I've already turned off the kettle, I've been waiting that long."

I let her get the last word—always a good idea with Mrs. Murphy.

Her kitchen table was picture perfect, with a green-and-white checked tablecloth, two dessert plates, cups and saucers, plus cloth napkins—cloth! She placed my Lenox dish in the center, and I was pleased to see the tissue paper complemented her colors.

"I know you're particular about these things, Nathan, so I bought some Twinings Scottish Breakfast Tea. Will that do?"

"Absolutely," I said. "In fact, it's one of my favorites."

"Well, of course I prefer Irish breakfast tea." She paused with a look of contemplation on her face, as if formulating a grand philosophical statement. "I think the Scottish tea has a bit more of an edge to it, if you know what I mean. Just like the Scots, I'd say."

I let that pass. The last thing I wanted to do was get into a discussion with her on the Scots versus the Irish.

Once we'd had some tea and I'd devoured four spiced wafers to Mrs. Murphy's one, I gave her a progress report on The Great Trash Bin Mystery. She wasn't pleased.

"So you're telling me you've come up short, is that it? And you haven't even looked into Jacob Weiszman's senility." Sometimes she was like a dog with a bone.

I ignored the Mr. Weiszman comment and tried to explain my thinking. "I'm still sorting things out, and I need more time, but I believe your trash bin situation may be more far-reaching."

That earned a raised eyebrow.

"I don't want to go into details until I have more evidence. You may not be the only one who's had their trash bins meddled with."

"Well, that sounds highly unlikely, Nathan. I mean, I would have heard something from my neighbors. Of course, the McErleans across the way aren't talking to me anymore, and I can only get a nod or a mumbled 'good morning' from that Mary Polanski. Still …"

"Give me more time, please." I searched her face for some encouragement. "I think there's more here than meets the eye … maybe."

She crossed her arms and raised her eyes toward the ceiling. "You do what you need to do, Nathan." Her gaze lowered to make direct eye contact. "But you know I'm not much for conspiracy theories."

I covered my laugh with a fake cough. Mrs. Murphy and conspiracy theories were like bread and Irish butter—impossible to have one without the other.

Chapter Twenty-One
Coming in Handy

I've been called a bookworm and an academic. I wear those labels proudly. But I'm also pretty handy at do-it-yourself projects. Repairing a damaged bookcase, replacing electrical fixtures, and changing a flat tire are, if not a cinch, certainly easy enough for me. In fact, I enjoy seeing the physical results of this kind of practical labor. It's a pleasant change from my more cerebral pursuits.

Since I don't have AAA, it was time to dig out my work clothes and change the flat tire on my Saab. The thought of "work clothes" was ironic. That used to mean a button-down shirt and a tie. Now it meant ripped jeans I couldn't bear to throw out yet, and an oil-stained flannel shirt. How many times was I going to change my clothes?

Fully attired in an outfit I didn't mind getting dirty, I stood in front of the offending tire and mentally calculated each step. Then got to work.

I pulled the emergency blanket, my P.I. kit, and a steel pipe from the trunk, lifted the trunk floor panels, and gathered up the jack, lug wrench, and tools from their Styrofoam holder. The temporary spare was more troublesome. I had to bend way over and reach in for it. Maybe I should consider AAA membership.

With everything laid out at the front of the car, I draped the blanket on the pavement and the curb, more for cushioning than cleanliness. After some contortions while positioning the jack in the right spot, I cranked it up just enough to make sure it was secure. Now comes the hard part, I thought.

It's not so much that the factory lug wrench isn't long enough; it's more that most tire stores use those noisy impact wrenches to tighten the lug nuts so no mere mortal can loosen them. Having faced this problem in the past, I was prepared. I carry a two-foot length of steel water pipe in the trunk. What was it Archimedes said? "Give me leverage and I will move the world!"

I slipped my Archimedes-inspired pipe over the lug wrench and gave it some muscle. Sure enough, the lug nuts came loose. Crank up the jack, off with the flat, on with the "donut" spare, tighten things up, and lower the car back down—ready to go. Almost. Hefting the full-size wheel and tire into the trunk sent a twinge of pain down my spine. Maybe Brad could recommend some aqua therapy exercises to ease that tightness in my back. I replaced the metal pipe and wrapped the blanket around everything.

Rather than take the flat to a local service station, I

texted Berni to ask if she had an air compressor to reinflate the tire. A quick thumbs-up emoji confirmed it.

While I could get by with torn jeans without being too embarrassed if I ran into someone I knew, the oil-stained shirt had to go. Back inside for another shirt, this time short-sleeved since it was getting a little warmer. Still, I threw my jacket into the back seat, just in case.

One of the joys of off-season Ocean City is the ability to park just about anywhere … except maybe on Asbury, which is crowded year-round. Berni's shop is at the South End of the island, so I pulled up to the bay door in the back alley without issue. The door was wide open, a hip-hop tune was blaring, and I caught the acrid smell of oil and hot metal. Berni was hard at work.

I popped the trunk, wrapped the blanket around the tire so I wouldn't get too dirty, heaved the thing out, dropped it by the door ... and stood there, transfixed. Deep into her project, Berni was oblivious to my presence. She had a rusty bicycle sprocket secured in the vise at her workbench, and held a ball-peen hammer in one hand and a butane torch in the other.

Watching her alternately heat the bearing in the rusty sprocket and then tap it with the hammer was fascinating. I'm not sure where she'd learned her skills, but Berni knew every aspect of bicycle repair. And I was reassured to see her wearing safety goggles and leather-palmed gloves.

She performed this heat-and-tap process over and

over. What patience! She was so immersed in her work, she probably didn't notice the glowing fibers on the back of one of her gloves. Couldn't she feel it?

I hesitated a moment, but when the covering started to blacken and smoke, I yelled out to her.

She dropped the hammer and turned to me. That's when the torch in her other hand ignited an oily rag on the workbench. Finally aware of the danger, she extinguished the torch, set it on the bench, and tried to tamp out the rag with her gloved hands. That just made it worse. The fire spread and engulfed the entire rag in flames.

They say time slows down in an emergency. In this case, everything happened fast.

I ripped the blanket off my flat tire and rushed toward Berni, half stumbling over a bike frame. She stood there paralyzed, a dull look in her eyes as she stared at her charred gloves and the burning rag.

Somewhere deep inside me, my old Red Cross training took over. I wrapped the blanket around her hands, held them tight for a moment, then looked around for some way to starve the oily rag of oxygen.

Berni had to have a fire extinguisher somewhere. She was always so safety-conscious. I glanced under the workbench. Nothing there but more tools and spare parts. Now I was frantic, my eyes tearing up from the oily smoke. But it was right in front of me on the pegboard. I grabbed it, pulled the pin, and sprayed the rag. Tears ran down Berni's face, either from pain or smoke. She started to say something, but I couldn't make it out over the ringing in my ears.

I had no idea what shape her hands were in, but I had to be sure her gloves weren't still burning. Grabbing her by the waist, I led her outside to a garden hose by the shop door. I soaked the blanket with water, then carefully pulled it from her gloved hands and ran more water over them. It took me a moment to figure out why the water spray kept moving up and down—my hands were shaking that badly.

Afraid that her skin might peel if I removed the gloves, I thought it best to leave them on. Did I do the right thing? Would my actions cause scars on her hands? In the moment, I just wanted to eliminate any chance of more fire.

Berni finally spoke up. "You saved me, Nathan. That could have been really bad."

Now my eyes were watering. "I hope I didn't make it worse."

What a strange turnabout. She put her arms around me and hugged me.

"It's okay, Berni. You've saved me any number of times. It's the least I could have done."

I felt her body shake with either laughter or relief. As comforting as that hug was, I knew there was more we had to do.

"Berni." I pulled away and held her by the shoulders. "Do you have a first-aid kit? Or gel packs for burns?"

She still wasn't thinking clearly; I could see it in her eyes. Maybe she was in shock.

"Berni. A gel pack for burns. You have to have them in the shop."

She tilted her head, eyes wide. "I must," she said.

I ran back to her workbench, searching the shelves, opening cabinets and drawers. The music was still blaring. Finally, I found a red zippered pouch stenciled with "First Aid" next to a stack of repair manuals. The zipper came undone when I tore it open. Never mind. There they were—burn gel packets. I grabbed two, but before I took them to Berni, I yanked the plug on her boom box.

I first met Berni when we were in group therapy together, about four years ago.

We were a gloomy lot. No one smiled. No one looked at anyone else. Since this was the start of a new group, the therapist called our names, one by one, and told us to introduce ourselves. When he said, "Bernadette, tell us about you," she replied, "Please, call me Berni."

Ah, a kindred spirit.

Once it was my turn, and I said, "Please, call me Nathan," Berni smiled at me. It was the first ray of sunshine I'd felt since the accident ... since Anna's death.

I was at "group" after months of grief counseling. Berni's situation was similar—her mom had died in a house fire. It was complicated. Her father was no longer in the picture. Her mother lived alone and was probably clinically depressed; I'm not sure. I do know she was an alcoholic and a smoker.

Berni had tickets to a show in Atlantic City that fateful night. It was her first date with a woman she'd met at the gym. She'd promised her mom she'd stay over afterwards. But she and the date really hit it off, and they ended up at a motel.

You can imagine the rest. If Berni were there, she might have saved her mother from the fire. Or she might have died with her mom. That kind of thinking can haunt you for the rest of your life.

I draped my jacket over Berni's shoulders and eased her into the passenger seat of my Saab before closing up her shop. She insisted that she didn't want to go to the ER, so I took off for the urgent care facility in Marmora.

Chapter Twenty-Two
An Illuminating Lunch

The clinic took forever with Berni. I'd paged through all the months-old magazines in the reception area, and watched several patients come and go after Berni had been led into an exam room. I stood and paced between the chairs, sat down again, and idly scrolled through photos on my phone, trying to kill time.

My frustration was interrupted by a text from Patrolman Bob. He had some news for us and wanted to meet at Yianni's Cafe on Asbury in thirty minutes. I sent a terse reply about Berni's injuries. After expressing his concern, he suggested I call when we were leaving Marmora.

Berni wore a half-hearted smile, but looked pale as the nurse led her back into the reception room. Both her hands were covered with white bandages. I almost dropped my phone in my haste to get up from the chair and go to her.

"It's okay, Nathan. You did the right thing."

"She's right," the nurse said. "When she first came in, I was about to call an ambulance to take her to Shore Memorial. But you followed all the right steps for burns with water and gel packs."

That praise didn't sit well with me. By calling out to Berni when she had the torch in her hand, I was partly to blame for the fire.

Berni had her own recriminations to work through. "I don't know why I didn't have a bucket of water by the bench," she said. "I always do when I'm working with a torch."

Better for both of us to deal with the present rather than dwell on the past. "So, what happens now?" I asked the nurse.

"They're first-degree burns on the backs of her hands. Her palms were obviously protected," she explained. "I applied ointment that should help the healing process and prevent the bandages from sticking. She'll need over-the-counter pain medication."

"Oh, I can handle it alright," Berni said. Always the brave one!

"Just keep the area clean and dry for a few days," the nurse continued, "and change the bandage daily. And as I said, avoid breaking the blisters. Come back if the pain worsens or if there appears to be an infection."

I thanked the nurse, put my arm around Berni, and led her toward the door. We were halfway out when the nurse came running. "You forgot your jacket!"

In all the excitement, my jacket ... and the note inside the front pocket ... were the last things on my mind.

By the time we walked into Yianni's, Bob was on his second cup of coffee. He was seated in a booth near the back, conspicuous in his police uniform. We'd tried to park on Asbury, but ended up in the lot on Central, across from the Police Department. It was easy enough to walk through an alley to the cafe.

Bob rose from his seat. "Let's see the burn victim," he said. He's not much for tact sometimes.

Berni walked over and showed him her bandaged hands. "It could have been worse. Nathan did a good job administering first aid."

"In much pain?" He asked.

"Not bad." She always seemed to downplay her discomfort.

An awkward moment passed with Bob looking at Berni's hands and me standing there like a sphinx. I kept waiting for him to say something sympathetic.

"Come on, sit down." He motioned for us to join him, then waved to get a waiter's attention. "We should order first and then talk. It's well past lunchtime."

Yianni's menu was as colorful as their decor. Tantalizing photos of pasta, burgers, crab cakes, and gyros made any luncheon choice tough, but I'd always enjoyed their chicken and cheese quesadillas. And they brewed real iced tea, none of that weak powdered-mix stuff. Berni ordered a Veggie Burger Delight and a Green Power smoothie. At least she wouldn't need a knife and fork for that. Bob picked a bowl of homemade chili with cheese, onions, and sour cream. I guess he was hungry, too.

As we waited for our food, I decided that recounting my day's adventures—starting with the flat tire and the Poe Puzzler note—could wait. I wanted to hear what Bob had to say, but he seemed fidgety. Berni got things started. "So, I texted Bob this morning and asked him to look into Eli Davis's death," she said. I had no idea she was doing some sleuthing on her own.

"Yeah," Bob said, "I wasn't sure I'd get anywhere, but it was worth a try. I found some info in our database and then got in touch with a Trooper friend in the Cape May barracks. That hit pay dirt."

Now he had my attention. "So, what did you find out?" I asked.

"Elijah P. Davis was killed in a one-car accident on the south end of the Garden State Parkway, near Cape May Courthouse. As you told me, Berni, it was in July, five years back. The accident occurred at around 2:00 a.m."

The implications started to sink in. It wasn't an overdose or gangs. But it could be suicide.

"What do you mean by a one-car accident?" Berni asked.

"The official accident report said that apparently no other cars were involved. He lost control of his car and ran off the road into a tree. They estimated he was driving over a hundred miles an hour."

"You're using some wiggle words, Bob." A slight smile on his face told me there was more to come.

"You're right, Nathan. And that's why I wanted to

talk to my buddy in Cape May. He remembered it well. And he said there was more to it than the accident report indicated."

"Well, come on, Bob, don't keep us in suspense," Berni said.

"Okay. Okay." He took a deep breath and held it a moment. "This is between us, got it?"

"Of course." Berni and I spoke at the same time. She smiled at me, then turned her attention back to Bob.

"So ... Eli Davis was part of a group of high school kids that were into street racing. They all had hopped-up cars, like turbocharged Subarus and VW GTIs. There was a strong suspicion that he was racing another kid when he lost control and ran off the Parkway. You know, like Harrison Ford in American Graffiti."

"Wow ..." Berni couldn't hold back her emotions. "Did they ever find out who was racing with him?"

"No, but as I said, they had their suspicions. Nothing they could prove, though." Bob rubbed the back of his neck.

"Was he drinking or high?" I asked.

Bob frowned and scratched his chin. He always looked like he needed a new razor. "There was a tox report, but like the rest of the accident details, it was subject to interpretation. The kid's body was pretty badly burned. Eli was definitely over the blood-alcohol limit, though. Anything beyond that was inconclusive." He glanced at his watch. "Sorry, guys. I've got to get back. I just wanted to give you the low-down."

He waved to our waiter and made some cryptic gestures to signal he wanted his lunch to go. He eats at

Yianni's a lot. "You okay picking up the tab, Nathan?"

"Sure. No problem." Bob is a master at never paying for a meal.

He looked like he was about to get up until I protested. "Wait! Before you go, I've got to tell you about the latest note from my Poe Puzzler."

I could see the indecision on his face, but when the waiter handed him his to-go box, it was all over. The hearty scent of hot chili with all the fixings swirled around us. "Let's catch up later." He slid out of our booth and disappeared through the kitchen entrance.

I was crestfallen. However, that feeling only lasted until our waiter placed the quesadilla in front of me. Its crispy, golden shell oozed melted cheese. My stomach growled. Everything else would have to wait.

The conversation died while we ate, and in a very short time, there was nothing left on my plate except bits of shredded lettuce. Berni, on the other hand, had hardly touched her veggie burger. At least she'd slurped down the last drops of her smoothie.

"So, what do you think about Eli Davis now?" She gave me one of her searching looks. "I can't see how you're in any way responsible for his death."

That seemed to let me off too easily. "Well, no ... but it's still a jolt to my ... I don't know, maybe my pride as a teacher that I let him down."

Berni banged a hand on the table and immediately winced, realizing too late what she'd done. She recovered quickly, though, and began to lecture me. "I don't know what your problem with this is, Nathan. The kid hit a tree driving like an idiot on the Parkway. That's not your fault! Get out of this funk."

Her vehemence surprised me, and I raised my hands in surrender. "Okay, Berni. I get it." I picked up my fork and absently pushed the lettuce around on my plate. "It's not about me. I'm not to blame." Trying to put my feelings into words, I tapped my fork against the plate. "So, why was Tammy Davis—Eli's mother—so upset with me?"

"Who knows? Lots of reasons, I suppose." Berni spoke just above a whisper. "She's still dealing with her grief. Maybe she found someone she could lash out at. Besides herself, that is. You can understand that, can't you? I know I can."

It was time to put an end to this conversation.

"Come on," I said. "Let's get back to your place and get you some pain meds."

"Wait a minute. What about the Puzzler—the new note you mentioned? Do you have it with you?"

I grinned. "As the Good Witch Glinda said to Dorothy, 'You've always had the power, my dear.'"

Berni gave me a wide-eyed look. She obviously hadn't seen The Wizard of Oz as many times as I had.

"My jacket. The one that's been draped over your shoulders for the past couple of hours."

She still didn't make the connection.

"I stuffed the note in my jacket pocket when I pulled it from the flat tire. It seems ages ago now."

"Oh. Wow. Let me read it." Again, she moved too fast. She flinched as she stuck her bandaged right hand into the jacket pocket. Either the pocket was too small or her bandages were too large.

I got out of my seat and rushed over to her side. "Really, it can wait. There's nothing new in the note. Just another classical allusion to my might-be ancestor."

My humor wasn't working. I couldn't even get a lopsided grin out of her. "Just take it out and read it to me," she said.

I retrieved the ripped and crumpled note, getting my hands dirty in the process. "The quote is from The Premature Burial, and the note is not addressed to me specifically, but it begins, 'For you' – kind of strange, isn't that? Anyhow, here's what it says: 'I remained without motion. And why? I could not summon the courage to move. I dared not make the effort which was to satisfy me of my fate.'"

"Sounds pretty ominous to me."

"I guess I'm getting numb to all this."

She shook her head and let out a long breath. "Okay. That's for another time. Get me home, please."

Chapter Twenty-Three
What Kind Monster You Are?

Once we got back to Berni's, I helped her climb the stairs to her apartment and got some ibuprofen from the bathroom cabinet. She sat at her small kitchenette table while I brewed chamomile tea. "You must be exhausted," I said.

"I'm doing okay," she replied.

Her pale complexion belied her words. Berni is quite the stoic.

Conversation ceased as I made the tea, stirring in local honey to give it more flavor. I'm not a fan of most herbal teas. Chamomile is the exception; however, good for calming the nerves or as a gentle tonic before bedtime. Once the tea looked strong enough—it's hard to tell with chamomile—I placed the teacup in front of her.

She downed the pills and sipped her tea, holding the cup with her two bandaged hands. We both let the minutes pass in silence. I decided to wait until she was finished to speak up. She beat me to it.

"You don't have to stay with me, you know. I'll be okay."

How did she know I was going to offer to do just that? Most people don't say what they really mean. Not so with Berni. I could always take her words at face value. Still, this didn't sit right with me.

"I'm not sure you'll be okay by yourself," I said. "We should probably redo your bandages later this evening and ..."

A wan smile and subtle toss of her head told me this argument was going nowhere. "Here's the deal, Nathan, my friend. You know I appreciate the offer, but I want some time alone. Maybe I'll lie down on the couch for a while and just chill."

"What about after that? How will you call for help with your hands all wrapped up?"

She lifted her purse from the floor and pulled out her phone. Because of her bandages, she struggled at first, but I never saw her flinch. She was either a very good actor or the painkillers were working. "See?" she said, wiggling her fingers in the air. "My hand may be bandaged, but my fingers work just fine. Besides, my friend Kathy's an RN ... you've met Kathy, no? I'll call her when her shift is done and ask her to tend to my wounds."

"You're really sure, Berni?"

"I'm really sure, Nathan." Her smile was genuine.

"Okay, let's get you comfortable." I walked over and gently eased back her chair. "Come on. Your couch beckons."

She shuffled toward the couch like an old lady, then

stood up straight and put on a false smile. "I'm not an invalid, Nathan," she said. "I can function just fine on my own."

"Yeah, sure." I fluffed up a pillow on the couch and motioned for her to lie down. "Let's be honest. You're not the best patient, Berni. Try to relax. Sleep is the best healer." I covered her with an old quilt she had draped on the back of the couch. "I'll call you later tonight. Text me if you need anything ... as you so aptly demonstrated, your fingers work just fine. Okay?"

"Okay, Dr. Nathan."

"Seriously, Berni, if you need anything at all, just let me know."

"I will," she mumbled and closed her eyes. I wanted to bend down and kiss her forehead, a surprisingly paternal urge. Instead, I brushed back a lock of her hair. By the time I'd walked to her door, she was breathing softly.

There were a few things I wanted to take care of before I left. First, I went into her shop, took the charred rag from her workbench, threw it on the pavement, and thoroughly soaked it using the garden hose. There were no glowing embers, but I didn't want to tempt fate. Next, I loosened the vise and dumped the bicycle sprocket into her metal recycling bucket. Maybe inanimate objects can't be jinxed, but why take the chance?

My flat tire was the last item to deal with. Rather than start up the noisy air compressor or just leave it for Berni to inflate, I hoisted it back into the trunk of my Saab and wrapped the blanket around it. As Berni said when we'd left Yianni's, "That's for another time."

It was late afternoon by the time I got home and eased my car to the curb. Quite a day! So, when I walked up to my front porch, the last thing I wanted to see was another note, this one lodged in my screen door. What now? I thought. Even though it was white rather than red, I still felt a shiver of trepidation as I pulled the note free and opened it. Not to worry, though—the small, looping cursive was unmistakable.

"Mr. Nathan. You come over. I make csirke leves."

Dear Mrs. G! I had no idea what csirke leves was, or even how to pronounce it, but it was probably some kind of Hungarian food, and that sounded good to me. Before I could indulge in her exquisite cuisine, however, I had to take another shower and change my clothes. At this rate, I was going through laundry like a high school football team.

"You sit," Mrs. G informed me. "We talk later."

While I rarely go against her bidding, I was drawn to the stove by the tempting smells wafting from a large soup pot.

The meaty aroma of chicken was just an undertone. What caught my olfactory senses more strongly was the sweet smell of cooked onions ... and maybe parsnips. When I asked about the pale-yellow chunks floating at the top, she told me they were kohlrabi. Not a vegetable I was familiar with, but it seemed to add an earthy note.

And with Mrs. G, there are always extra spices, so I wasn't surprised to see the cut-off stem and pointy tip of a wicked-looking pepper on the counter.

I stepped back a few paces while she continued cooking. She raised the heat and soon a light-colored foam began to form on the surface of the soup. With quick, practiced motions, she picked up a teacup from the counter and skimmed the foam away, emptying it into the sink. I leaned in closer to see the result. The broth was now a clear, golden brown. And if anything, it was even more aromatic.

"That smells great, Mrs. G. Is it some kind of Hungarian chicken soup?"

She huffed out a breath, obviously perturbed by my question. "Csirke leves!" As if everyone should understand that meant chicken soup.

"Help me pronounce it."

She eyed me, maybe to make sure I wasn't joking. "Okay," she said. "Like this – cheer, ke, lev, esh."

I tried it. That brought a smile to her face. "Not bad for English boy." She returned to her culinary ministrations. "Now go sit. Not done yet."

Heaven knows I'm not a neat person, but my house is relatively uncluttered. That's not the case with Mrs. G's home.

Her living room is about the same size as mine, but it felt much smaller. Her overstuffed couch, loveseat, and an enormous china cabinet reduced the floor space to a narrow aisle between the furniture. And every square inch of wall was covered with pictures.

While I'd been in her home before, I'd never had the chance to really examine things without her looking over my shoulder. So while she was occupied in the kitchen, I did a quick circuit of the room.

There were gilt-framed prints of famous landscape paintings—from the Hudson River School of artists, I believe—dramatic and romanticized images of nature untouched by humankind. Several faded photos were probably of her Hungarian ancestors. Each picture showed a man with a full mustache seated in the foreground and a woman standing behind him, her hand on his shoulder. No smiles, just wide-eyed stares. No one looked happy.

Small shelves with ornate flower vases dotted the walls, with wall sconces on either side holding thin wax tapers. She even had one of those pseudo-Colonial barometers on the wall – the kind that's shaped like a banjo. A miniature red, white, and green Hungarian flag was tucked behind it.

The display of wall art ended at the china cabinet, a tall, imposing piece made of dark wood. It must have weighed a ton. In addition to carved cabinet doors and solid-looking drawers with ornate silver hardware, two glass enclosures on either end presented another opportunity for Mrs. G to display her keepsakes. Inside each were Lladro figurines of country girls with lambs or ducklings.

I'd almost completed my survey of all this when I noticed a more modern photo on the wall between the china cabinet and the hallway—a place of prominence. It pictured a man wrapped in chains, gazing up at the camera. I was pretty sure it was a promotional photo of Harry Houdini. What a strange addition to her landscapes and family photos.

"He was Magyar." As usual, I was startled by Mrs. G coming up behind me. How does she do that? After the brief shock of her appearance, I gathered my wits enough to ask what she meant.

"You mean Harry Houdini was actually Hungarian?"

"Mm-mm. Hungarian Jew. Name was Weisz. Father was rabbi." She could be a real fount of knowledge sometimes.

"I always thought he was Italian," I said.

"No. He was Magyar. Man of mystery. Just like you. Ha!"

I couldn't be sure if that interjection was a joke, a compliment, or a slight. You never know with Mrs. G. But I didn't have time to ponder that thought before she announced, "Soup ready. You sit and eat now."

I could have had a third helping, but Mrs. G whisked away my bowl and cleared the table before I could ask for more. What an incredible meal! Nothing from Lipton and Campbell comes close. This was chicken soup, ne plus ultra.

Sitting in a blissful state of satiation, my mind a blank, I was totally unprepared for Mrs. G's question.

"You tell me, what kind monster you are?"

She might as well have been speaking in Hungarian. "What do you mean?"

A loud huff escaped her lips, her shoulders drooping with apparent frustration. "You tell me you dream. So, I say you dream monsters. Maybe you the monster. So, tell me, what kind monster? Bear? Wolf?"

"Oh. That. Um, let me tell you about the entire dream before you go analyzing it."

"You wait. I get Zoltan Dream Book."

She got up from the table and disappeared down the hallway. For someone her size, Mrs. G can move briskly. When she returned, at a much slower pace, she was clutching the large book of dreams to her bosom. She slammed the book onto the table—for emphasis, or just because it was heavy—then sat opposite me again. "Zoltan Dream Book," she announced, as if I didn't know. "Zoltan tell you what dream means."

I smiled. Might as well play along. "Let me recount as much as I can remember. Dreams fade with time, you know ..."

"Okay. You talk."

I related the details of my dream ... my nightmare ... of grading student papers and seeing my arms turn into paws with sharp claws that ripped the papers to shreds.

"Igen. Igen." Mrs. G repeated the word. I'd spent enough time with her to know that was Hungarian for "yes."

"That's it," I said. "That's the dream."

She nodded and paged through the thick tome. "You arms get hairy, like fur, yes?"

"That's right."

She stopped and leaned down to examine a passage in the book more closely. "So, maybe bear."

"I guess."

"Hmph. Bear means you afraid. Danger. Maybe not secure."

I shrugged. "That fits."

She didn't appear satisfied with my response—too easy?

"Or maybe paws like wolf. You think you wolf?"

"I really don't know, Mrs. G. More like a monster, I'd say."

She pounded a hand on the book. "So, which? Bear or wolf?"

"Let's go with wolf."

She flipped through more pages, mumbling to herself. "Okay. Wolf. In dream, wolf means you trapped. You no trust people. Maybe you hide something inside."

That got my attention; it seemed to hit home. But then I realized that, just like a good fortune-teller, all of Zoltan's interpretations were vague enough to apply to my situation. "Look, Mrs. G, it was like I turned into a wolf ... a wolf monster."

"Jo Isten!"

I couldn't translate that, but it didn't sound good.

"You werewolf!"

"Only in my dream, Mrs. G! I'm not a real werewolf. Honest!"

"Werewolf in dream mean big fight. Good. Evil. Big fight. Not good dream. Bad things coming. Very bad."

It was time to bring this Hungarian dream

interpretation session to an end. "Calm down, Mrs. G. I know what my dream was about. It was about my students, when I was teaching, and how I let some of them down. I really don't need Zoltan to tell me that."

Deep in thought, Mrs. G seemed deaf to my response. She closed the book and got up from the table, this time moving more slowly than before. "Bad things coming," she said. "I give you something special."

She walked down the hallway again, and I heard a loud scraping sound, like she was moving heavy furniture, and then a sharper noise that sounded like a wooden box being pried open. I got up and walked toward the hallway. "Are you okay, Mrs. G? Do you need my help?"

I heard her mumble something in her native tongue, but it didn't sound urgent, so I just stood there, waiting. When she returned, her hands were clasped in front of her, as if in prayer. She walked up to me and looked me squarely in the eye before talking. "Give me you hand," she said.

I reached out my right hand. She grabbed it and turned it palm-side up.

"You keep on you." She placed something cold and hard into my palm. It was the size of a saucer—a demitasse saucer, that is, maybe three or four inches in diameter.

I opened my hand to see a large, ornate medallion. It looked very old, like a museum artifact. Four horse heads were depicted in the shape of a cross, with a braided circle of silver surrounding them.

"Protect you from bad things, from evil," she said.

So, it was some kind of talisman, some ancient-looking good luck charm, no doubt Hungarian or at least Eastern European. I'm sure it had special meaning for Mrs. G and her tribe. I didn't feel right taking it.

"This looks precious," I said. "I'm not sure I should accept it, Mrs. G. Is it a family heirloom?"

She didn't respond, but looked down at the floor and shook her head. "You keep 'til evil pass. You keep with you all the time." She raised her eyes to stare at me again. "You promise."

I let out a held breath. Taking possession of this medallion would only put more weight on my shoulders. But when Mrs. G asks you to promise, it's best to comply. "Okay, if you say so. I'll guard it and keep it safe. Don't worry."

"I worry for you, Mr. Nathan. Bad things coming."

Chapter Twenty-Four
The Meaning of Horses

It only takes a minute to walk home from Mrs. G's. That night, it seemed much longer. The moon hadn't risen yet, and dark clouds scuttled across the sky, hiding the stars. Streetlights only made the shadows seem darker, and the rustling of bushes in the ocean breeze seemed to hide the sound of something else out there. Something following me.

I reached into my pocket and grasped the strange talisman Mrs. G had given me. Whatever protection it might offer was welcomed. As I reached for my keys to unlock the front door, my hand shook. There was no doubt about it. Her Old World juju had spooked me.

Once inside, I locked the door, flipped on the kitchen lights, and leaned against the counter, trying to calm my nerves. Lenore came prancing down the hallway from one of her hiding places, but skidded to a stop when she saw me. She knew something wasn't right. I'm confident cats are sensitive to human emotions, and Lenore and I have developed a special bond over the years. If I was spooked, she would be, too.

I bent down and put my hand out to her, rubbing my fingers against my thumb. "It's okay, Nori," I said. "Come over and let me pet you." Her eyes grew bigger, and one ear twitched.

I tried to clear my mind and push the darkness away, then gently called to her again. Lenore wasn't buying it. She let out a little mmrrip and started to backtrack, ready to retreat at a moment's notice. The sound of loud voices out on the street was the clincher—she literally high-tailed it back down the hallway.

When I looked out my living room window, I saw three kids on bikes, their flashlight beams swinging wildly as they rode up the street, yelling back and forth to each other. They stopped at each parked car and placed something on the windshields. Unlike the almost balletic choreography of the Bin Busters, this was chaotic free-form, with what appeared to be periodic arguments among the kids about which car was "theirs" to service versus their buddy's.

It was too late in the season for local stores to be distributing flyers; I figured it probably had something to do with the wind-farm protests. Either way, there was nothing suspicious or ominous to the kids' actions, so I shrugged it off.

A glance at my watch made me realize I hadn't followed up with Berni. It wasn't too late to call—only a few minutes after eight. I pulled up a chair at the kitchen table, grabbed my cell phone, scrolled to her contact screen, and dialed. It rang so many times, I was sure it would go to voicemail. When she finally picked up, I could hardly hear her over loud music and voices raised in conversation. "Berni? Berni, can you hear me?"

"Oh, hi, Nathan. Hold on a sec."

I heard her place a hand over the phone, muffling the noise. There was a squeak of a door opening and then the noises stopped. She must have walked out to her back deck. "Sorry for all that, Nathan," she said. "A few of my gym friends are over, and I guess we've gotten a little rowdy."

This is not what I'd expected. When I'd left Berni, she was asleep on her couch. And now she didn't sound the least bit tired or in pain. I had to ask, though. "How are your hands?"

"They hurt, which I guess is normal, but nothing too bad."

"I was going to drive over and check on you …"

"Oh, no need for that, Nathan. Kathy took care of it. Like I told you, she's a nurse."

"Okay." I felt deflated. Maybe it was my ego ... probably. Berni had lots of friends; she made friends easily. Me? After the accident and my retirement from teaching, I'd lost track of so many people. Sure, I was friendly with people in town, like Nickie at the library and Patrolman Bob, not to mention all my clients. Berni was my one true close friend, however. And I just didn't know if she'd say the same about me.

"How about I stop by tomorrow sometime?" I asked.

"That would be nice, Nathan."

She paused, waiting for me to say something more, but I couldn't come up with anything else.

"Anyhow, thanks for checking up on me. Really."

"Of course," I said. "Enjoy your impromptu party."

"Yeah, you bet."

I shook my head as I disconnected, trying to deal with all the emotions packed into the day. As I paced back and forth in the living room, my hand almost involuntarily reached into my pocket and felt the cool heft of the horse-head talisman. What a strange piece!

Do certain metals lend personality to an object? Or maybe we endow them with meaning based on their worth. This will sound absurd, but that ancient Hungarian medallion felt solid and trustworthy. It could've been my imagination running wild. Given the events of the day, that was surely a possibility.

Still ... horses' heads ... four of them. Rather than continue to conjecture, it was time for some online research. I strode into my back office, turned on the desk lamp, and fired up my laptop. With the medallion resting against the base of the lamp, I began to fall down the rabbit hole of the internet.

In ancient cultures, horses were associated with gods and goddesses, symbolizing power, fertility, and speed. In Greek mythology, the horse was linked to Poseidon, the god of the sea, who was said to have created the first horse from a wave. And so it went. From the winged steeds of Greece to the shape-shifting kelpies of Celtic lore to spiritual horses in Native American mythology, there were plenty of meanings to choose from. All of these, however, were in the wrong part of the world.

I narrowed my search to Eastern Europe. The three animals that appeared most often in Slavic myths, I found, were the bear, the wolf, and the horse. Zoltan would approve of the first two, especially in dream interpretation. No doubt Mrs. G would object to grouping Hungarian Magyars under Slavic tribes, so I typed in "ancient Hungarian folklore"—probably where I should have started. To the Magyars, horses' heads symbolized good luck, something I could have guessed. From that rosy result, things got decidedly charnel.

Magyar shepherds would place horses' skulls around their farmyards as talismans to keep wolves away. If a meadow or hilltop was suspected as a gathering place for a witch's coven, the skull of a horse would be buried there. And gypsies of the region placed horses' skulls on fence posts to ward off evil spirits. Yikes! That's a lot of dead horses.

I decided I'd be better off not knowing a lot of this, and I'd just keep the medallion in a safe place in my office, hoping it could do all the warding off I'd need. What better place than up on the bookshelf by my raven statue? I pulled a chair over to the shelf and carefully placed Mrs. G's heirloom at the raven's feet, mouthing a silent wish for my protection. Some people had St. Christopher medals. I had a raven and a horse-head medallion. Hey, whatever worked.

Chapter Twenty-Five
On the Scent

The morning was wet, with a cold, gray drizzle blowing on the wind. A certain slant of wintry light escaped through a gap in my drapes and found me in bed at 7:30.

The weather wasn't giving me much enticement to get up. Lenore, however, had other ideas. She made a circuit of the bedroom, complaining all the while, then attacked an imaginary foe in my slippers. I got the message. Time to feed her and face the day.

I zombie-walked into the kitchen, dished out a can of cat food for her, and put the kettle on. No dreams of monsters or wolves in the night ... or horse skulls, for that matter. I brushed away the cobwebs of sleep and began to think about my to-do list.

First, of course, was to check on Berni. While she sounded like she was in no pain last night—I'm guessing shots of tequila were involved—an injury often hurts more the day after. I glanced at my phone. It was still early, but Berni rarely slept in. I called.

Just as it had done last night, her phone rang and rang. When Berni finally picked up, her voice was garbled. "Hahlow ..."

"Jeeze, Berni. Did I wake you?"

After a few deep breaths, she sounded more coherent. "I'll be honest with you, Nathan. Yes, you did." She probably wasn't recriminating; just stating the obvious.

"Sorry, Berni. I was worried about you. How are your hands?"

Another loud breath was followed by the sounds of her bed creaking. "Well, I wasn't feeling any pain last night. And I'm not awake enough to say right now."

She was laying on the guilt, and I suppose I deserved it. "Sorry, Berni. Sorry to call so early."

No response.

"Is it okay if I stop by to check on you? Say, mid-morning?"

"Yeah." She stifled a yawn. "You mean like 10:00 or 10:30, right?"

"Not before then. I promise."

"Fine, Nathan."

I've come to despise the word "fine." More often than not, it's used sarcastically ... even by matter-of-fact Berni. This was not a good start to the morning.

After I hung up, I brewed a cup of Yorkshire Gold black tea. It's strong and flavorful without being bitter, a good way to get the wheels turning in the morning. Oatmeal didn't sound appealing, so I put two slices of bread in the toaster, and pulled the butter dish and a jar of thick-cut English marmalade from the fridge.

As I waited for the toast, I made mental notes of what I wanted to accomplish before checking on Berni. It was still early, so nothing would be open in town.

The toaster dinged, pulling me out of my reverie. I placed the slices on one of my favorite Portmerion plates and put thin pats of butter on each. I always wait for the butter to melt into the toast ... like they serve in diners. The Wilkin & Sons marmalade doesn't spread easily; that's part of its appeal. Little slivers of orange peel in slightly tart jelly make this more of a spread than a jam. I savored each mouthful and sipped my tea, putting aside my worries to live in the moment—as my counselors always suggested.

With breakfast complete and a reasonably full stomach, I got to work. First, I went into the office and fired up my laptop. There was no email response from Brad. I'd just have to talk to him when I saw him at aqua therapy. I sent a quick note to Nickie at the library, telling her I'd stop by later in the day.

That left the issue of my flat tire. I still didn't want Berni to deal with it, so I decided to drop it off at the local tire store on the north end of Asbury. I was a frequent customer—flats seem to be a regular occurrence these days—and I hoped that Dan, the store's manager, would be on duty. He always treats me well.

A glance out the window confirmed it was still raining. I donned a raincoat and put on my Irish knit cap, ready for whatever Mother Nature had in store. Before leaving, I always look around to make sure I haven't forgotten anything. If Dan was going to suggest waiting at the tire store, I should bring something to read. A book was out of the question—too wet outside. Nothing else came to mind, so other than my phone, I left empty-handed.

As I walked onto my porch and locked the front door, I took a moment to glance up and down the street at the parked cars. Each one had a flyer on its windshield. That, at least, helped dampen any suspicion that the Poe Puzzler was involved with those kids on bikes last night.

I still hesitated when I pulled the soaking wet paper from my windshield. But it was just another call to arms by the wind-farm protesters. I really was becoming paranoid.

"Why don't you have a seat, Nathan? I'm sure we can take care of that flat in just a few minutes." Dan was as cordial and professional as always.

Now I wished I had brought along some reading material. The hard plastic chairs in the waiting area provided little comfort. I was surrounded by tire displays of all sizes, for everything from motorcycles to trucks. The place reeked of rubber. A more sensitive individual would likely have a hard time breathing. Me? I got used to it, even though the smell was far from pleasant.

A few minutes later, Dan returned with a frown at the corner of his mouth. "This is pretty strange, Nathan. How did you say you got that flat?"

"I didn't, but it was nothing out of the ordinary." This was not exactly a lie, but certainly not the whole truth. "I noticed it when I went out to my car yesterday morning. I assume a vandal zeroed in on me for some reason." Okay, I was really leaving out the most important parts. No reason to unload my troubles on Dan.

"Well, here's the thing," Dan said. "Your tire is missing its valve."

Now I was the one frowning. "I didn't know tires had valves ... at least I didn't know they were called valves."

Dan laughed. He motioned me over to one of the displays. "You've put air in your tires at some point, right?"

I nodded.

"You know the little rubber stem that sticks out of the wheel?" He ran his hand over the nearest tire display, pointing out the valve stem. "That's how you put air in the tire, and the valve makes sure it doesn't come out."

"I guess I never thought about it."

"Most people take their tires for granted," Dan said. "Take care of your tires and they'll take care of you. That's what I always tell my customers."

He had a twinkle in his eyes, and I was getting ready to hear a treatise on the proper treatment of radial tires. I was saved by one of his technicians, who popped his head in the waiting-room door. "All set!" he said, then disappeared back into the shop.

Dan looked deflated. I think he actually enjoyed talking about tires. I wasn't free to leave just yet, though. He opened the door again and called after the young mechanic, yelling over the machine-gun-like noise of an impact wrench. "YO, RYAN!" The racket stopped. "Why don't you bring Mr. Poe's car into the bay and mount that tire?" He turned to me, his foot still propping open the shop door. "You've got time, Nathan, don't you?"

I hesitated, not wanting to spend more time than I had to in that noisy and odoriferous environment. But it would save me the trouble of mounting the tire myself. "Oh, sure. That's fine."

Now I was using the "fine" word.

After everything Dan had explained, it took a moment for me to connect the dots. My flat tire. The Poe Puzzler. And that odd little valve. "So, how does that tire valve work?" I asked Dan. "I mean, how does one remove a valve from that rubber stem?"

He shrugged. "It's easy enough if you have a valve-stem puller."

"Is that some kind of tool?"

He looked around the waiting room. There were no other customers on that cool, October morning. "I'm not supposed to allow customers in the shop. You know, liability and all that. But I can trust you, right?"

"Of course."

He opened the door wider and motioned me into the working end of the business. Thankfully, Ryan was busy bringing my Saab into the bay, so my ears weren't assaulted by the cacophony of his tools. Dan walked over to a workstation and picked up a small turn key. It looked like something you'd wind an old clock with, but the central tube was longer and had an unusual fixture on the end. "Here it is," Dan said. "This is a valve-stem puller. It's a simple device. Heck, you could probably buy one on Amazon for ten or twelve bucks, but they wouldn't last … and most people wouldn't know how to use it. Now, this," he rubbed his thumb over the tool, "is a commercial valve-stem puller."

I bent down to look more closely. Dan took that as a sign of interest.

"You just remove the valve cap and screw this baby into the valve stem. Unscrew it and out comes the valve with all the air. Simple, right?"

"That's interesting. I guess it's not something your typical shade-tree mechanic would have in his toolbox."

"Oh, no. It's pretty specialized. It's best to leave tire work to the professionals!" He cocked his head and smiled. He might have been putting me on, but Dan is usually a straight-shooter.

"So, I could buy one of these valve pullers online, right?"

"Well, you could. But what are you going to do with it?"

He had me there. Unless I was planning to give someone a flat tire, that is.

I drove away from the tire store feeling good—about "taking care" of my tires, about dealing with the flat without asking for Berni's help, and especially for being able to breathe without smelling rubber.

Although it was still drizzling, I opened both front windows to clear my head. I needed my sense of smell to be in top shape to pick out Berni's get-well present.

It was well past 9:00 by the time I parked in front of the Artisan Body Products boutique. I said hello as I walked in, then went straight past the mermaid paintings and frou-frou lotions to the back of the store where an oasis of pleasant aromas greeted me. The multi-colored bars of soap were tastefully arranged and clearly labeled. And there were so many appealing choices. Some smelled good enough to eat.

With the salesperson's help, I narrowed my selection to "beach bum," "Mexican coffee," or "French toast." The first one seemed redundant, since Berni could open her apartment window and breathe in the same scents from the salt air. I really don't know coffee. Was Mexican anything special? "French toast" emerged as the clear winner. I put my face next to the soap and wafted its aroma to my nose—sweet, eggy bread with a hint of vanilla, sizzling warm butter, a whiff of cinnamon, and the lingering scent of maple syrup. Yum!

Tastefully wrapped with multi-colored tissue paper in a small yellow bag, the little gift was sure to put a smile on Berni's face. I got into my car and placed the bag on the passenger seat. With a glance at my watch, I realized it was still too early to call on her. No point making the same mistake twice. I had some time to kill.

The rain had stopped, but gray clouds scuttled across the sky. I decided to take in the drama of the morning with a quick stroll on the boardwalk. Even though Shriver's Salt Water Taffy was open, the large parking lot behind the store was mostly deserted. I parked my Saab, zipped up my raincoat, and trudged up the long ramp from Ninth to the boardwalk.

What I hadn't accounted for was the wind. It funneled through the opening between Shriver's and Manco & Manco Pizza with a ferocity that made me lean into it, taking far more energy than I'd expected. I held onto my cap so it wouldn't end up in Somers Point.

I found shelter from the wind at the top of the ramp under Shriver's awning. My efforts were rewarded by a spectacular display of white-capped waves. There must have been a storm at sea. Every other wave announced its arrival with a boom that echoed against the storefronts. Gulls swooped and screamed above the surf. As nature proclaimed its presence, I took in the panorama of beach, birds, waves, and clouds with a silly smile on my face. This is why I loved Ocean City!

I don't know how long I stood there, reveling in Mother Nature's drama, before my phone vibrated in my pocket. With a loud sigh for being disturbed at that special moment, I pulled it out and answered.

"Nathaniel? Nathaniel, are you there?"

"Yes, Mrs. Murphy." I had to shout to be heard above the wind and waves. "Give me a minute to find a quieter place."

I ducked into the only open door at Shriver's and found a quiet corner near a large display of gift boxes.

"Okay. I can talk now."

"I know it's none of my business, but why are you looking for a choir? I mean, the weather's pretty nasty, and you sound like you're outside somewhere, but that still doesn't make sense to me. Nathan? Are you there?"

The trouble communicating with Mrs. G is her broken English. With Mrs. Murphy, I sometimes have no idea what she's talking about.

"I'm sorry, Mrs. Murphy, but I'm not following you. What about a choir?"

"Well, you said it yourself. You said you were looking for a choir place. I certainly don't know of any place like that on a wet October morning."

It took me a moment to connect the dots. "Not a choir. I said a quieter place."

"Oh. Well, never mind. That's not why I called, anyhow."

I waited. It was always a good idea to give Mrs. Murphy free rein.

"So. I noticed some paper stuck under the windshield wiper on my car this morning, so I went out in the rain and got it. I don't know why people think it's perfectly okay to put things on cars like that. I mean, it's an invasion of privacy, don't you think?"

"Yes, I agree. I got one of those protest flyers as well, Mrs. Murphy. I think everyone up and down the street did."

"Right. Well, what do you think of the poem inside?"
She'd lost me again. "Poem?"

"Yes, the one about the wind killing a woman named Lee. I mean, that's not very nice, is it?"

My mind was reeling, trying to make sense of all this—the wind, Mrs. Lee. It was out of context, a confused jumble. Then it hit me like a thunderclap.

"The wind came out of the cloud by night, chilling and killing my Annabel Lee."

"Yes! That's it. You mean you got it, too?"

I took several deep breaths.

"Are you there, Nathan?"

"I didn't get a poem. Just a protest flyer."

"Then how are you able to recite it? That's pretty

spooky, Nathan."

I steadied my breathing and rolled my neck before speaking. "It's a poem by Edgar Allan Poe ... a famous poem. Annabel Lee. That's how I know it."

"Oh, well, they didn't teach us that one in school."

All I could think was, my Puzzler had messed up. The poem was delivered to her instead of to me. Maybe he was changing his tactics ... or targeting her ...

"Nathan? Are you still there?"

"Here's the thing, Mrs. Murphy. I think that poem is a message from my Poe Puzzler. And for some reason, you got it instead of me."

"Oh, my lord! You mean this is from that man who's harassing you? And now he's going after me?"

Chapter Twenty-Six
I Can't Believe ...

I rapped my knuckles on the door. Tap-tap ... tap. Berni and I had a secret knock. It's not something we did consciously or even spoke about; it just sort of happened.

"Come on in, Nathan!"

A gust of wind followed me as I opened her door. Located on the second floor and with no larger buildings around it, Berni's apartment got the brunt of the weather. I shut the door and hung my wet coat and cap on the doorknob.

She was sitting in the middle of her couch in pink-and-black PJs, immersed in a TV show. It was an old Columbo, the one with Patrick McGoohan as a CIA spy. She glanced back at me. "You've got hat hair," she said with a smile. I brushed my hands over my head. "It's pretty blustery out there. I almost lost my cap." She muted the show, slid over, and motioned for me to sit next to her.

"Just getting some sleuthing tips from Lieutenant Columbo," she said.

"Sleuthing?"

"Yeah, I thought you'd like that word."

There's something mesmerizing about a TV show with the sound turned off. You have to watch it. I've seen that episode any number of times, so I knew the plot. But I was still glued to the set as I stood there. McGoohan and Leslie Nielsen were strolling among carefree kids and indulgent parents at an amusement park, discussing espionage and murder. It was a classic juxtaposition.

"Yo, Nathan. I'm over here!" I came out of my TV trance when Berni shut it off and waved her arms at me.

"Sorry, Berni. I do love a good mystery."

"Speaking of which, what do you know? What's the latest on your Puzzler?"

Where to begin? I thought. "First things first. How are your hands? Are you in much pain?" I sat down beside her, the little gift bag on my lap.

Now, she was the one distracted. "What's in the bag?" Her smile was refreshing.

"Oh, just a little something to say 'I'm sorry' and 'I hope you feel better.'"

She ran her fingers along the collar of her pajamas, her smile getting bigger. "And who's it for?"

"Someone I care about."

She leaned over and gave me a peck on the cheek. "Hand it over, big boy!"

I placed the gift bag in her lap. She rustled the tissue paper and pulled out the soap. "Mmmm. Smells nice."

"It's called French Toast," I said, stating the obvious.

As glad as I was that the soap was a hit, Berni hadn't answered my first question. "Tell me how you're feeling. How are the burns healing?"

"I'm doing okay, all things considered. Kathy stopped by this morning and put some salve on them … redid the bandages. She said they were 'superficial burns' … just on the outer layer of skin. What's it called? Epidermis?"

"Sounds right, but I wouldn't call any burn like that superficial."

"A medical term, I guess."

She shifted in her seat and turned to me. "Smelling that soap made me hungry. I've got some leftover sticky buns that I could heat up in the microwave. How about it?"

"Sounds good to me."

She got up and gave me a hard look, but I could see a twinkle in her eye. "I'll be in charge of setting the table and heating the buns. You, Mr. Tea Snob, are in charge of our liquid refreshments."

"I prefer 'Tea Connoisseur,' but I accept your proposition."

"So … that leaves one more tough decision. Which is it going to be? With nuts or with raisins?"

"One of each, of course!"

After indulging in the truly scrumptious sticky buns, accompanied by a pot of cinnamon spice tea, I brought her up to speed. There was a lot to tell her, starting with the previous night at Mrs. G's. When I got to the part about the ancient Hungarian medallion, she stopped me.

"Okay, let's see it," she said.

"I don't have it on me. It's at home."

She looked down and blew out a breath. "Nathan, my friend ... I can't believe it."

"What?"

"Here you're given this super weird talisman, told to keep it with you to ward off evil, and where is it now? Is it in your pocket, keeping you safe? No, it's in your house. And nobody's home."

My face reddened. She got me on that one, but I wouldn't admit it. I pushed back my chair and crossed my legs. "Well ... I mean ... come on, Berni. You don't believe in that stuff, do you?"

She got up from the table and walked over to her apartment door, pulling the little drapes aside to look out at the weather. When she spoke, she didn't turn to me. "There's power in believing. Whether or not that medallion does anything ..."

"Okay. Okay. Let's get past that. There's more. Sit down. Let me explain." I told her about the kids on bikes putting flyers on all the cars, and finding nothing more exciting on my car in the morning than a pamphlet protesting the proposed wind farm.

"You thought there was going to be another note from your Puzzler, didn't you?" she said.

"There was a note, but it wasn't delivered to me." I explained about the call from Mrs. Murphy, and the Puzzler's note with a line from "Annabel Lee" stuffed into her pamphlet. "Curiouser and curiouser, isn't it?" I let all this sink in.

"So ..." She got up and paced in her cramped kitchen. "Either the Poe Puzzler is targeting Mrs.

Murphy now ... as well as you ... or the kids made a mistake. Right?"

"Assuming the Puzzler told the kids to put a note on my car, I can't believe they'd mistake a Saab convertible for Mrs. Murphy's car."

Berni stopped pacing and looked at me. "What kind of car does she have?"

"A Buick. Some kind of old Buick sedan."

She continued pacing, then stopped again. "Just a minute. What color is her car?"

"It's green." I knew where she was going, but I wasn't convinced. "Sure, it's green, and my Saab is green. But she's got a sedan and my car's a convertible."

"Here's the thing, Sherlock," she said. "Your convertible top is black, right?"

"Yup."

"And does Mrs. Murphy's Buick have a black vinyl roof, like you see on some old cars?"

I pushed back my chair and walked around the table. When I looked out her kitchen window at the cars parked along the curb, almost all of them were white or silver or gray—no green cars. "I don't know. Kids aren't into cars these days, but I can't believe they'd mistake a green Saab convertible for a green Buick with a black vinyl roof."

"It's just kids, Nathan. What do they know about Saabs? They were probably told to put the Poe note on a green car. And they did. Just not the right green car."

I sat down again and motioned for her to do the same. "Let's put that aside for now. There's more." I filled her in about my visit to the tire store and how I learned the Poe Puzzler had flattened my tire using a valve-stem puller. "Do you know what that is?" I asked.

"Sure," she said. "I've got valve removal tools for Presta and Schrader valves. They're for bikes, but it's similar for cars."

I couldn't believe I was the only one who didn't know about valve-stem tools.

"The thing is, Berni, Dan at the tire store told me that not too many people have valve-stem pullers in their toolkits. It's not that common ... except at tire stores." She nodded as I talked, her face brightening.

"And that means," she said, "your Puzzler might work at a tire store."

"You nailed it, Berni!"

"Wow, we're getting closer to figuring out who your archenemy is."

We sat in silence, pondering the implications. The only sound was the wind rattling the windowpanes. She spoke first. "There aren't that many tire stores in the area."

"True, but he could always work in Somers Point or Atlantic City or ..."

"Still," she said, "let's start local first. Did you ask Dan about any of his younger employees?"

I tugged at my ear. Was that too obvious? I certainly had the opportunity when Dan was explaining the wonders of tires. "Um, no. I didn't. I could stop back there later today."

"But did you see any other workers there?"

"Well, yes. There was a young guy who moved my car into the service bay. I think his name was Ryan."

Berni sprang up, almost knocking over her chair in agitation. "Nathan! I can't believe you might've had the Poe Puzzler right in front of you and you didn't do anything about it!"

Chapter Twenty-Seven
All at Sea

Duly chastised, I walked down the steps from Berni's place with a growing sense of unease. If Ryan were my Poe Puzzler, he could have done something to my car while it was in the tire shop.

Rationally, it was easy to dismiss this feeling. Ryan looked shorter than the guy we'd seen at Waverly and Seaspray the other night. And Ryan was blond, without any facial hair. No glasses, either. None of his physical characteristics appeared to match.

Emotionally, however, I wasn't so sure. Telling myself I was only motivated by a sense of road safety, I popped the trunk, grabbed the lug wrench and my handy two-foot pipe, and double-checked all twenty lug nuts. They were tight.

Satisfied that my Saab's wheels had not been sabotaged, I checked the trunk for any telltale red notes. No notes. I closed my eyes and let out a sigh. Ryan could not be the Puzzler. Still, I might have a conversation with my buddy, Dan, at the tire store ... just to be sure.

I'd told Nickie I'd stop by the library before noon, so I was calling it close—my watch read 11:52 a.m.

It took less than ten minutes to drive there, but by the time I'd parked my car, it was after twelve. Knowing Nickie, she'd be punctual, and right then, I was not. I hurried up the ramp, held the big glass door for a woman struggling with a baby stroller, and came to a huffing stop at the circulation desk. "Is Nickie around?"

I didn't recognize the librarian—they have several part-timers I hadn't had much contact with—but she smiled at me. That's always a nice start with a stranger. "I'm pretty sure Nickie's at lunch." The disappointment must have shown on my face. "She should be back in about thirty minutes. May I help you with something?"

I stood there for a moment, undecided. Should I come back? I needed to go home to shower and change before my aqua therapy session later that afternoon. Then again, I could put the time to good use. "Do you have old high school yearbooks here, not from Ocean City but from Mainland Regional?"

"We have a small collection…" Her smile faltered. "I'm afraid they're not very well organized—some missing years." She waved an arm over her shoulder. "Go to the back corner, past the line of computer kiosks, and you'll find them on an open shelf."

Her directions were clear enough. Halfway between the circulation desk and the yearbooks, however, I was intercepted. "Nathan! Mr. Poe. We need to talk."

This was a different side of Nickie than I'd seen before. And it didn't bode well. She spoke between clenched teeth. "Come with me ... please." She marched me into a small conference room, closed the door, and pointed toward a chair. "Sit. The tables are turned now. I'm the teacher and you're the student. Understood?"

Her cheeks were red, her hands in tight fists at her side. It was pretty obvious I was in for a tongue-lashing. I pulled out a chair, sat down, and looked up at her. "You appear to be upset," I said. My comment didn't help her mood at all.

"You could say that. You could definitely say that. Your ... your request has gotten me into hot water. I never should have let you talk me into it."

I raised both palms in surrender. "Slow down, Nickie. Please. What happened?"

She blew out a breath that lifted the pink locks from her forehead. "You want to know what happened? Well, let me tell you what happened. I started looking into patrons who had taken out books on Poe, as you requested. I was trying to do it discreetly. Let's just say I was bending the rules a bit. Well, the director found out, and she reminded me in no uncertain terms that what I was doing was illegal, unethical, and just plain wrong."

I felt my face flush. "I didn't mean to get you in trouble, Nickie. And I wasn't asking for patron names ... not exactly ..."

"Stop right there. You know the rules, probably as well as I do." She shook her head back and forth several times. I could almost hear her counting to ten before continuing. "Look at me." She sat down across the table and made direct eye contact. I felt like I was backed into a corner. No way out of this one.

"I can almost quote, word for word, what the library director told me. She said, 'Librarians must take patron privacy very seriously. We cannot share information about someone's borrowing history. Unless we have some kind of legal mandate or the permission of the patron, we cannot reveal anything—not titles, dates, or anything else. It's forbidden. Verboten. Absolutely not allowed.' Now, do you get it?"

She was right, of course. I had overstepped the bounds of our friendship. "I'm very sorry, Nickie. The last thing I wanted was for you to get into trouble. Please forgive me. And let me know if I should speak to your supervisor and tell her this was all my fault."

She pulled back her chair and stood, finally breaking eye contact. "No. That won't be necessary." As she walked toward the meeting room door, her voice softened. "I never should have let you talk me into it."

"And I never should have asked you. I'm really sorry."

She left me sitting in that small room, alone with my thoughts and recriminations. I'd messed things up pretty badly. Some would say I took advantage of a former student. My intentions were good ... well, you know what they say about good intentions. Nickie got into trouble because of me. I couldn't see any way to make this right, to mend my relationship with her. No amount of artisanal soap would help. It was probably best to lie low and hope that time would heal her wounds.

What's more, this certainly didn't help my

investigation into the Poe Puzzler. I could sit there and sulk or take action. I chose the latter. Isn't that what C. Auguste Dupin would do?

I found my way to the shelf of local high-school yearbooks and pulled out one from my last year of teaching at Mainland Regional, plus a couple of earlier volumes. It was a long shot, but maybe something would trigger a memory. Maybe I'd see a picture of Ryan from the tire store ...

It was past 1:00 pm, my eyes were bleary, and my stomach was growling. An hour of poring over student photos had led me nowhere. After a while, they all looked alike. I found several Ryans, but none that looked like the tire-store kid. Maybe my Poe Puzzler wasn't a disgruntled student. Or I simply didn't have enough to go on.

It was turning into a very down day. First, Berni questioned my investigative skills. Then Nickie got into trouble with her boss because of me. Then I spent a fruitless hour paging through yearbooks. Maybe I should go home and get that Hungarian good luck medallion. Or jump into bed and put a pillow over my head.

I realize that my "Small Mysteries" company is more of a hobby than a business. Still, was I delusional in thinking I had some genuine "sleuthing" abilities? Being my own client was turning into a very hard case.

With the yearbooks back on the shelf, I trudged toward the exit, but stopped to say hello to Dawn, the reference desk librarian. We go way back. After exchanging pleasantries, a thought occurred to me. Yes, I wrestled with it, not wanting to get yet another librarian into trouble, but I couldn't help myself.

"So, Dawn, do you mind if I ask you a question?"

"That's what I'm here for, Nathan."

I tried to get the wording right before opening my mouth again. "Is there a chance that you've seen greater interest in books by and about Edgar Allan Poe lately?"

"In fact, we have," she said.

Now I was getting somewhere! "So, you've noticed someone, um, some people, ask about Poe's short stories, poems, and maybe even biographical information?"

"Yes, indeed, Nathan."

I felt my excitement grow. Maybe I should have started with Dawn first.

"It's perfectly natural," she said.

Wait. Where was this going? "Why do you say that?"

"Nathan! It's October. We always get more interest in Poe around Halloween."

That took the wind right out of my sails.

Chapter Twenty-Eight
Have You Seen Tammy?

I'd spent so much time at the library that I had to rush home to shower and change before my aqua therapy class. I was calling it too close to enjoy a proper lunch, so I gobbled down a couple of ham-and-cheese roll-ups with some unsweetened iced tea, leaving me full if not fully satisfied. Then it was back to the Community Center pool for my session, with 15 minutes to spare. Since Brad, our coach, had never answered my email about prescriptions, I wanted to ask him in person.

His answer was vague, but reassuring. "I suppose someone could join our group without a prescription..." He drew out the word "could" for emphasis. "As a rule, I require one. You know, for insurance and such. Everybody wants to sue somebody these days."

That meant Tammy Davis must have had a prescription for aqua therapy. She didn't join the group just to confront me about my dealings with her late son. I put aside that bit of information so I could concentrate on making amends. After five years, she was still mourning her son's death, searching for blame wherever she could find it. Although I doubted it would mean much to her, the least I should do was apologize for Eli's perceived slights.

After changing into my swimming trunks in the men's locker room, I waited for Tammy by the shallow end of the pool, breathing in the sharp scent of chlorine, watching each person come through the doors. The minutes ticked by. Brad issued his usual rah-rah speech and blew his whistle. Everyone got into the pool except me. I sidled up to him. "Have you seen Tammy Davis today?" I asked.

"Tammy? No, she called in," he said. "Some kind of stomach bug. We don't want to spread that around!"

He shooed me into the pool, where I joined an older gentleman who introduced himself as David. Between Brad's shouted encouragements and the heavy breathing of all but the younger participants, David regaled me with stories from his research into Ben Franklin's London years and the new information being uncovered at Franklin's former residence there. David was an interesting conversationalist, but my mind was elsewhere—was Tammy really sick, or was she avoiding me? My movements were half-hearted, and at one point, Brad chided me for "not keeping up."

Back in the locker room after our session, I tried to come up with logical next steps in my search for the Poe Puzzler. When I played out the pluses and minuses, I decided not to talk to Dan about his young tire-store employee. It was a long shot. The Tammy Davis situation, however, required further resolution. Exactly how to proceed was not clear.

I needed some "alone time" to think. But after my

minimalist lunch, my growling stomach reminded me that I also needed groceries—my cupboard was bare. On the drive home, I detoured to the local Acme, putting together a mental shopping list as I drove.

Why is it always so cold inside grocery stores? My hair was still damp from aqua therapy, and with so much on my mind, I'd left my jacket in the car. Even though I needed to visit the refrigerated section, I saved it for last, giving me time to walk around and warm up. I wove my way through the aisles, picking up blueberries, salad mix, chicken breasts, and bread. Finally, more or less adjusted to the store's climate, I wheeled my cart to the far aisle to pick up milk and yogurt.

And who did I see perusing the soy milk selections but Tammy Davis! She presented a curious tableau—still as a statue, one hand reaching out to select a carton from the shelf, a look of concentration on her face. As I stood and stared at her, I realized how pretty she was, how slender and graceful her hands and fingers were. But even at a distance, I noticed a sadness at the corners of her eyes.

I called out to her, and she smiled as she turned to the sound of her name. The smile faded quickly, however. "Oh, it's you," she said.

Was it anger I saw in her expression or annoyance? I knew I had little time to make my point, so I soldiered on. "Tammy, I wanted to apologize to you and try to explain..."

She was having none of it. "Why are you following me?"

I wasn't expecting that. Did she really think I was stalking her? "I just happened to see you here. This is where I get my groceries. It's a coincidence."

That may have mollified her. At least she didn't bolt away or call for help. But I realized I only had a few minutes to say what I wanted ... and ask a question or two.

"Please don't take offense at my intrusion," I said. "Again, I want to apologize. My last semester teaching, well, I wasn't myself. I'd lost my wife, my wife Anna, in a car accident. I'm sure you can understand. You, more than anyone."

Her expression softened. That's what I thought I saw in her eyes. "I'm sorry for you, for your loss. But I don't see any reason to talk to you. I told you how my son felt about you. I don't need to know any more than that."

I'd come far enough with what I'd hoped would be received as a sincere apology and explanation. Now it was time to try to make some connections, to see if Eli Davis had anything to do with my Poe Puzzler. "I'd just like a few minutes of your time. Maybe we could sit down over a cup of coffee ... or tea. Maybe you're like me and you don't drink coffee. I'm sure we could find someplace nearby. I'd like some time to talk to you about Eli and maybe Eli's friends from when he was in high school."

She narrowed her eyes and glared at me. Any advantage I may have gained was lost. "Why do you want to know about my son's friends?"

Oh, boy, how to proceed?

"It's complicated. A long story. There's someone who's been contacting me ... anonymously. I think it's a former student. I'd like to find out more about some of the kids in my classes that last year teaching."

"You're asking the wrong person." She shut me out, just like that. Without even considering the dairy products she'd been pondering so intently only a few minutes before, she grabbed a carton of soy milk at random and tossed it into her grocery cart. As she reached for the milk, the sleeve of her jacket pulled back, and I noticed a series of scars on the inside of her wrist. My God, what had that woman gone through?

She'd already turned her back on me and started to wheel her cart away. There was one more thing I needed to know, however, to help me gauge her level of disaffection. "Wait. Please. Am I the reason you didn't come to aqua therapy today?"

She looked over her shoulder and laughed. It was a cynical laugh. "Not everything is about you," she said. "I don't like our coach, Brad. It's that simple. And I've found another class in Pleasantville."

I opened my mouth to say something more, but I couldn't come up with an appropriate response.

With one more verbal barb directed at me, she brought our brief conversation to an end. "Why don't you just leave me alone?"

As she reeled back to her cart and walked away, her gait was stiff and forceful, a march rather than a walk. That was the last time I saw Tammy Davis. And I'm sure that was perfectly fine with her.

Chapter Twenty-Nine
What's in the Stew?

A construction truck was blocking the street in front of my house, so I drove around back to the alley and parked by the steps to my office door. I often pull into that tight space when I need to unload groceries or other packages, simply because it's a shorter path to my house. And I was glad I did, since it took a couple of trips back and forth to the car before I had set my bags on the small landing.

Then I had to deal with my storm door. You wouldn't think something so mundane could be such a nuisance, but it often sticks. The aluminum frame isn't bent, and the hinges aren't loose. The problem is inside the latch. I've tried lubricating it with 3-in-1 oil and WD-40. I've even pulled the mechanism apart and adjusted the springs, but the latch jams ... or not, depending on the weather ... or its mood. It can have good days and bad.

This wasn't one of its good days. Powerful gusts were still coming off the ocean, and when I finally yanked the door open, the wind pulled it out of my hand. The door is fitted with safety glass, so I wasn't too concerned about it breaking, but I was tired of this constant battle—would it stick or wouldn't it? Even though I didn't want to spend the money, I needed to find a handyman to replace it. One more item on my to-do list.

As I unlocked the office door and hauled the groceries inside, Lenore scampered out to greet me. She put on her cute cat act, rolling onto her back, paws curled upward, and an adorable expression on her face. Who could resist that? "Okay, Len-Oreo, I'll give you some treats." Yes, she and I have our routines.

Once I'd fed my furry companion, I placed the grocery bags on the kitchen counter and started to unpack. Halfway through this chore, my phone rang. It was Mrs. Murphy. With everything else going on that day, I'd forgotten to get back to her about the Poe Puzzler note. As usual, I could hardly utter "hello" before she launched into me.

"Well, Nathan, I expected to hear from you sooner. I mean, that note! It's very upsetting, I can tell you. You've got to come over. We need to talk about this."

I paused before replying. It's always a good idea to phrase things the right way with her. "Yes, of course, Mrs. Murphy. I understand how you feel. Just let me finish putting away ..."

"I was so worked up this morning, I had to do something to get my mind off it," she continued, talking over me. "You know the old saying, right? 'Idle hands are the devil's workshop.'"

"I don't think that applies in your case, Mrs. Murphy," I said. "I'm pretty sure it refers to idle people getting into trouble."

"Trouble? What are you saying, Nathan? Of course I'm not getting into trouble. Well! All I wanted to tell you is that I needed to do something with myself rather than sit alone and fret."

"I meant no disrespect."

I heard a grunted "harrumph!" and a sharp intake of breath. The last thing I wanted was to upset her. Even a perceived insult could lead to days of repercussions.

"So, as I was saying … when I get bothered, when there's a problem gnawing at me, I cook. That's what I do. And since you took your time calling me back, I've made quite a meal, quite a feast, I have to say."

Was this leading up to a dinner invitation? I didn't want to assume, so I came up with a generic comment. "That sounds like an excellent strategy to deal with stress."

My words made her pause—a rare occurrence. "Well, if you say so. But what's my point? My point, Nathan, is that I've put together a delicious Irish stew, my grandma's recipe. It's too much for one person. So, finish up what you're doing and come over."

I don't think Mrs. Murphy heard the low rumble from my belly. At least I hope not. "That sounds delightful," I said.

"And then after we eat," she continued, "we can talk about this Annabel poem and the line about the wind killing her. How dreadful!"

Hungarian cuisine and Irish cuisine—I'm lucky to

have two older neighbors who ply me with a delectable variety of comfort foods. Could it be their maternal instincts? At this rate, I'd probably put on a few pounds. But I wasn't thinking about calories when Mrs. Murphy opened her front door and invited me in.

The rich, savory smell of beef was complemented by an earthy fragrance, no doubt from carrots, onions, and potatoes. There was something else, though, a sweet, almost malty scent. "My heavens, Mrs. Murphy, what a comforting, homey aroma!"

"Yes, it does make the whole house smell … like home," she said. "Well, come in, Nathan, come in!"

Even though the anticipated feast was foremost in my mind, I noticed that Mrs. Murphy wasn't in her usual plain dress. In fact, she was pretty dolled up, with a maroon and gray pleated skirt and a pale gray blouse. I even detected a touch of lipstick. If I'd known this was going to be a formal dinner, I'd have put on something else. Not only that, but I'd forgotten to bring a hostess gift.

She ushered me to sit at her large dining room table and poured us each a glass of red wine. I had a moment of foreboding when I glanced at the label—no raven on this one, though.

"So, what's in your grandmother's secret recipe, if I could ask?"

She narrowed her eyes, and I thought I might have crossed a line. Family recipes are often closely held. When she didn't object, I plowed on. "Other than beef and vegetables," I said, "I can detect the scent of some other interesting ingredients."

"Then you have a good nose," she said, with a twinkle in her eyes. "I put in rosemary, thyme, and a bay leaf. But I bet what your detective nose is detecting is the cup of Guinness I've added." A pun from Mrs. Murphy! Had she gotten into the wine before I'd arrived?

A timer went off in the kitchen, and she excused herself to check on our meal. A few minutes later, she returned with a large soup tureen. "One more thing," she said as she hurried back to the kitchen and emerged carrying a loaf of brown bread and a breadboard. She sat opposite me with a look of complete satisfaction on her face. I waited for an awkward minute—should I serve her? Would she say grace? She rescued me with a wave of her hand. "Don't stand on ceremony, Nathan. Dig in!" She didn't have to say it twice.

We'd scraped each delectable morsel from the bottom of the soup tureen, finished most of the bread, and killed off the bottle of wine. I slid my chair back and basked in the glow of being pleasantly stuffed.

Mrs. Murphy looked equally sated. While we had to "get down to business," as she'd told me several times, I didn't want this moment to pass too quickly. I'd known her for over four years, lived just down the street from her, but I didn't really know that much about her, including her first name. The envelopes I'd seen in passing were all addressed to "Mrs. F. Murphy." I wasn't sure if the F stood for her late husband's first name or hers.

Since we were both pretty mellow from the meal and the wine, I thought I'd broach the subject. "Mrs. Murphy. We've gotten to know each other pretty well, and I greatly appreciate your wonderful cooking and all you've done for me."

That elicited a gentle smile and a nod from her. Compliments, especially when they're valid, go a long way when you're building up to a personal question. "All this time, I've always addressed you as Mrs. Murphy. That's out of respect, of course. But, I'm curious. What's your first name?"

Her smile disappeared, and she broke eye contact. "Oh, I don't use it much," she mumbled. "Except with my old friends, people I've known for a long time ... before that movie ruined everything."

Now I was totally baffled. "What movie? I'm sorry, but I don't follow." In my tipsy state, I wasn't connecting the dots. I went through a mental list. The F could stand for Frances, Frieda, Florence, Faith, Faye, Francesca, Felicity. None of them sounded very Irish. Oh, no! Was she talking about Shrek?

She must have seen the look of recognition on my face. "Yes, Nathan, that rather heavy and homely love interest for the troll or ogre or whatever Shrek was. She's ruined my name!"

"But Fiona is a beautiful name, Mrs. Murphy. It's Gaelic, right? I'm trying to think ... something about purity or ..."

"Yes, you're on the right track, Nathan. Some say it originated in Scotland, but I think the Scots stole it from the Irish. And it does have a Gaelic meaning ... 'fair' or 'white.' I've always liked my name. I was proud of it, but now that movie has sullied it."

For some reason, this made me angry. And it didn't seem fair. I stood and came around to her side of the table. It might have been forward of me, but I put a hand on her shoulder. "You can be proud of your Irish heritage and your beautiful name ... Fiona." She looked up at me with the sweetest smile I'd ever seen from her.

The moment passed, and as I removed my hand from her shoulder, she gathered herself back up. "Enough of all this emotional clap-trap," she said. "Now let's get down to business and deal with that horrible poem." She rose from her chair, adjusted her skirt with a swift flick of her wrists, and strode out of the dining room.

> It was many and many a year ago,
> In a kingdom by the sea,
> That a maiden there lived whom you may know
> By the name of Annabel Lee;
> And this maiden she lived with no other thought
> Than to love and be loved by me.

I recited the first stanza of "Annabel Lee" for Mrs. Murphy—Fiona—as she came back into the dining room carrying the bright-red note. We both knew what was written there. She had told me over the phone.

When I was a child, I'd memorized several poems by Poe. I could recite this one in its entirety when I was a teenager. It was always one of my favorites ... long before my wife's death.

"Is that how the poem begins?" Mrs. Murphy asked as she sat down again at the table. "That part sounds beautiful. But then he talks about her death, right?"

"The poem recounts a beautiful story, but a tragic one," I said. "It's about love, jealousy, and death. It was the last poem Edgar Allan Poe wrote before his own death in 1849."

"The nuns probably didn't appreciate that one. We never studied it in school." She laid the note between us on the table. I wasn't looking at her when she spoke; my eyes were fixated on that red piece of paper. "We read 'The Raven' and a couple of short stories by Poe," she continued. "You know, the one about the madman who cuts out his neighbor's heart and hides it in the floorboards. Pretty gruesome stuff, if you ask me."

I reached over and opened the note. It was folded in three, like a business letter, but more precisely. The creases were sharp, the edges aligned with no overlap. Even though I knew what I was about to read, I was still trepidatious. When I saw what the Puzzler had underlined, my hands shook with rage.

"The wind came out of the cloud by night, chilling and killing my Annabel Lee."

"Nathan, what's wrong? Your face is all red."

It took me a moment to find my voice. "It's what he's underlined. He knows. He knows about Anna and how she died. Why did he have to bring her into this?"

Mrs. Murphy pulled back her chair, stepped around behind me, and placed both hands on my shoulders. Now it was her turn to comfort me. "Try to calm down, Nathan. It's just a note ... not a very nice note, but just a note."

She eased her hold on my shoulders, and I slumped forward. "You don't understand," I said. "This has been a sort of game, an odd but stimulating game. Other than the bloody wine bottle, that is. But all these quotes and questions about Poe. I kind of enjoyed it. A game of cat and mouse. The Puzzler trying to outwit me, outmaneuver me ..."

She drifted over to a corner of the room and absently pulled dead leaves from a potted spider plant. Her tone was soft as she spoke without facing me. "That's a pretty peculiar way of looking at things, Nathan." Then, as if she'd decided to make a stronger point, she whirled around and looked me in the eye, her expression adamant. "Don't you find all this kind of creepy? And you're enjoying it? That's just plain weird!"

I stared at the red note on the table. "Then maybe I'm weird," I mumbled.

She shook her head, either refuting me or in disbelief, I couldn't tell. "But here's the thing, Mr. Private Investigator. Why was that note placed on my car and not yours?"

I got up; I always think better when I pace. "It was a mistake, that's all."

With hands on her hips, she gave me a look. Mrs. Murphy didn't have to speak to express her skepticism.

"It was just young kids on bikes," I said. "Who knows what they were told to do ... maybe just to put the red note on the green car with a black top. That seems the most logical explanation."

She wasn't buying it. "That's not very logical at all,

Nathan. My Buick is a lot bigger than your little foreign car."

That made me laugh. "Yeah, a Saab convertible is not a Buick sedan. I get it. But they're both green and they both have black tops. It's the only way this makes sense to me." I rolled my neck, trying to relieve the tension in my muscles. "I didn't tell you this before, but I saw the kids last night. They were putting the protest flyers on all the windshields. A couple of them were arguing with each other. Maybe they were squabbling over which car should get the 'special' flyer, the one with the red note in it?"

She pursed her lips, and I heard her foot tapping on the oak floor. As I said, Mrs. Murphy clearly telegraphs her emotions. "This is all too much," she said. "Here. Sit down again. I've got something to help put the world right."

I had no idea what she was talking about until she returned with two shot glasses and a bottle of Jameson Irish whiskey. Since we'd already finished off a bottle of red wine, this was not a good idea. I had little choice, though. She filled both shot glasses to overflowing and pushed one across the table to me. As she raised her glass in a toast, she paused, waiting impatiently for me to do the same.

A smile brightened her face, and she spoke with an Irish accent I hadn't heard from her before. "May neighbors respect you, trouble neglect you, and the angels protect you!"

That made me chuckle until I realized she'd downed the whiskey in a single gulp. She slammed her empty glass on the table, scrunched her brow and nodded to me—an obvious signal I was a laggard. I'm not much for hard liquor, but I was cornered. To refuse would have been most impolite, so I closed my eyes and chugged the whiskey. No way would I admit how much it burned going down—I've got my pride.

"To your health," I uttered in a gravelly voice. Maybe we hadn't put the world right, but it didn't seem to matter anymore.

Chapter Thirty
The Shadow

I'd only had two shots of whiskey—it's hard to say no to Mrs. Murphy—but I walked home on unsteady feet. The wind was still howling, pushing me back as I struggled to cover the short distance to my front door. The construction truck that had blocked the street was no longer there, so I considered moving my Saab from the back alley … then thought better of it. I probably wasn't sober enough. Besides, no one would complain in off-season October.

The red note was stuffed in my back pocket, ready to join the others in the "evidence folder" in my desk drawer. Whatever doubts I may have had about the Puzzler's motives were no longer valid. It was past time to take him seriously … and my gut told me it had to be a "him" … had to be a former student … had to, in some way, relate to Elijah Davis, even though the facts didn't point that way.

I vowed to call Patrolman Bob in the morning, maybe go to the police station downtown and make a formal complaint. Didn't the underlined words in this note justify that? Wasn't it clear evidence of harassment or even stalking?

I unlocked the front door, glad to be back in my sanctuary. With sleepy eyes, Lenore perked up from her place on the green chair, jumped down for a big stretch, then issued a plaintive meow, saying she'd missed me. At least that's how I interpreted it. "Yes, Lenny-Oh, it's good to be home."

My body was feeling mellow from all the food and drink, but my mind was racing. This Poe Puzzler game had to stop. After his reference to Anna, I no longer wanted anything to do with these strange notes. The only way to stop them, however, was to uncover his identity and confront him. The germ of an idea began to form in my mind … but it wouldn't coalesce. What I needed was something to pull me out of this food and alcohol stupor.

I put the kettle on and rummaged through my tea cabinet to find just the right blend. After Irish stew, red wine, and whiskey, Japanese Sencha didn't seem right. So I chose my old standby, Darjeeling, which has a delicate blend of black tea with milder caffeine.

Lenore was eyeing my movements in the kitchen, her head cocked to one side. Treats were out of the question—it was too close to her dinner time. A gentle belly rub would do for now, and it would make me feel better as well. She knew what was coming, because when I eased myself down to pet her, she circled around and flopped on her back, her paws relaxed, waiting for my affection.

They say that cats don't like their bellies rubbed. That may be true for some, but Nori and I have our own rules. With soft, gentle strokes, all in one direction, I ran a hand over her silky fur. She does purr very loudly, but I could see she enjoyed it by the slow flexing of her front paws. That, and of course, she let me do it! "Okay, best white cat in all the universe. Thanks for being my buddy."

The tea kettle whistled, startling both of us. She twisted upright and bolted under a kitchen chair. I turned off the stove, waited a few seconds for the boiling water to subside, then poured it over the tea bag in my Black Cats & Barn Owls mug. There are some amusing online discussions about whether one should put the sugar and milk in before or after the hot water. Me? I'm not that fussy! It really doesn't matter which comes first as long as you put in just the right amount of each—that's my secret to a nice cup of tea.

Grasping the mug with both hands, I wandered into my study. The easel with its large clipboard was still set up, but I had no new insights to add to it. I've seen way too many detective shows where everything comes together on the evidence board, maybe with strings of yarn pulled from one spot to another. That's fine for fiction, and I suppose writing things down could help organize one's mind. Staring at what I had written, however, wasn't helping me at all.

I set the mug on my desk—using a coaster, of course—and cleared off everything except the desk lamp. The top drawer held my laptop, and in a haphazard pile, my collection of Puzzler notes. Maybe some organization wouldn't hurt. I pulled them out and placed each one in chronological order on top of my desk.

Since I'd mailed the first note with my response to the Puzzler's P.O. box, I pulled a blank sheet of paper from my printer, labeled it #1, and placed it first, on the left. I'd made a photocopy of the second and had the originals of all the others. Of course, that awful bloody wine bottle acted as a note, so I positioned another sheet of paper, labeled #5, in its place.

This exercise got the wheels turning in my head. The first two notes asked basic biographical questions about Poe—where he died and why he hated Griswold. My "invitation" to meet him at Waverly and Seaspray was in the third note. The fourth was about the Black Death, and from there things descended into more and more macabre topics.

After the wine bottle, the sixth note referenced Poe's "Premature Burial"—the note that accompanied my flat tire. And then the seventh note, the one that still unsettled me. Annabel Lee. "Chilling" and "killing." I pulled it from my pocket and set it on the desk with the others.

Seven notes. Seven taunts. I stared at this odd collection. What had I done to provoke the ire of the Puzzler?

The wind was still howling outside, with occasional gusts strong enough to rattle the window panes. The only other sound in my office was the click-click-click of the heat registers as they labored to take the chill out of the room.

"Enough!" I slammed a fist on the desk and shouted in my frustration.

I was tired of being on the receiving end of all this, of

being a man of inaction rather than action. How C. Auguste Dupin would chide me for that! I had the Puzzler's P.O. address. Now, I could turn the tables on him.

I gathered the notes in a neat pile and looked for a paperweight. My eyes strayed to the raven on top of my bookcase … and then to the Hungarian medallion. It was about time I put that talisman to good use.

Moving my guest chair closer, I stepped up and grabbed the ancient roundel. It felt strangely cold to my touch, as if some sort of energy had sucked the warmth from the room. I hadn't noticed that when I'd first brought it home.

As I stepped down, I balanced the heft of this strange totem in my hand. Was it made of silver or nickel? Or maybe some obscure alloy? Its considerable mass didn't match its size. In any case, it would make a fine paperweight for the Poe Puzzler notes. Perhaps it could cast its magic spell over them and lead me to a solution.

Ever the curious cat, Lenore pranced into the room and leapt onto my desk. With cautious steps, she approached the medallion, ears flattened, nose sniffing the air. All cats possess a primal discomfort with anything new in their environment. She may be a house cat, a pet, but Lenore's feral instincts surface when she faces a suspicious object in her domain.

"It's okay, Lenori," I whispered to her, trying to ease her fears. "Yes, that's certainly an odd piece, but it's from Mrs. G, so I'm sure it's okay." Her ears twitched at the sound of my voice, but her eyes stayed glued to the talisman. Rather than curling up for a nap on my desk, her usual routine when I'm working, she jumped down and sat, wide-eyed, at the entrance to the hall. It was about as far from me and the medallion as she could go while still keeping watch on us.

Brushing aside Lenore's odd behavior, I settled into my office chair, pulled my laptop from the top drawer, and closed my eyes, waiting for inspiration. How could I challenge my nemesis to a meeting? It had to be handled carefully. I had to lure him in the same way he had strung me along. After launching Word, I stared at the blank, white screen, devoid of words. Nothing came to me.

When in doubt, turn to Poe—Edgar Allan, that is! I searched my mind for a Poe reference about meeting someone, ideally an antagonist. "The Casque of Amontillado"? The first line was a classic. No, that wouldn't do. Talking about revenge was not the right angle. As my kindergarten teacher used to say, "You catch more flies with honey than vinegar."

Surely there was something in "The Murders in the Rue Morgue," I reasoned. In that story, the narrator first meets Dupin as they both reach for the same book in a Parisian library. Then again, I didn't feel good mentioning "library," not after my conversations with Nickie. Besides, I wanted a secluded meeting place. More research was needed.

When I got up to retrieve one of my many volumes of Poe's writings from the bookcase, I was jolted to a stop at the sound of the storm door banging open. Lenore arched her back like a Halloween cat, her tail as fat as a squirrel's. "Just the wind, Nori," I whispered. Far from being mollified, she looked over my shoulder and hissed.

That sent a chill down my spine.

I turned to see what had frightened her. A dark shadow was cast against the small glass panes of my office door. The shadow of a man in a hoodie.

I froze. The shadow leaned in closer, blocking most of the light from the alley. Had I locked the door? In the dim light of my desk lamp, I zeroed in on the doorknob. Yes, it was locked. But then I saw the knob turn, ever so slightly. He was testing it. He was trying to see if he could open the door … to barge into my home, my sanctuary.

Something snapped in me. I yelled and scrambled back to my desk. The small drawer on the right slid open without a sound, and I grabbed my antique letter opener. It could inflict as much damage as a dagger.

He must have heard me and even seen my movements through the glass. He had the advantage over me there. All I could see was his shadow.

I brandished the letter opener like a hunting knife, its sharp point glinting in the dim light. With my arm out in front of me, I inched closer to the door, yelling out to him. "I'm armed!" He was standing mere inches from me, with nothing between us but my weather-beaten door.

His movements stopped. Was my challenge enough of a deterrent? No. He was still there, his shadow cast large by the sole streetlight in the alley. He hadn't moved.

Fumbling with my left hand, I pulled my phone from my pocket. My clumsy thumb struggled to input the code. Then I saw the "emergency" icon. I swapped hands—dagger in left, phone in right, and hit the icon to dial.

"9-1-1. What is your emergency?"

"Someone's trying to break into my house. He's right at my back door!"

Chapter Thirty-One
Hobson's Choice

"So, you say you saw a prowler?"

Officer Lamb and I did not get off to a good start. "No," I replied. After what I'd been through, I had no patience with her skeptical tone. "It was an intruder. He was trying to break in."

She shrugged her shoulders. "And did he?"

She had me on the ropes, but I wasn't going to give in. "No, but he was about to."

She looked down at her highly polished shoes and paused a moment before meeting my eyes again. "There's a difference between trespassing and B&E— breaking and entering."

The situation probably called for me to be polite, even obsequious. I was in no mood. "Look. Words matter to me. But in this case, I don't care what you call it. All I can tell you is I felt threatened. If my back door wasn't locked, he'd have pushed right in. I know it."

"You're that retired English teacher, aren't you?"

I knew the rest was coming, so I gave her time to get it out.

"And you've got that private investigation business, don't you?"

If this were a schoolyard, we'd be nose to nose, itching for a fight. The words came out of my mouth before I had time to think. "What of it?"

"Nothing. Just asking."

I closed my eyes and counted to ten; I only got as far as five. "Maybe we should start over."

"Sure. So, where did you see this ... this person?"

My pulse still hadn't returned to normal. "Follow me. Please."

Officer Lamb's police cruiser had burst onto the scene with a screech of tires, red and blue lights pulsing, and siren wailing. She'd checked to see if I was okay, then did a perimeter search around the house, but found nothing. I didn't expect her to. The Poe Puzzler's shadow disappeared from my office door as soon as I'd called 9-1-1. He was too cunning to stick around. I knew that much about him.

While I should have been grateful for the quick police response, all I could think was what the neighbors must be saying. Mrs. G was probably looking out her living room window. Mrs. Murphy was no doubt at her front door. This was more excitement than they'd seen in some time.

I led Officer Lamb down the hall and into my private office, now fully lit with a floor lamp and overhead light. Seeing my inner sanctum with fresh eyes, I was surprised at the cobwebs on the ceiling and the dust bunnies under my desk. I needed to do a better job of cleaning ... and brushing Lenore.

After a cursory look around the room, more than likely noticing its untidiness, Officer Lamb walked up to my office door and jiggled the knob. I joined her. She was only about five-foot-three, so I towered over her.

Since it was still early fall, the "shoulder season," she could have been one of the dozens of Special Law Enforcement Officers the city hires to deal with the tourist population. With all the gear she had clipped to her navy blue uniform—gun in holster, flashlight, radio, and I don't know what else—I figured her to be a regular. She was professional, nothing frivolous about her, but a certain attitude sometimes seeped through.

"Don't have a deadbolt on this door?" she asked.

"No. As you can see."

"Hmm." She stood on tiptoe to get a better view out the small window panes placed high in the door. Her dark auburn hair was clipped back and mostly hidden by her police cap. As she craned her neck, I caught a glimpse of some freckles. I bet I'd never recognize her if she was in her "civvies." She turned from the door, and the look on her face made it clear I was going to get another wrist-slap about home security. "That storm door doesn't look very secure," she said.

I let out an exasperated breath. "Yes, I know. It's on my list."

She leaned in closer to me and wrinkled up her nose. "Mr. Poe, have you been drinking?"

This was too much. I'd called for help, and now I was being interrogated. "Yes, I had some alcoholic beverages at dinner. At a neighbor's."

"You didn't drive, did you?"

Counting to ten was no longer an option. "Look," I said with an edge to my voice. "I called 9-1-1 because a man in a hoodie was trying to break into my house. I saw him wiggle the doorknob, testing to see if it was locked."

She stared at me, her eyebrows raised.

"And no," I said, "I didn't drive after dinner. I walked home."

Her pursed lips and a slight shake of her head made her attitude clear. I just wanted her to get on with her job.

"Let me take a better look outside this door and in the alley," she said. "I may have missed something."

As skeptical as she appeared to be, at least she was being thorough.

No sooner had she stepped out of the office door than my phone rang—Mrs. Murphy. Of course.

"Are you okay, Nathan? I saw the police car pull up in such a hurry. Surely they don't have to drive so fast down our street. Unless it's an emergency. Was it an emergency, Nathan?"

"Slow down, Mrs. Murphy." I took a moment to breathe, willing myself to achieve some semblance of composure. "It was and it wasn't … an emergency, that is. A man in a hoodie, likely my Poe Puzzler, tried to break into my house."

"Oh my. That's horrible, Nathan!"

Patience is a virtue. That's what my grandmother used to say. I wasn't feeling it just then. "Let me get back to you after I talk to the police officer. I'll call you in the morning."

"Are you sure you're okay, Nathan? I'd feel horrible

if anything happened to you, especially after our little tipple this evening. I was even a bit concerned about you walking home alone. And now this—an intruder. Dear Lord!"

"I'm fine. Please, Mrs. Murphy. I'll call you tomorrow. Okay?"

After she reluctantly agreed, I hung up and closed my eyes, trying to compartmentalize the evening's events. That's when I felt a presence in the room. I hadn't heard her come in—Mrs. G, of course. On little cat feet, as usual.

"Bad things happen?" she asked. I got the impression she'd be disappointed if I said no.

"Yes … I guess you could say that."

I explained what had occurred and how I'd reacted, finally calling 9-1-1 when I felt my nemesis would actually break into my home.

"Bad man. Same bad man who leave you notes?"

"Yes, I'm sure. He was wearing a hoodie, just like we'd seen the other night when Berni and Bob chased him."

She glanced over at my desk and pointed to the Hungarian medallion. "You keep that with you. Protect you from bad man."

Officer Lamb chose that moment to walk back in, so of course her ears perked up when she heard Mrs. G. She gave us both an icy stare, then cleared her throat before addressing my neighbor. "Excuse me, but who are you and what 'bad man' are you talking about?"

Mrs. G's face reddened. This was the first time I'd seen her confronted by authority, and knowing her as I do, I was sure it wouldn't go down well. She squared her shoulders and stiffened her back before responding. "I'm Gyulalyi, Klara. I'm neighbor to Mr. Poe. Good friends."

Officer Lamb turned to me, as if to verify her statement.

"She's a dear friend, Officer Lamb. And she's always keeping an eye out for me."

The officer didn't speak for a few moments, just slowly nodded her head, her eyes darting back and forth between us. "I'll tell you what, Mrs. Goo … ma'am. You should go back to your home. I need to talk to Mr. Poe in private."

She mumbled some words in Hungarian. I wouldn't be surprised if they were cuss words. Then, with her back to the officer, a clear signal of her dismissiveness, she spoke directly to me. "You come see me later. Okay?"

"Tomorrow, Mrs. G. Please."

She strutted back down the hallway to my front door. I started to speak, but was interrupted by my front door slamming shut. If she were Mrs. Murphy, I would have said she'd gotten her Irish up. I don't know the Hungarian phrase for that.

"I can see why you call her Mrs. G," the officer said. "What is that name? Russian or something."

"No, it's Hungarian. And what difference does that make?"

"Just making conversation with you. That's all. You know, communicating."

I tried to steer her away from Mrs. G and back to why I'd called the cops in the first place. "So, what did you find out there?"

She turned down the corners of her mouth before responding. "Nothing out of the ordinary," she said. "A few garbage-can lids flying around in the wind. Are you sure that's not what you saw?"

It wasn't easy, but I kept my temper when I responded. "Yes, I'm sure. A garbage-can lid can't wiggle a doorknob."

"Hmm." Her eyes still held that suspicious gaze whenever she looked at me. "So, tell me about this 'bad man' you two were talking about."

I gave her the Reader's Digest Condensed version, leaving out plenty of details—like Patrolman Bob's involvement … and the bloody bottle on the beach. She took it all in, and even though she glanced at my desk—the Hungarian talisman and my letter opener were clearly in view—she didn't ask me any follow-up questions. That surprised me. I shouldn't have been so easily fooled, however. She noticed everything.

"We'll monitor the alley; have a patrol car drive through a few times tonight," she said. "But maybe you ought to come down to the station tomorrow and talk to a detective. Sounds like you've got a stalker." She pointed to the Puzzler notes. "And bring that pile of notes you have under that silver medallion. That's the only hard evidence you've got." No mention of the antique letter opener. Maybe it was innocuous enough to avoid her scrutiny.

She walked down the hallway to my front door, then turned around as if she'd forgotten something. "Just one more thing, Mr. Poe," she said. Someone must have watched too many episodes of Columbo.

"Oh, what's that?"

"I assume that's your Saab convertible parked back there?"

Here it comes, I thought. "Yes, that's mine."

"You can't park in the alley," she said. I caught a twinkle in her eyes. Was she toying with me? "Even in the off-season."

"I thought about moving it," I explained, "but as you said, I'd been drinking."

"Well, that leaves you with a choice, doesn't it? Pay a parking ticket or risk getting arrested for DUI." She was enjoying this conversation too much.

"That's a Hobson's Choice, isn't it?" From the look on her face, I could see she didn't get it. And I found some small satisfaction realizing I'd stumped her.

"What does that mean?" she asked.

Now it was my turn to smile. "It's an old English saying," I explained. "Basically, it means even though there appear to be options, you really only have one choice."

"I get it," she said. "It is what it is. That's what I say. And you've already been ticketed, so it's no choice at all. Have a good night, Mr. Poe." She walked through my small living room, out the front door, and got into her police car … and finally turned off those blinding strobe lights.

But I was left with a nagging thought.

I ran into the kitchen and pulled the big Maglite from under the sink, then hurried back to my office. Not only did this metal-case flashlight cast a bright beam, but worse comes to worst, it could be used as a weapon. I considered grabbing my letter opener, but that seemed too extreme.

As I opened my office door, though, I had a moment's hesitation. Officer Lamb had checked everything, but what if my Poe Puzzler was hiding somewhere in the dark? I let out a held breath, switched on the flashlight, and stepped out into the night.

Chapter Thirty-Two
A Perfect Counterfeit

After patting my pocket to be sure I had my car keys, I shoved the office door shut. It was unnerving knowing that the Poe Puzzler had grasped the same doorknob less than an hour before. And Officer Lamb hadn't even checked for fingerprints! To her mind, this whole thing must have seemed trivial. If I weren't so shaken, I would have been angry.

The wind was still blowing hard, so I struggled to latch my intractable storm door. After tonight's episode, I really needed to get it fixed, not to mention installing a deadbolt on my office door. I swung the flashlight beam wide before venturing down into the alley, looking for anything out of the ordinary. The only sound was a nearby street sign creaking back-and-forth with each gust of wind.

Just as Officer Lamb had said, a couple of garbage-can lids had blown into the alley. I scurried to pick them up and put them back where they belonged.

As I'd come to expect living on the North End, no one was about—no pedestrians walking in the alley, no loud music from passing cars, not even one of our year-round rabbits scampering for cover. At well past nine o'clock, everyone was in bed, quietly reading a book, or watching their favorite TV show. It's such a peaceful neighborhood. And that made the actions of my Poe Puzzler even more unsettling.

I swung the flashlight beam over to my car. Sure enough, a parking ticket was stuffed under the windshield wipers. I'd received one or two in the past, so I knew what to expect. Without paying much attention to the ticket, I stuffed it into my shirt pocket and gave the area one more quick scan with the light. Everything was ordinary, neat, and tidy, as usual. There was nothing to indicate a crime had been perpetrated, or nearly so.

And yet, a chill ran down my back, either from the cool night air or the lingering suspicion that my nemesis wasn't done with me yet. It may seem silly now, but I did a 360-degree inspection of my car, shining the light on each tire and crouching down to look underneath. Getting down like that is no problem for me; it's the getting back up that's difficult.

As satisfied as I could be under the circumstances, I unlocked my car and slid into the driver's seat. Then I realized my mistake. Maybe I've seen too many horror movies, but I gazed into the rearview mirror and then whipped around, directing the flashlight beam onto the back seat. Nothing. I took deep breaths to calm my racing pulse … and hit the power lock switch.

There was certainly enough adrenaline coursing through my system to sober me up. So, I had no qualms about driving around the block to the front of my house.

My Saab had other plans. A slow rrr-rrr-rrrr was all I got when I turned the ignition key. Oh, come on! I said to myself. Not now!

I mouthed a silent prayer to the Norse Gods, then tried again. I heard the same slow grinding sound from the starter, but then praise be to Odin, my long-suffering Swedish steed sprang to life with a cough.

A new battery—another item for my long to-do list.

I waited for the engine to settle down to a smooth idle, put the transmission in Drive, and eased my way out of the alley and around to my street.

When I walked in the front door, I expected to see Lenore greeting me with wide eyes after the night's events. No Lenore. She must have been hiding in one of her usual spots. I couldn't blame her. She was used to a calm and relaxed atmosphere in our house. Not tonight.

"Come on out, Nori," I called to her. "It's almost dinnertime." I opened a few closet doors that were slightly ajar, places where she might have fled for sanctuary, then bent down to look under the kitchen table. No sight of her. Lenore would emerge when she was ready, I reasoned. There was no use crawling around trying to find her. The crinkle of paper in my shirt pocket reminded me to take a better look at the parking ticket. The town's fines might have gone up since my last one.

I walked into my now brightly lit office and unfolded the ticket on my desk. I really have to hand it to my Poe puzzler. The guy was clever. Very clever. Everything about this ticket looked official. But it wasn't. He'd left another note. And this time he'd made sure it was on my windshield and not Mrs. Murphy's.

He must have studied parking tickets closely to make such a perfect counterfeit—it looked just like the real thing. In large block letters at the top, it read, "COMPLAINT AND SUMMONS." There was even a court ID and ticket number. Listed below were my Saab's color and its New Jersey license number. After a bunch of legal boilerplate, it read: "You are hereby summoned to answer the complaint charging you with the offense listed." All of that was typeset like the real thing. But then he got creative. My offense? It was handwritten below.

"Failure to teach."

Ouch! That hurt. So, as I'd suspected, my Poe Puzzler was more than likely a former student, and one I'd offended somehow. I hadn't taught for years, though, so why take it out on me now?

In pondering all this, I almost didn't read the rest of the ticket, this part also handwritten:

"You are hereby ordered to appear at the Life Saving Station tomorrow night at 11:59 p.m. Come alone."

Of course, he would tell me to come alone. As my students used to say, "As if!"

And it wouldn't be a Puzzler note without some reference to Poe and his works. In Times Roman Bold at the bottom of the ticket, it read: "And the revel went whirlingly on, until at length was sounded the twelfth hour upon the clock." That sounds quite pleasant until you realize it's from Poe's "The Masque of the Red

Death." It's the scene near the end when a ghastly masked figure—the Red Death personified—enters Prince Prospero's masquerade ball.

Pretty grim, but then again, this was another chance to meet my adversary.

To think that earlier that night, I had been crafting my own invitation to meet him in person. He always seemed to be one step ahead of me. Time to put an end to that.

It was pretty late for a call, so I ventured a text to my two sleuthing partners, Berni and Bob. "New note! Meet for breakfast at Positively 4th Street. 8 am."

Within moments, I got a "do not disturb" reply from Berni. Good! Sleep is the best medicine, and I hoped her burns were healing. Bob took longer to respond, but I finally got a thumbs up from him.

As Sherlock Holmes would say—and, of course, he was fashioned after Poe's C. Auguste Dupin—the game's afoot!

Chapter Thirty-Three
We Make Our Plans

I awoke tangled in bedsheets, my pillows scattered on the floor. It was a restless night, grappling with thoughts of locks and doors, and how involved I wanted the police to be. I assumed my Puzzler was a former student, and even though he despised me … well, I had a certain responsibility to him, as I do to all my students.

Something had driven him to take action against me. What had I done that made him seek such revenge? Surely, if I could only talk with him, we could sort out our differences.

Looking back now, I should have realized I was being naïve. I was blind to how damaged my Poe Puzzler was.

After showering and dressing for the day—it looked like a cool but clear autumn morning—I put some krinkles in a bowl for Lenore. She hadn't responded to my calls; with cats, you have to be patient. Knowing her as well as I do, she'd probably emerge from her hiding place once I'd left the house, then eat her food … and just as likely return to her secret cubby until she felt safe enough to come out again.

It was too early for my meeting with Berni and Bob, so I brewed a strong cup of Irish Breakfast tea and crunched on a couple of spiced wafers to settle my stomach.

I'd chosen our breakfast meeting place well. The old U.S. Life Saving Station is diagonally across from the Positively 4th Street Cafe. We could eat pastries and make plans for our midnight encounter at the same time.

The Life Saving Station was built in the 1880s, when shipwrecks off the Ocean City coast were common … and the beach was closer to Atlantic Avenue than it is today. The station is now a museum and a registered historic building. The architecture is pretty unusual. Can a wooden structure be called Gothic? That certainly fits. It has steep gables and wide, heavy overhangs. A narrow, spindly watchtower pokes through the center of the roof like a spear. In bright sunlight, this small structure looks impressive. In foul weather, it looks eerie.

Most locals associate the station with the famous 1901 wreck of the Sindia. It ran aground during a strong nor'easter. At the time, the Sindia was the largest cargo-carrying sailing ship in the world—329 feet long. And in an interesting bit of synchronicity, it was built in the same Northern Ireland shipyard as the Titanic. But unlike that better-known catastrophe, surfmen from the Ocean City Life Saving Station rowed out to the floundering ship and saved all hands before the Sindia's hull broke apart.

Why my Poe Puzzler chose it for our rendezvous, I

couldn't imagine … other than its name. It would certainly be deserted late at night. Why he specified a minute before midnight was also a mystery.

Once it was time to leave, I placed all the Poe Puzzler notes, plus Mrs. G's strange Hungarian medallion, in my messenger bag and stepped out on my porch, breathing in the fresh, salty air. The wind had died down, and it was a perfect jacket-and-hat October morning. As I unlocked my Saab and slid into the driver's seat, I had a moment's trepidation. I knew I couldn't put off getting a new battery much longer, but I'd hoped to get to my breakfast meeting without drama.

Maybe my twenty-year-old Swedish car enjoyed sitting in the morning sun, or maybe I was just in luck. It started without hesitation. Some cars have personality. Mine, maybe too much.

I found a parking spot on 4th Street, on the south side of the Life Saving Station. It was still early, and I didn't see Berni's truck or Bob's bright yellow Mustang. So, I tried to envision where my Puzzler was going to confront me.

White wooden fences enclose the property on all sides. On the east side, facing toward the beach, a brick-paved driveway leads to a launch ramp. A replica surfboat, the kind used by the rescuers, was displayed nearby. While the lot used to be relatively wooded—for Ocean City—all but one tree had been felled during the building's four-and-a-half-year renovation.

Since it was off-season, the museum inside the station was closed, and there was no sign of activity. Surprisingly, there were no "keep out" warnings and no obvious security cameras.

I locked my car and ambled around the building, getting a mental picture of what it would look like at midnight. What caught my eye at first was the remnant of the Sindia's rudder post, mounted in front of the south side porch. This huge cast-iron piece gave an idea of the mammoth scale of the ship.

From that vantage point, I scanned the surrounding neighborhood. The entire property was so open, with unobstructed views from the streets, that I had a hard time figuring out how my Poe Puzzler would surprise me; I was certain he wouldn't just walk out onto the porch one minute before midnight.

That is, until I ventured around the north side of the building. There, I found an ADA-compliant wooden ramp running between the building and a dilapidated shed. As beautifully restored as the station was, the shed was badly in need of paint and had delaminated sheets of plywood covering the windows. The shed doors were secured with a large padlock, but it looked like the plywood over the windows could be pried off easily enough. This seemed to be an ideal spot for the Puzzler to hide, scoping out our arrival.

I went back up the ramp and leaned over to pull at a corner of one of the plywood coverings. A floorboard creaked behind me, and a gruff voice called out. "What are you doing there?"

I swung around, red-faced, until I realized who it

was. Berni is quite good at mimicking a male voice, deep and authoritative. Seeing my reaction, she bent over, laughing. "Gotcha!" she said when she'd caught her breath.

I shook my head. Yeah, she'd really spooked me. "I didn't hear you pull up."

"I parked right behind you," she said, "and when I got out of my truck, I caught sight of you walking around the other side of the building. You seemed lost in thought."

I looked down at her bandaged hands. "So, how are the burns? It looks like you've got smaller bandages on them."

She glanced down, as if she'd forgotten all about the shop incident. "Actually, they're doing okay." She looked up with a coy smile. "Kathy came over and tended to my wounds."

I nodded. "It must be nice to have an on-call nurse."

"Uh-huh. She's really good at what she does."

Was there more than friendship at play here? I was about to chance a personal question when Berni caught me off guard with some out-of-character vocabulary. "So, what were you reconnoitering?"

I'm sure she saw the quizzical look on my face.

"That's a pretty good English-teacher word, isn't it?" she said with a grin. "But, seriously, why are you casing this place?"

"It's the latest note from the Poe Puzzler. He wants to meet here at midnight tonight."

"Ha! The witching hour!" She was certainly in a good mood.

"Don't joke, Berni. If we play our cards right, we can corner the guy."

She shrugged. "Maybe. He's pretty wily."

"There's more. He tried to break into my house last night."

Her eyes widened in alarm. "What!? What happened? Why didn't you call?"

Our conversation was cut short by the sound of Patrolman Bob's Mustang GT pulling up to the curb. Bright yellow and with unmuffled exhausts, his car was loud—to the eye and ear. No sneaking up on culprits in that vehicle!

"Let's get some breakfast and I'll tell you all about it," I said.

What a gem the little café at the corner of 4th and Atlantic is! Walking into the place is a delight to the senses. First, of course, is the wafting smells of freshly baked goods and coffee. It's an odd thing about coffee; I don't drink it, but the smell is enticing. Once inside, you notice the tile mosaics that adorn the walls and tables. Most of these are in an aquatic theme, but now and then you'll see one that's more abstract.

Since the place is called Positively 4th Street, the owner must be a Bob Dylan fan. I have no idea how Dylan managed to win the Nobel Prize ... in literature! But never mind. In a tribute to the singer/songwriter, there are two colorfully painted guitars mounted on the wall. Each one has a little sign that says they aren't for sale, but if you want to play one, you're welcome.

As we gathered around the counter, eyeing the menu, I told Berni and Bob it was my treat. I got no argument from either one.

The drink choices were plentiful. You could get all manner of hot and cold coffees, everything from a macchiato to an Almond Joy espresso. Hot tea, on the other hand, was only listed once. I felt somewhat discriminated against, but then the perky young woman behind the counter offered me a choice of several different tea bags. I selected the most unadulterated black Tetley tea—no citrus or flowery enhancements for me.

Bob got a large mug of coffee—no flavorings for him, either—but he did ask for three sugar packets. Berni, no surprise, ordered a smoothie, one called Oh Kale Yeah! Besides the aforementioned kale, it contained banana, apple, quinoa, and other healthy-sounding stuff. She declined to order anything else—"the smoothie will fill me up," she said. In contrast, Bob let us know he was "ravenous."

I played a little mental game, trying to guess what he'd order. Since he got a plain mug of coffee, I thought he'd go for something equally ordinary, like an egg and Taylor pork roll sandwich. I was wrong. He chose the Godfather Bagel, which was liberally garnished with cream cheese, pesto, pine nuts, and sun-dried tomato. I have to admit, it sounded tempting.

For me? Well, I simply love their pastries. I selected an apple walnut fig-jam muffin and a slice of pumpkin pie coffee cake. Yum!

They also make scones, but after Mrs. Murphy's authentic delights, I just couldn't.

Once we got our food, we settled at a round table in an adjoining room. The nearby window offered a clear view of the Life Saving Station. I was patient, letting Bob and Berni enjoy their breakfasts before diving into the events of the previous evening and my midnight invitation. I eased into the conversation with an apology.

"Sorry to text you guys so late last night," I said. "I thought it was safer than calling, given the hour."

"Ah, no problem, Nathan," Bob said. "I was watching the Phillies game … and I needed an interruption from yelling at the TV. What a night!"

I turned to Berni with raised eyebrows, hoping she'd say she was in the land of nod when I texted. "I had my phone on 'do not disturb,'" she said. I caught a slight smile at the corners of her mouth. "Kathy and I were at the movies last night."

It sounded like Berni and Kathy just might be an item. Bob interrupted my musings before I could ask.

"Look, I'm on duty at nine," he said. "What's this all about? Another note?"

I filled them in on everything that had happened the night before—the Puzzler attempting to open my back door, Officer Lamb's inquiry, and the fake parking ticket with its "invitation." Bob only interrupted once to comment about Officer Lamb. "Yeah, she's a stickler for protocol," he said.

Once I'd related all the details I could think of, the group sat in silence, with only the click of coffee cups and the hiss of an espresso machine filtering in from the other room. "So, what do we do now?" Berni asked. "Come back here at midnight and wait for the Puzzler to waltz down Atlantic Avenue? And he wants you to go alone."

"Yup," said Bob, "and I'd bet he's certain you won't!"

"I've got an idea," I said.

They leaned in closer, and we spoke in soft, conspiratorial tones as we made our plans.

Chapter Thirty-Four
Rescue Operation

With a bark from his Mustang's dual exhausts and a squeal of the rear tires, Bob took off for the police station. Who was going to give him a ticket? Berni and I had more time on our hands, so we wandered back to the Life Saving Station.

I'd explored the place a few years earlier, simply because I was intrigued by the building. Now, we were looking at it from a different angle. We took in the wide porches that would be deep in shadow at night, the open surfboat in back, and the run-down shed, each one offering a good midnight hiding place.

"If Bob is right," I said, "my Puzzler will expect the three of us to show up early and wait for him to arrive."

Berni slowly shook her head. "We were early the other night at Waverly and Seaspray, but that guy was fast."

"True. This time, however, we've got a better plan than sitting in your truck with pizza on our laps."

She gave me the side-eye.

"I know. I know. I was the laggard who couldn't even

get out of the truck in time."

She shrugged, and we continued to inspect the property, retracing our steps to ensure everything I'd laid out in the cafe would work.

"The alley on the north side is his most likely escape route if he gets spooked," she said.

"Probably the way he'll come, too. But he has to park somewhere. Even if we only get a license plate number, it will be progress."

We surveyed the alley. It was narrow, with houses tucked in tight on either side. Plenty of opportunities to duck between them or even hide under a porch. And in mid-October, most of the houses were empty.

There didn't seem to be anything more we could do until later.

Berni rested a hand on my shoulder, a frown tugging at the corners of her eyes. "A lot depends on your visit with the police," she said. "You are going to go see them, aren't you?"

I let out a dry chuckle. "No choice. I'm sure Officer Lamb has already filed a report about last night's events. They're expecting me."

A smile returned to her face, and she gave me a quick pat on the back. "Okay, Frodo. On to our next adventure."

Berni waved goodbye as she jumped into her pickup truck, parked right behind me. I eased into my Saab, totally unmindful of the sorry state of my old battery. Sure enough, when I turned the key, all I heard was a slow rr … r. Then nothing.

The sight of Berni's truck in my rearview mirror as it

backed away made me panic. Like a fool, I hit the power window switch. Obviously, nothing happened. I opened my door and frantically waved an arm. She got the message.

With a grunt and a sigh, I stepped out of my car. Berni jogged over. "Car trouble?" she asked.

"Yeah. Dead battery."

"Are you sure?"

I wasn't in the mood for a discussion of my automotive diagnostic skills, so I stepped aside and motioned for her to have a seat and try it herself. The only response to her efforts was a muted click. She looked up at me. "Yup. Dead as disco."

She got out of the car and rubbed the back of her neck as she looked down at the pavement. "I assume you don't have a set of jumper cables," she said in a quiet voice.

My filters came off. "And I assume you do!" I spat back at her.

She looked back up at me, a smile in her eyes. "Gotcha, again!" she said, smacking me on the shoulder. It must have hurt her bandaged hand, but she didn't let on. "Of course I have jumper cables! I travel prepared ... unlike some people." Her mood was the polar opposite of mine.

An English teacher's brain works in mysterious ways. That's all I can attribute to what came out of my mouth next—a slow chant as much as a recitation of one of Poe's poetic couplets: "Resignedly beneath the skies, the melancholy waters lie."

She scrunched up her face, arms out in a "what are

you talking about?" gesture. "Okay, Mr. Poe. How 'bout you put those melancholy waters aside, and pop the hood. I'll swing my truck around to bring us nose to nose."

Look under the hood of a Saab of my vintage, and you won't be able to spot the battery. It's hidden by a large plastic cover. But Berni knew what she was doing. She pried loose a rubber seal, then unscrewed the cover and handed it to me. "Put it in the trunk," she said. "You won't need it for a while."

With the Saab's battery uncovered, Berni performed the dance of the cables, going back and forth between the two vehicles. Red to red—positive to positive—and then the black grounds. I offered to help, but Berni told me to sit in the car. Once the cables were secure, she started up her truck, and signaled for me to wait a few minutes. When she gave me the go-ahead, my engine sprang to life with only a minor complaint. Relief flowed through me as I slouched in the driver's seat.

Once she'd coiled up the cables and placed them back in her truck, Berni ambled over and gestured for me to lower the window.

"You were lucky I was here," she said.

"Don't I know it!"

"Look, you can't get complacent now or you'll find yourself stranded. Here's the deal. Follow me over to my place. We'll pull that tired battery from your Saab, take it to the **NAPA** store over the bridge, and get you a new one. They usually want a 'core' in return."

I paused to consider. "That sounds fine, Berni, but what about your hands? You're surely not going to remove the battery in the state they're in."

She beamed down at me. "No, I'm not," she said. "You are! You know the old saying ... teach a man to fish ..."

Berni was an excellent teacher. She made me don a shop apron and safety glasses, and eventually found a pair of XL work gloves for me before we began. Looking over my shoulder and with gentle encouragement, she gave me step-by-step instructions.

Could I have done the job myself? Doubtful. Not only do I lack the right tools, but I probably would have snapped off the rusty bolt holding the battery bracket.

"Now comes the heavy lifting," Berni said. She wasn't joking. It's not so much that the battery was heavy; it's leaning over the fender and getting a good grip on it that made it hard. "Set it on the ground for now," she told me. "You've got to clean up some of the corrosion in the battery tray before we go any further."

She disappeared into her shop, but soon returned with a small metal bowl, a chip brush, and a box of baking soda. As I've said, Berni's a pro.

While the baking soda did its thing, I hefted the battery into the back of her pickup truck, and we headed for the auto parts store in Ocean View. It was a golden opportunity to find out more about her new friend.

"So, tell me about Kathy," I said.

She grinned, but waited a moment to respond. "What do you want to know?"

It was going to be a slow game of give and take. I could play that one. "Where did you meet her?"

Her smile broadened. "We met at the gym a couple weeks ago. It was kind of cute … and kind of stupid."

"Go on."

"I was pedaling pretty hard on a stationary bike. I saw her get on the bike alongside mine. She had on tight-fitting yoga pants and a blue 'Hello Kitty' t-shirt. What adult wears that?"

By the way she talked about Kathy, I could tell this was more than simply friendship. "Okay," I said. "I get the cute part. What about the stupid part?"

"Soon, I realized Kathy was matching my speed. Her hair was pulled back in a ponytail, and it swished back and forth with each thrust of the pedals."

Rather than ask a follow-up, I let the silence do the job for me.

"Well, as you know, I'm kind of competitive. So, I started pedaling faster. Sure enough, she matched my pace and went faster still. Pretty soon, we were standing on the pedals, both bikes creaking on their mounts. I was the first to break up laughing. It was insane! We both cooled down, slowing to a more sedate pace, and then she introduced herself."

I got the picture. And it was good seeing Berni so happy. Was I a little jealous? Sure, but Berni's my best friend. She had room in her heart for a companion … and room in there for me, too.

"That's sweet," I said.

Our conversation stopped as we crossed the Roosevelt Boulevard Bridge, her truck tires whining over the grooved surface of the road. The noise subsided as we rolled along the concrete road into Marmora. The little restaurants we passed on either side looked deserted, but the liquor store parking lot was crowded. No booze in Ocean City; it's either Marmora or Somers Point if you want beer, wine, or something stronger.

"So, when am I going to meet this Kathy?"

"Oh, you'll meet her soon enough," she responded.

"Tell me more, Berni. You're being tight-lipped."

She shrugged. "Kathy's a year or two younger than me. And she has a much younger brother. He got into drugs and ended up in juvenile detention. When he got out, he went to live with an aunt in Virginia. So, they're not close."

"How sad." I have no siblings, and I've always envied people who do. Then again, I've heard too many stories of family problems like this.

"It gets worse. Her mom died last month. And her brother never showed up for the funeral."

I stared out the window at the passing strip malls, gas stations, and liquor stores on Route 9. I wanted to offer some words of comfort, but all that came to mind were empty platitudes. We rode in silence for the rest of the trip.

Berni's phone buzzed as we pulled into the parking lot of the auto parts store. She turned off the engine, reached into her back pocket, and smiled when she saw the caller ID. I opened the door to get out, but she raised an index finger—the universal sign "for wait a minute."

After she said hello, all the talking was on the other end of the line. Her smile drained away. "Hold on, Kath," she said. "Just a sec." Berni's face was ashen; I knew this was not good news. She covered the phone with one hand and turned to me. "Carry the old battery into the store and get a new one. They'll help you out. I've gotta take this call."

With a foot out of the truck, I hesitated. I wanted to stay with Berni, to support her in any way I could. But, obviously, this was private. I got out and eased the door shut.

My mind was elsewhere as I carried the old battery into the store. A helpful young clerk took one look at me and relieved me of the heavy weight. When he asked me for the make, model, and year of my car, at first I couldn't think.

What was going on with Berni and Kathy?

Chapter Thirty-Five
Fiona and Klara

I got the story in bits and pieces as we drove back to Berni's shop. Kathy's wayward brother had returned to New Jersey, and things weren't going well. Berni didn't fill in all the details, but apparently there were heated arguments between the siblings about their late mother's house in Marmora.

When we pulled up to her shop, she gave me terse instructions for installing the new battery, then got back into her truck to drive to Kathy's. I stumbled through the process well enough. At least the wind had died down and the October sun felt warm on my back as I clamped everything down. My dear old Saab started right up, and after a moment, all the warning lights disappeared.

All of that should have made me feel better, given me a sense of accomplishment. Berni's mood when she left, however, hung over me. I felt useless, not knowing how to comfort my best friend. After she and Kathy had talked, I thought I'd come back to Berni's and get us some takeout dinner. There was no point in insinuating myself between the two of them. I hadn't even met Kathy yet.

With all these thoughts weighing on me, I drove back into town. At the red light at 9th Street, which always seems timed too long for cross-traffic, I considered making a right turn toward the police station to talk with a detective, as Officer Lamb had instructed. But I just wasn't up for it. Good thing. When I pulled up to my house, who did I see emerging from Mrs. Murphy's front door but Mrs. G and her. By the way they both looked at me, it was apparent they had been waiting for my arrival.

It's hard to imagine a more unlikely pair, both in stature and personality. Sort of like the nursery rhyme about Jack Sprat and his wife, or if you're into old movies, Laurel and Hardy. Besides, I thought they'd had a falling out before I'd even moved into town.

I grabbed my messenger bag from the front seat and walked over to greet them. Judging by their body language, this was not a friendly visit. Mrs. Murphy stood with arms crossed. Mrs. G put her hands on her hips. No doubt about it—I was in the doghouse.

"Good morning, ladies!" I smiled, hoping to lighten the mood. "It's still morning, isn't it? And what brings the two of you here today?" My feigned pleasantries got me nowhere.

"We must talk," Mrs. G said, tapping a foot in a harsh staccato.

"Did you forget to call me?" added Mrs. Murphy. If she were a grade-school teacher, the look on her face would have made the kids cringe.

Oh boy. I had promised to call her to explain the

commotion last night. Mrs. G had witnessed most of it … okay, maybe just some of it. It might be time to tell them everything about my Poe Puzzler. You never know, I reasoned. They could have a different way of looking at things.

With a promise to reveal all, I invited them into my home. It was almost noon, so I knew I had to provide some refreshments. Luckily, I'd gone shopping the day before; I had a few options.

They sat opposite each other at my humble kitchen table, giving each other knowing looks, but surprisingly, not talking. No doubt about it—they were up to something.

I filled the kettle and put it on the stove, then decided to forgo teabags and brew my best loose tea—Fortnum and Mason Royal Blend. It takes a little more time with tea leaves, but this rich, golden-amber tea is worth it. Assuming our forced meeting required a degree of formality, I pulled out my Portmeirion dessert plates— I'd broken one a few weeks before Christmas, so I was lucky it was only the three of us. Digging deep into the pantry, I found an unopened box of water crackers. Thinly sliced salami, English cheddar, and fresh grapes were the best I could do for my makeshift charcuterie board. It would have been nice to add figs or dried apricots, but I wasn't prepared for anything that elaborate.

Mrs. Murphy broke the silence. "You're taking an

awfully long time, Nathan. You don't have to go to all this trouble for us."

Right!

I was saved from replying by the whistling kettle. Then I realized I hadn't primed the teapot. I had to slow down. Was I nervous? Mrs. Murphy and Mrs. G were always open, friendly, and supportive whenever I needed help. Their attitude as they sat at the table, though, put me on edge.

I couldn't let that distract me from making a proper pot of tea …

Pour hot tap water into my little red pot. Wait a few minutes for it to retain some of the heat, then drain it. Measure out three-and-a-half heaping teaspoons of Royal Blend. Turn the stove back to high, and when the kettle begins to whistle, turn it off. With the water still hot but not boiling, pour it slowly over the tea leaves. Then set a mental timer for three minutes.

There were a few more things to do before I could sit down. Both my neighbors took sugar in their tea, but their preferences varied from there. My sugar bowl had a slight crack in the lid; I turned the offending edge toward me as I set it on the table—no point making it obvious. A splash of two-percent milk went into the cups for Mrs. Murphy and me. Mrs. G preferred lemon, so I cut a couple of slices and placed them on a saucer in front of her.

Finally, I joined them at my kitchen table and poured the tea.

"Nathan. You have horses heads?" Mrs. G gave me a hard stare.

Horses heads? I didn't understand at first. All that came to mind was an Emily Dickinson poem, "Because I could not stop for Death." It was the last two lines: "I first surmised the horses' heads were toward eternity."

"Nathan!" Mrs. G jarred me out of my reverie. "You have horses heads?"

"Oh. Sorry, Mrs. G. Of course. They're in my messenger bag, over there on the couch."

"Hmph! You keep horses heads with you. Always! Protect you! Understand?"

"Yes, I understand." Wow, she was pretty adamant about that strange talisman.

"Okay," she said. "Now you talk."

"Yes, Nathan," Mrs. Murphy added. "Leave nothing out. We want the whole story."

As we're often told, it's best to start at the beginning. For me, that meant the very first note I'd received from the Poe Puzzler almost two weeks prior. They were silent as I laid out the chronology of events with all the details I could recall.

When I'd finished, I waited for their response. It didn't take long. Mrs. Murphy wanted to know more about the Edgar Allan Poe quotes, and the stories and poems they'd come from. Mrs. G asked a few pointed questions about what kind of teacher I'd been and how I'd gotten along with my students.

It's only when they questioned me about meeting the Poe Puzzler that night that I hesitated. I didn't so much mind them knowing. It was more that I was worried they'd want to change my plans or, worse still, to get involved. My fears were well justified.

"You realize there's a long alley behind that station," Mrs. Murphy said. "It runs all the way to Corinthian Avenue. It's an obvious getaway route." She delivered this with a smug look on her face. "Well? Have you thought about that?"

Some blocks on the North End are significantly longer than those farther south on the island. Maybe it's because the beach had cut much further inland a century and a half ago. Or maybe the town fathers simply hadn't established a grid when the streets were laid out. Mrs. Murphy had a good point, but Berni, Bob, and I had already considered the alley in our plans.

There was no use getting into a back-and-forth. I asked for a time-out, and pulled a bottle of raspberry wine from the fridge. Since I lacked anything resembling dessert wine glasses, I set three shot glasses on the table and poured our first taste. Quite a few more followed.

When the mood had mellowed, I tried to bring an end to the conversation.

"Look. Berni, Bob, and I have a solid plan," I said. "I believe we've covered all the bases." How could I have been so naïve to think that my two endearing but nosy neighbors would accept what I'd told them, wish me a pleasant day, and leave me in peace?

Mrs. Murphy dropped the bombshell, directing her question to Mrs. G as if I weren't even in the room with them. "Well, Klara. Is your car in running order?"

"Ha! My Mercedes-Benz in good shape, always. Very good shape!"

Mrs. G was lucky to have a plus-size lot with a narrow driveway that ran alongside her house to a one-car garage. She kept her silver Mercedes sedan—it had to be at least thirty years old—in pristine condition, although she rarely drove it.

"Good!" Mrs. Murphy pushed back her chair, barely hiding a Cheshire cat smile. "We have an interesting case here, don't we, Klara?"

That got a somber nod from Mrs. G, and her usual Hungarian affirmative: "Igen."

My mouth hung open. They have an interesting case?

The two of them rose from their chairs in unison.

"You come over to me, Fiona. We talk about this some more."

As they headed toward the front door, Mrs. Murphy turned to me. "It's clear you need our help, Nathan," she said.

What kind of Pandora's box had I opened?

I had to call Berni and tell her about this new twist to our carefully laid plans for the night. As well-meaning as they were, my neighbors could create all manner of unintended consequences.

When I dialed Berni's cell phone, it rang a few times, then stopped. I heard a series of electronic clicks, some muffled words, and the line went dead. Technology is great when it works. I do wish cell phone service was as reliable as good old landlines. Try again. This time it went to voicemail, so I left a brief message for her to get back to me.

What was really weighing on me was what I had to do—go to the police station and show them the Puzzler's notes. I'd been procrastinating all day, and it was already past three o'clock. I paced back and forth in my living room, mentally sorting out what I'd tell them and what I wouldn't. In my worst imaginings, this would turn into an investigation into me rather than the Poe Puzzler. Would they believe me, or assume I was delusional?

My musings were interrupted by Lenore prancing into the room and stretching out her front paws. As if disappearing for the better part of a day was nothing unusual! "Nori, where have you been hiding?" I bent down and put out a hand for her. She ambled over and rubbed her cheeks against me. "I was worried about you, you little fur ball."

I scratched behind her ears—a favorite spot of hers—then eased myself up and went to refill her food dish. As I stood at the kitchen counter, she wove between my legs, making mewing sounds. When I put her dish down, however, she sniffed at it and walked away. Not a good sign.

"What's the trouble, Lenoreo? Bad stomach?"

She looked up at me, her head cocked to one side. I'm convinced we can communicate with each other, but whatever she was trying to get across at that moment didn't translate.

"Did you eat something you shouldn't have?" Ignoring food that's right in front of her is not normal Lenore behavior. If this continued, I'd have to call the vet in the morning. "I know," I said to her. "The vet is not your favorite place, Nori, but something ails you."

I freshened her water dish, then picked her up and brushed my hand over her sides and belly. No complaints from her, so there were no obvious pain points. "It's a mystery, little buddy."

When I set her down, she lingered for a moment at her food dish, then sauntered down the hallway, no doubt seeking another hiding place. As concerned as I was, there was nothing to be done about it ... and nothing more to keep me from the police station. I donned a jacket and grabbed my messenger bag. My cell phone trilled before I got to the front door—it was Berni.

"Hey, Nathan. Sorry I missed your call. I left my phone on the kitchen counter. There was no place to set it down in the garage."

This threw me for a moment.

"Are you there, Nathan?"

"Yes. I guess I'm not following. What garage?"

"At Kathy's house. Helping detail her old Chevelle for tomorrow's parade."

"I'm still a little lost, but you sound okay. Is the ... uh, situation sorted out with Kathy and her brother?"

She took in a deep breath. "Hardly. Casey was here earlier, and I excused myself so the two of them could talk in private. It got heated. Lots of shouting. Then he left."

That didn't sound good, but Berni's mood seemed positive enough. "Look, we've got a wrinkle in our plans for tonight," I said. "Mrs. Murphy and Mrs. G insist on joining us ... helping us in some as-yet-to-be-determined way."

That stopped the conversation for a beat as Berni

mulled this over. "You know, we might be able to use their help. We could position them at either end of the alley."

Trying to hem in the Poe Puzzler was not a bad idea. Still, I had my doubts that we could "direct" my two neighbors in ways they hadn't thought of first themselves. Not to mention the danger they might be in. I still didn't have a sense of how far the Puzzler would go.

We needed more time to discuss this. "How about I stop by later this evening?" I asked. "We can sort this out over some Mexican takeout."

"Not tonight, Nathan. I'll be helping Kathy with her car. And she needs someone to talk to right now."

I was disappointed, but tried to hide it. Change the subject, I thought. "So, Kathy has an old Chevy?"

The smile in her voice was obvious. "It's really cool. A 1970 SS Chevelle with a big block V8. Blue with wide white stripes. It's her pride and joy."

The conversation dwindled, so I reminded Berni about our "tactical" meeting before my rendezvous at the Life Saving Station.

"Of course!" she said. "I'll be there as planned."

We said our goodbyes, and as I slipped my phone into a pocket, I realized I'd been standing by the front door with my jacket on the whole time. No more excuses. The Ocean City Police were waiting for me.

Chapter Thirty-Six
The Triage Room

I parked in the lot behind Yianni's and gazed across the street at 835 Central Avenue. The three-story police building looked like an old high school, and indeed, that's how it started out, in 1883. No doubt it had been repurposed several times over the decades.

As I crossed the street, the lowering October sun reflected off the top-floor windows, but left the bottom of the dark-brick building in shadow. A chill ran down my spine. While I'm familiar enough with City Hall on 9th Street and its classic stone-and-pillars architecture, I'd never once stepped foot in the police building. After all, I'd only been an Ocean City resident for about five years.

What appeared to be the original entrance, a tall, curved opening with bold letters spelling out "Ocean City Public Safety Building," had been cemented over years ago. An unlikely addition jutting out on the left had an ADA-compliant ramp and the only door facing the street. That's where I headed.

Black lettering at this modern entrance told me it was for the Ocean City Municipal Court. "Court" and "public safety"—that fits with "police," right? Had to be the right place, I reasoned.

After going through the glass doors, I found myself in a small foyer with one locked door, another door marked "stairway," and an elevator. A large placard informed me that the police department was on the first floor. Something didn't make sense; I was on the first floor. It was only after I turned around in a circle, looking for an obvious entry, that I noticed the fine print under the sign—"Public entrance on the south side." I was on the West side.

Outside again, I walked past several parked police cars and saw yet another sign affixed to the bricks at the corner of the building. I was heading in the right direction. Looking down a wide alley on that side, I finally spotted a clearly labeled OCPD entrance a dozen yards away.

The entry foyer was much smaller than the one for the municipal court, and it was crammed with hefty-looking police bicycles. Straight ahead, I saw a bullet-proof glass enclosure and the back of a police officer, busy at a computer. A blinking red light on a ceiling-mounted security camera confirmed I was being watched. I cleared my throat.

"Hello," the officer said, as he turned to me with a smile. "How can I help you?"

"Well, um, I guess I want to talk to a detective about this intruder at my house last night ... you know, you've probably heard about it from Officer Lamb, or I guess she's written up a report about it ..." Why hadn't I rehearsed what to say before I'd arrived?

To his credit, the policeman nodded encouragingly, as if he dealt with this sort of thing every day. Maybe he did.

"Okay, let's begin with your name and address."

I gave him the information, and he was well-read enough to comment, "Poe, as in the famous mystery writer?" I confirmed his assumption and felt the tension ease from my neck and shoulders. It's easy to start a friendly conversation when two people are on the same wavelength.

His smile wavered with the next question. "And what's in the bag you have over your shoulder, Mr. Poe? There's nothing hazardous in it, is there?"

That put me on edge again. But why? All I'd brought with me were the Puzzler notes … plus Mrs. G's talisman.

"Just notes," I said, "pieces of paper."

He gave me a quizzical stare.

"It … they show how I've been … what I want to talk to the police about."

"Nothing more in there?"

"Well, there's also this strange Hungarian medal." I lowered my gaze and closed my eyes. How to explain it?

"A Hungarian medal?"

"Like a good luck charm. It's nothing hazardous or lethal or anything like that."

The officer was not convinced. I couldn't blame him.

"Why don't you pull it out and show me?"

I rummaged through my bag and brought the horse head medallion up to eye level. He took his time staring at it through the bulletproof glass. "That's not for some kind of Satanic ritual, is it?" he asked.

"Oh, no! It's for good luck, good juju, whatever the Hungarians call it."

A long moment passed in silence. Was I going to be frisked? Would I have to swear allegiance to the laws of the State of New Jersey before I could go any further?

"Okay, we're good, Mr. Poe," he said, and I saw his hand move beneath the desk. A loud buzzer sounded and the metal door on my right popped open. "Have a seat in the Triage Room. Through that door. Detective Rietti is on duty. He'll be with you shortly."

The walls inside the Triage Room were painted a drab, industrial green. The only decoration was a "Scenic Ocean City" calendar, still showing August. I had to fight the urge to flip it to the correct month.

A long metal table with three folding chairs—two on one side, one on the other—took up most of the floor space. On my left, an identical door to the one I'd come in probably led into the police station. The opposite wall framed a tinted, plate-glass window, muting what little afternoon light remained in the alley outside.

I sat on one of the folding chairs and ran my hands over the table. It looked like a cast-off from some commercial laboratory, with a dull, dented steel surface reflecting years of use. Mounted near the ceiling was another security camera, its red light blinking at me.

Was this supposed to be an interrogation room? It certainly felt like one. If I were in charge, I'd place some large Shore posters on the walls, and maybe put cushions on the hard folding chairs. Just like wooden pews in churches, I guess the chairs were designed so you wouldn't get too comfortable.

The only thing I'd decided before coming to the police station was not to mention the bloody wine bottle. While it may have been the most startling move by my nemesis, I had absolutely no evidence that it ever took place. For a time, Berni didn't even believe me. With nothing to show the police and a lingering dread that I'd be thought delusional, that part of the story would remain untold.

So I opened my messenger bag, found the sheet of paper about the bloody bottle, folded it in half, and shoved it into my pocket. The detective didn't need to see the Hungarian talisman, either. That had nothing to do with the notes. It was probably best to lay out everything else on the table—everything I wanted to share, that is.

I'd just completed that task when an electronic buzzer startled me, and Detective Rietti entered the room. He seemed preoccupied, with a quiet smile but a certain world weariness in his eyes. His navy blue tie was pulled loose, and the top button of his shirt was undone. A paper cup of coffee was in one hand, and in the other, he carried a clipboard.

"Mr. Poe? I'm Detective Rietti." He nodded as I introduced myself, but didn't offer to shake hands, even after he'd set the coffee cup and clipboard on the table. I couldn't tell if this was normal procedure for police detectives or if he was concerned about germs ... or appearing too friendly. He sat opposite me and slid the clipboard across the table.

"Before we start, could you please confirm your name and address, and sign this disclosure form?"

There was no point reading the lengthy legalese, so I scrawled my signature and sat back, waiting for his lead.

"Here's the thing," he began. "I've read Officer Lamb's incident report, so I have a general idea what occurred at your home last night." He placed both hands on the table, glanced down at the papers, then looked into my eyes. "I gather there's more going on here. Why don't you tell me about it?"

Since I'd just recounted the whole chronology to my neighbors, it was easy enough to do it again. Unlike Mrs. Murphy and Mrs. G, however, Detective Rietti interrupted me repeatedly with pointed questions: Exactly where did I find each note, what I felt the overall message was, and was I afraid for my safety?

Answering the first one was easy. As to the overall message and any fear I felt, well, I found those questions hard to respond to. Yes, the notes had become more and more ominous, even personal. It's only when the Poe Puzzler alluded to my wife that I became rattled. Afraid? No, I wouldn't admit to that.

Once I'd told him all the details—minus the wine bottle—and answered his questions, he sat back in his chair, looking at the array of Puzzler notes on the table. He drummed the fingers of his right hand on the dented table, as if listening to some internal rhythm, but didn't speak. Time dragged on. The lingering silence got on my nerves.

Finally, he looked up at me. "Who do you think is doing this?"

Ha! As if I hadn't spent the last ten days trying to figure that out. "I don't know," I said. "I can surmise that it's a former student. But I've been retired from teaching for years."

"No one in particular comes to mind?"

"No."

More silence and finger tapping from the inscrutable Detective Rietti. He gazed out the plate-glass window for a moment, then turned to me. "Here's the thing, Mr. Poe. Someone is harassing you. That much is clear. But there's not much we can do at this point."

Why was I not surprised? "So, is there no way you can help me?"

"Okay. Two things. The fake parking ticket is clearly fraud and possibly more than that—impersonating a city official comes to mind." He picked up the ticket and scrutinized it more closely. "Mind if I hold on to this?"

"Not at all," I replied. "I've made a copy."

He attached the ticket to his clipboard, pushed back his chair, and stood. "My bigger concern is this invitation to meet at the Life Saving Station tonight." As little space as there was in that room, he paced back and forth as he continued. "I strongly advise against that. There doesn't appear to be any obvious physical threat, but things could escalate. Plus, we're too short-staffed to assign someone. We're expecting more than our usual October crowd tomorrow. A lot of our officers are getting overtime working security at the parade."

"I wasn't looking for any police support."

He smiled, a broad smile for the first time. "I know you're some kind of small-time private investigator …"

I started to respond to his characterization. He raised the palm of his hand to stop me.

"I also know you're friends with Bob. If I was a betting man, I'd guess he plans to join you tonight in an unofficial capacity …"

He pushed his chair in, picked up the clipboard and coffee cup, certainly stone cold by now, then set them back down again so he could pull a card out of his front pocket. "Here's my card. If you have anything else to add or if anything else occurs, let me know. As for tonight, I hope you won't have to call 9-1-1."

Chapter Thirty-Seven
The Calm Before

As I drove back home along Atlantic Avenue, I glanced to my right at the roiling bank of clouds over the ocean. It had been an unseasonably warm October day, but the view to the east appeared ominous. I recall a fellow teacher trying to explain "temperature inversion" to me over lunch one day. Much of his meteorological lecture didn't stick, but the sky looked like a recipe for heavy fog. Just the right cover for my Puzzler.

All this brought to mind the issues I was facing. How could I control the actions of Mrs. Murphy and Mrs. G? What was wrong with Lenore? Should I make a vet appointment for tomorrow morning? And since it seemed likely I'd be eating alone, what should I have for dinner?

I parked in front, and in the gathering dusk, my eyes were drawn to a yellow sheet of paper stuck in my door. No! The Poe Puzzler could not have delivered yet another taunt. I glanced right and left as I walked up my porch steps, trying to discern anything out of the ordinary, anything that might indicate his presence.

I slid the paper from the door and opened it. With a

sigh of relief, I saw it was from Mrs. Murphy. "We're in this together now. Let's talk." That would have to wait. My first concern was for Lenore.

All my usual tricks did not work. Lenore was once again in hiding, and by the look of her food dish, she still wasn't eating. At least she appeared to be drinking from her water dish. Better to be safe than sorry—I called our local vet. It was after hours, but I left a message with their answering service, requesting a morning appointment. They were very thorough, asking how serious her condition was. As far as I could tell, it wasn't serious. Something, however, was certainly awry.

Next on my list was calling Mrs. Murphy. I had to sit down for that. It only rang once before she picked up.

"Nathan? Is that you? I hope so. I've been expecting your call."

Conversations with her are never short, but I did my best. And I had little choice but to invite her and Mrs. G to our 10 p.m. meeting. I'd have to warn Bob about that. Berni was already aware of the situation. Last Bob knew, however, it was just going to be Berni and him reviewing our plans for midnight at the Life Saving Station.

Mrs. Murphy promised to call Mrs. G ... or should I say, Fiona promised to call Klara. For the life of me, I could not think of them that way. Sure, they were many years my senior. It was more than that, more than just respect for my elders. In the few years I'd lived on the North End, I'd always known both ladies by their family names ... okay, maybe not Mrs. Gyulalyi, but my Hungarian pronunciation never met her standards.

After disconnecting, I sent a brief text to Berni and

Bob, confirming our meeting and "introducing" our new team members. The group dynamics would definitely be interesting.

It was time to conduct a more thorough search for Lenore. My house is too small to have many hiding places. Some of them are just harder to get to.

Into my bedroom I went, and with a grunt, got down on my hands and knees, and looked under the bed. I don't know what's under your bed, but mine has all manner of detritus. There are old shoes, a slim cardboard box with an extra set of sheets, a notebook or two, a dead flashlight that I hadn't realized had rolled under there, and innumerable dust bunnies. One of those bigger dust bunnies might've been Lenore; I couldn't be sure.

With another groan, I got up and went into the kitchen to get my large flashlight. Back in the bedroom and back on the floor, I turned on the light and scanned under my bed, all the while softly calling Lenore's name. I doubt any famous philosopher has ever said this, but sometimes dust bunnies are just dust bunnies.

The next likely hiding place was my bedroom closet. Maybe I shouldn't detail everything that was on the closet floor or how disorganized it was. Suffice it to say, Lenore could easily hide there. This time, I only needed to bend over and move some things around to confirm this wasn't the place.

The bathroom was another possibility, but the pantry door was firmly shut. That left the hall closet, which is long and deep, its doors always slightly ajar. I suppose I should've looked there first. Sliding the door fully open, once more on all fours, I shone the flashlight and reached around. In only a moment, I touched something soft. And heard a mild complaint—not a cry of pain; more just a "why are you bothering me?" sound.

I'd found her, but I didn't want to pull her out. If she needed time alone or time to heal, I'd grant her that. She'd come out when she was ready. Still, I was glad I'd contacted the vet.

All this up and down and agita had piqued my appetite. It was probably my previous suggestion to Berni—I had a hankering for Mexican.

There are very few restaurants on the North End, and most are closed in the off-season. Although I rarely splurge on food delivery, tonight would be an exception.

I'm not a Luddite, but I guess I'm old enough that using a smartphone app to order food is not second nature. I'd done it once before without mishap, so I only hesitated for a moment.

I launched the DoorDash app on my phone and searched for Mexican restaurants. There's a decent one on West Avenue in the center of town, so I zeroed in on that. Some items on their menu seemed too heavy, like their overstuffed burritos. Eventually, I found a chicken molé that looked appetizing. I selected it and added a bottle of Mexican Coca-Cola, then continued to complete my order and pay. Once I'd double-checked everything and added a healthy tip, I hit submit and received a confirmation. Now it was just a matter of waiting.

Thirty minutes later, I heard a knock at my front door. I turned on the porch light and was startled to see a young man with glasses in a gray hoodie waiting for me. Does every twenty-something guy look like the Poe Puzzler? He handed me a bag with my food, thanked me, and jogged down the steps to his car. As he drove away, I had the unsettling thought that he could have been the Puzzler. How could I be sure one way or the other? And had I noted the license-plate number? No, I did not.

The delectable aromas of chocolate and cilantro brought my attention back to dinner. If a restaurant does molé well, it's a symphony of flavors ranging from dried chiles to sweet raisins. I dug in. As tasty as the meal was, I couldn't finish it. There was too much on my mind.

After cleaning up the kitchen, I decided to take a nap in the green chair. I rarely stay up late, and I certainly had to be sharp for our midnight rendezvous. To be sure I wouldn't oversleep, I set my phone alarm for nine p.m. That would give me time to mentally prepare for the briefing with my four investigative partners.

"To sleep, perchance to dream?" Ha! What I needed was rest. What I didn't want were any dreams about werewolves or bloody wine bottles.

I was just drifting off when the lost Lenore, my emotional support kitty, jumped into my lap. She circled twice, kneaded me softly, then settled down. I laid a hand on her side as she nuzzled her face into my other palm. Soon we were both in the land of nod.

The rumble of a truck trundling down the street startled me awake. Lenore jumped off my lap and ran down the hallway. As my eyes adjusted to nightfall, I realized I hadn't turned on any living room lamps before napping. Other than the soft glow from a light above the stove, my house was in darkness.

I pulled back my arms and stretched … and felt something sticky on my palm. With a growing sense of unease, I rose from my chair and hobbled into the kitchen. When I extended my left hand under the light, what I'd feared became obvious—blood. Blood from Lenore.

"Nori, you poor girl, what's wrong with your mouth? Did you bite into something you shouldn't have?" She probably couldn't hear my mumbled words, but my heart went out to her. I should have seen the signs earlier. I should have called the vet sooner. Unlike humans, cats hide their pain.

It was just a small spot of blood, the size of a dime, but a reddish-brown stain remained on my palm even after scrubbing with hot water and dish detergent. Why is it always blood? Blood from Lenore. Blood on that wine bottle. Blood in Anna's car….

After blotting my hand with a paper towel, I called the vet's answering service again. My need for an appointment was more urgent, I explained. Any time tomorrow would work. They agreed to let the veterinarians know.

I turned on the lights throughout the house to brighten my mood. And to help Lenore feel more comfortable, I placed an old towel on the floor by her "nest" in the hall closet and brought her water dish closer.

Now what? It was a bit past eight. Our meeting was still two hours away, and I had to find something to occupy the time. I started pacing in my small kitchen, just as Detective Rietti had in the Triage Room. Does walking back and forth help you think? I doubt it. It only made me more agitated.

I could try to work on my library presentation, but I knew I wouldn't be able to concentrate. Perhaps painting? I hadn't touched the canvas in days. If I could clear my mind of worries about Lenore and my upcoming encounter with the Poe Puzzler, it could ease the tension in my body. Zoning into a creative outlet might be just the ticket.

Natural daylight is always best for painting; I didn't have that luxury. I set up the easel and work-in-progress canvas in the middle of my bedroom, removed the shade from a lamp on my nightstand, and angled the easel to minimize shadows. It would do. Without bothering to don my painter's smock, I retrieved the palette board from my kit, fingered a couple of brushes to make sure they were clean and dry, then took a step back and stared at my artwork.

A deserted pier illuminated by the full moon. A man standing alone as the wind whips up the waves. What had seemed like an intriguing, even romantic scene before now looked eerie. How did I think this would take my mind off my worries?

It was no use. I packed up the painting kit with a resigned sigh. Sherlock Holmes played his violin when he wanted a distraction … or to gather his thoughts. Poe makes no mention of a similar trait in Detective Dupin. Maybe what was needed wasn't distraction but rather illustration.

Placing the canvas aside, I mounted my large sketchpad on the easel, the same pad where I'd tried to build a profile of my Puzzler. Flipping that page over, I grabbed a marker and drew horizontal and vertical lines—a grid work, a map of the streets around the Life Saving Station.

Most people are visual learners, I reasoned. Even with our age differences and something of a language barrier for Mrs. G, my well-meaning neighbors would surely understand our plans if I used this map to explain them. It was all straight lines, no curves. All geometric and logical. How could anything be misunderstood?

Chapter Thirty-Eight
Coffee vs. Tea

Mrs. G was the first to arrive—fifteen minutes before the agreed-upon hour. She carried in the largest French press I've ever seen. My awestruck expression must have forced her to explain. "You drink tea," she said. "I like coffee better. I bet Bob like coffee, too. I make it."

"I've got a coffeemaker in the cabinet," I said. "You didn't have to bother."

She let out a huff. "This is very good coffee press. Steel, not plastic. Made by Germans." She pronounced that last word as "chermans," which caught me off guard. Well, it certainly looked like the ultimate coffee machine.

"Okay, I've already got the kettle on for tea. Looks like I'll need a lot more hot water." I made some room on the kitchen counter and motioned for her to set the coffee press down. "Um. I don't know if I've got coffee in the house, though."

"I think of that." She reached into her voluminous pocketbook and pulled out a foil-wrapped package the size of a small loaf of bread. "I just grind it. Exact right grind for coffee press." She came prepared, I'll give her that. I shook my head in amazement. "You're something else, Mrs. G."

"What that mean?"

Oh boy. It's not simply that English is her second language … maybe even her third. It's the common phrases or idiomatic expressions that trip up communications. "I mean … it's a nice way of saying I'm impressed!"

That seemed to mollify her.

While she busied herself with the surprisingly elaborate process of making coffee—rinsing the French press with hot water, measuring the coffee grounds into the press, adding just enough boiling water to cover the grounds, and then waiting about a minute before filling it up—I made a pot of tea.

For our late-night meeting, I selected a simple but premium black tea—Tetley British Blend. It has a rich and rewarding flavor, and the right amount of caffeine to keep us alert until midnight. Besides, the little round tea bags are so appealing. For a snack, I resorted to my perennial standby, spiced wafers, arranged in a pleasing spiral on a large dessert plate.

As my tea was brewing, Mrs. G decided her coffee was ready, and she ceremoniously pressed down the stainless steel plunger. "You have big coffee pot?" she asked.

"Well, there's the one from my coffeemaker."

She shook her head and frowned.

"Okay, I have two other teapots. Will they work?"

She put a hand on her hip and clucked her tongue at

me. "No coffee pot. That figure!"

Is there really any difference between a coffee pot and a teapot? Okay, maybe in their traditional shapes, but they're both designed to keep liquids hot and pour them out easily. Still, her comment made me feel ashamed. Was I discriminating against coffee drinkers?

I walked down to the hall pantry and retrieved two large teapots that I'd stored on the top shelf. With the pots in hand, the thought struck me—if she put coffee in these, my tea would taste like watered-down coffee for weeks to come. Coffee seeps into the pores of porcelain. It would take a significant effort to rid the pots of that essence of coffee. From past experience, I knew I'd have to use vinegar and baking soda, and maybe even resort to bleach to do the job.

Was it worth mentioning this to Mrs. G? Asking her to go back and get her own coffee pot? No, that would be rude. I plodded back to the kitchen, resigned to deal with it. After dusting off the pots and rinsing them with hot water, I asked Mrs. G if I could fill them with her just-brewed coffee.

"Nem," she said. That's Hungarian for "no," as I was aware by now. "You do tea. I do coffee." This was getting on my nerves. After all, I was the host. Let it be, I told myself.

After scooping the tea bags out of the pot—tea gets bitter if you leave the bags in too long—I put a tea cozy over the pot and watched as Mrs. G manhandled the large coffee press to fill my little pots. Not a drop was spilled.

At the stroke of ten, the doorbell rang. It was Mrs.

Murphy.

"Good evening, Nathan. I must say, it's rather late for me. I'm usually in bed by this time. My, that coffee smells wonderful! I suppose I should have a cup to stay awake."

The initial score was Coffee: 2, Tea: 1. But I could try some persuasion.

"I've also made a nice pot of British Blend tea, if you'd prefer." I put on a winning smile. "It doesn't have as much caffeine as coffee."

"Oh, that's sweet of you, Nathan, but I think coffee is just what I need."

While my strong-willed neighbors poured coffee and kibbitzed with each other, I dragged a kitchen chair into the living room and moved the furniture around so everyone would be able to see the easel with my hand-drawn map. For now, it was covered with a drop cloth. I stepped back to examine the setup. Everything was in place. And right on cue, I heard Berni's truck pull up outside—the team was coming together!

Bob should be in the truck with Berni, his police patrol bike in the pickup's bed. The last thing we needed was his loud Mustang waking the neighbors and alerting the Poe Puzzler to our presence. And Berni should have had her beach chair and blankets back there as well. This was going to work out, I thought. But I had to talk with them before they came inside, first to discuss what to do with the newest members of our team, and second to put my thumb on the scale of the coffee versus tea competition.

Between the two of them, Berni would most likely go

for tea. In the time I've known her, I've never seen her drink coffee. That could even the score. Bob was probably a lost cause—coffee has to be the official beverage of police departments everywhere. I walked out onto the porch to greet them.

The night was chilly, and those roiling clouds I'd seen earlier had dissipated. It appeared we'd have clear skies and a bright half moon for our midnight encounter. When Berni and Bob climbed out of the pickup, I called them over. "Hey, guys, let's talk a minute before we join Mrs. Murphy and Mrs. G."

"What's up, Nathan?" Berni asked as we huddled on the front porch. Bob looked like he'd just gotten up from a nap. He didn't say a word, but joined Berni and me as I opened my arms to bring them closer.

"Two things," I said. "We've got to find something for my neighbor ladies to do tonight. They're seriously invested in helping out. I don't want them to get into harm's way, and I'm not sure how to explain that to them."

"Yeah," Berni said. "They can be pretty headstrong, can't they?"

Bob looked down at his feet and blew out a breath. "The alley is our weak spot. Why not have them park at either end? They could be our eyes and ears for your Puzzler's entry and exit from the Life Saving Station."

I'd been thinking along those same lines, so I voiced my agreement.

"We have to give them clear signals on what to do and what not to do," Berni added. "I mean, if they're sitting in their cars with the engines running and headlights on, it's not going to work."

"Agreed," I said. "Let's see if we can make them part of that decision … you know, make it seem like it was their idea."

"Easier said than done," Berni agreed, "but I'll try."

Bob reached for the front door, then turned to me. "Wait a minute. You said two things. What's the other one?"

I shrugged and acted as if it really wasn't of any consequence. "Oh, I just wanted to let you know that I've brewed a nice pot of British Blend tea, and I have some spiced wafers for a snack. To help keep us awake … unless you'd prefer something different … I can always…."

"Oh, no tea for me," Berni said. "I'm going to be camped out in my pickup bed for quite a while. If I drink anything, I'll probably have to pee."

Darn! My last hope of a tea victory vanished.

Bob moved his head back and forth, looking undecided. Could he actually choose tea? "That sounds good, Nathan, but do you have something stronger? I need some wake-up juice."

Final score: Coffee: 3, Tea: 1, Teapots: 0.

Chapter Thirty-Nine
Mapping It Out

After the coffee, spiced wafers, and chit-chat, plus two cups of tea for me, we gathered in the living room and I laid out our plans.

Mrs. Murphy and Mrs. G sat together on the couch. Berni got the best seat in the house—the green chair. And Bob made do with one of the kitchen chairs, straddling it back to front in traditional cop fashion.

A bit of theater always helps; I knew that from teaching. So, I stood by the cloth-covered easel until the conversation subsided. When I whisked off the cloth, all eyes were on my map.

The prime objective of our plan was simple enough—to identify the Poe Puzzler. If I could get a good look at him, it might jar my memory. If Berni could get a clear photo, better yet. And it would also help if Bob got his license-plate number. Not to mention that by talking with him, I hoped to find out why he was stalking me.

Black marker in hand, I began our "briefing." In my imagination, I saw flashes of every police procedural TV show I'd ever watched. But this wasn't some fictitious trope; it was my reality.

"Here, at the corner of Atlantic and Fourth, is the Life Saving Station," I began. "It's where my Poe Puzzler wants to meet." I put an "LSS" on the map. "The old rudder from the wreck of the Sindia sailing ship is a good spot for me to wait for him. It's visible from the street, and there's no place to hide around it."

All eyes were on the map and me. No one spoke; I continued.

"Berni will be parked on Atlantic, lying on a beach chair in the back of her pickup truck so she can see and hopefully shoot some photos of the Puzzler."

"But it's dark out." Mrs. Murphy interrupted. I knew I wouldn't get too far without some objections.

Berni saved me from trying to explain. "I've got my Nikon with a long lens, and I set the ISO at thirty-two hundred."

"I'm sure I have no idea what that means!" Mrs. Murphy declared, and I had to agree with her on that one. It sounded impressive, though.

Berni laughed. "It just means I can shoot in low light. It will work."

"And the bandages on your hands?" Mrs. Murphy continued. "How will you operate the camera with those bandages?"

"No problem," Berni said. "The camera is fully automatic—focus and exposure. All I have to do is point and shoot."

Now it was Mrs. G's turn. "You be warm enough?" she asked Berni. "I have big wool coat if you want."

"That's sweet of you to offer, but I'll be fine. I've got some old blankets in the pickup bed, and I'll bundle up."

"Back to the map, please." I wrote the letter B on Atlantic Avenue, just down from the Positively 4th Street Cafe. "Berni will have a direct line of sight to the Life Saving Station."

Bob cleared his throat and gave me the high sign. "Why don't I let Bob describe his role." I handed him the marker and sat on the arm of the green chair, next to Berni.

"I'll be cruising the entire area on my patrol bike," he said, and drew a circle that encompassed the alley behind the station and the surrounding streets—3rd, 4th, Atlantic, and Corinthian. "Even though my bike has a bright LED headlamp, I'll be running dark, so I won't give away my position. Don't forget, there are no streetlights in the alley."

"Hmm!" It was Mrs. G again. "This all sound good, but what you do if Mr. Puzzler walk up when you riding somewhere else?"

"And what are Klara and I supposed to do?" asked Mrs. Murphy. "I hope you've thought of that, Nathan. Just because we're older doesn't mean we can't be part of this secret plan of yours."

Things were getting out of hand. I stepped back over to the map and motioned for Bob to let me speak. "When we first made our plans," I began, "we thought it would just be the three of us—Bob, Berni, and me. But now … now that we have your help, you can play an important role, indeed, a vital role." I let that sink in. "If you're not afraid, that is. It could be dangerous." I knew my dauntless neighbors would take the bait.

"Ha!" Mrs. G threw up her hands. "Nobody afraid here!"

"We want to help you, Nathan," Mrs. Murphy added. "Not only that, but I think you need our help. How are you going to corner this nasty person?"

I smiled, and my confidence in our impromptu detective team swelled. Mrs. Murphy and Mrs. G were in. Before I gave them their assignments, however, I had to make sure they understood what we wanted to accomplish, and what we didn't want to happen. "Please keep in mind … everyone … we don't want to corner this guy. We don't want to get him agitated. We just want … I just want to talk to him and figure out what he's really up to."

"Of course, Nathan," Mrs. Murphy said. "I understand."

I turned to her neighbor. "How about you, Mrs. G? Everything clear?"

She frowned but mumbled, "Igen."

I saw the questioning look on Bob's face, so I translated. "That's Hungarian for yes, Bob."

"Yeah, okay," he said as he turned to Mrs. G. "As to your question, I'll hear everything Nathan says— through our phone hookup—so I'll know when this perp appears." He looked down, as if to gather his thoughts, then wagged his index finger at the group. "Understand this, too. I'm helping out, and my supervising officer knows what I'm doing, but I'm off duty. I'm not acting in any official capacity."

I was surprised by his little speech, but I also

understood he was sticking his neck out for me. "I appreciate that, Bob," I said. "We all do."

I turned to the map and tried to get back on track. "Where were we? Oh, yes, the alley." I tapped the marker on the map. "The alley is the obvious choke point for the Puzzler." I made direct eye contact with Mrs. Murphy and Mrs. G. "The alley is where we need your help."

That got their attention. "The Puzzler will probably park somewhere nearby and walk up the alley to the station. We were hoping that the two of you," I pointed at my neighbors, "would position your cars on either end—the west and the east end. You can park there with your engines running to keep warm, but with your doors locked and all your lights off. Use your cell phones to keep in touch with each other. If you see anything suspicious, turn on your lights and drive into the alley."

Another thought occurred to me. "And ladies, please keep your phones low, maybe down on your laps. We don't want the glow from your phones to tip off the Puzzler."

Mrs. Murphy and Mrs. G looked at each other. I expected some comment, some complaint, but they appeared to be mollified.

"Here's the way this can work," I continued. "Mrs. Murphy, you park on Atlantic, north of the alley, but within sight of it." I wrote an M on the map. "And Mrs. G, you park at the other end, near Corinthian Avenue." I scribbled the letter G there. "That means we've got both access points controlled."

The wheels were turning in their heads, I could see

that. I counted to ten, waiting for an objection. I got as far as six.

"Why I park so far away?" Mrs. G asked. "How I see what going on?"

"We need to control access to the alley, and you'll be at the other entry point—on Corinthian Avenue. You and Mrs. Murphy will be on the phone with each other at all times."

"That's fine, I'm sure, Nathan," Mrs. Murphy said. "But how will I know when to turn on my headlights and drive into the alley? I won't be able to see any of the action in front of the Life Saving Station from where I'm parked."

I raised a palm to address her issue. "Berni will use a flashlight to signal you. When you see that light, turn on your headlights and drive." I turned to Berni. "You've got that, right?"

"All good, Nathan." She patted her jacket. "It's right here."

I let out a breath. Our plan probably wasn't foolproof, but it seemed pretty solid. It was time to wrap things up.

Bob read my body language. He stood and took the floor. "Let's be clear on the timing," he said. "Mrs. Gyul … Mrs. G, you and Mrs. Murphy should be in position by 11:30. The same with you, Berni. I'll be riding up and down, looking for this Puzzler guy to park somewhere. And I'll be on a three-way call with Berni and Nathan— on mute, of course. He'll have his phone in his shirt pocket, so the guy won't be able to tell he's on the call."

He paused and nodded to me, so I finished up for

him. "I'll arrive and park on 4th Street just a few minutes before midnight," I said.

In the silence that followed, I had to stop myself from saying, "Be careful out there." Again, too many TV shows.

Berni stood and did a little jig with her feet. "Excuse me," she said, "but I need to pee." And unlike the rest of us, she hadn't even had any coffee … or tea.

Chapter Forty
One-Man Debate

Once we'd said our goodbyes, I cleaned up the kitchen and started the laborious process of de-coffee-ing my two teapots. After a thorough rinsing, I poured in white vinegar and warm water, then added a spoonful of baking soda. A miniature Mount Vesuvius erupted, but I caught the overflow in the sink. I left the pasty residue to dry in the pots until I got back from my rendezvous with the Puzzler.

Lenore hadn't surfaced the entire evening, so I tiptoed to her hiding place in the hall closet to check on her. She was all curled up in the back. It looked like she'd drunk some of the water, and she raised her head and made a small complaining meow. "We'll take care of you at the vet tomorrow, Nori girl," I told her.

I eased myself up and corralled my thoughts around the upcoming encounter. With all the planning and our team's clearly defined roles, we still didn't know the Poe Puzzler's true intentions. What did he hope to accomplish with a face-to-face meeting? While I'll admit to being anxious, I didn't think he'd resort to violence.

All the same, I felt paranoia creep up behind me and tap me on the shoulder. It was hard to convince myself that there wouldn't be some bizarre twist to the night's encounter. And what if he'd arranged this meeting at the Life Saving Station only to draw me and my friends away from my home? What if he planned to break in?

Standing between the kitchen and living room, I cast a fresh eye on my humble abode. There was nothing worth stealing; nothing of any real value to the outside world, only to me. But given what I knew of my nemesis, would he try to break into my place just to vandalize it? And how could I stop him?

An endless reel of old movies and TV shows played in my head. I'd never tried this trick in person, but I decided to give it a shot. I grabbed the lonely kitchen chair that I'd moved into the living room and dragged it into my office. Wedging the chairback under the knob of my office door gave me some satisfaction. It looked like it might at least slow down a forced entry. What else could I do?

All my angst sprang from ignorance of the Puzzler's intentions. Maybe, I reasoned, it would help to "rehearse" our upcoming conversation—sort of like how politicians prepare for a debate. I'd play both sides, the Puzzler and me, and try to anticipate what he'd say and how I'd respond.

I stood in the middle of my office, closed my eyes, and put my imagination into gear:

"And so we meet face to face!" I'd say.
"I'm through with taunting you, looking up quotes from Poe,

just to prove a point. It's time to confront you."

"What sin did I commit that warrants retribution?"

"You failed me! And you probably failed other students."

*"So much of my last semester teaching is a blur. My wife …
my Anna had just died. You … you have to understand what I was
going through."*

*"Ha! What about what your students were going through?
What about your impact on our futures?"*

Shaking my head, I opened my eyes and put an end
to this strange, improbable theater. He'd told me, in that
fake parking ticket, that I was guilty of "failure to teach."
That was the best insight I had into his motives. But what
led him, after five years, to start harassing me?

My gaze fell on the raven statue at the top of the
bookcase. Surely Poe and his fictional detective, C.
Auguste Dupin, had no insights into my predicament.
This was a modern-day issue between a disgruntled
student and me. Or was it?

The story of revenge in "The Cask of Amontillado"
wasn't that dissimilar. I certainly hoped I wouldn't end
up behind a brick wall, screaming for mercy! On the
other hand, maybe classic literature did echo my
situation. Insults, perceived or real, were as old as
humankind.

I took in a sudden gulp of breath at the thought of
another Poe story—"Hop Frog." The court jester's
revenge was brutal, burning the king and his council
alive. Surely, I told myself, I was letting my imagination
get the better of me. On the off chance that some Magyar
voodoo would help protect me, however, I grabbed the

talisman and put it in my back pocket.

A glance at my watch made me realize I had to get moving. It was time to leave my fantasy world and face the music, whatever tune my Puzzler happened to be playing.

The sky had been clear when Berni and Bob drove away, only about an hour or so earlier. I remember looking up at the faint twinkling of stars, trying to compete with the lights on the boardwalk. When I stepped outside as midnight approached, however, the world was gray. Halos crowned the streetlights, and a dull silence blanketed the town.

I stood on my front porch, trying to assess how this would impact our plans. Berni wouldn't be able to get a clear photo through the mist. Bob couldn't see well enough to detect any unusual movements. And the Poe Puzzler would have a much easier time eluding us. The weather had thrown cold water on our plans. At that eleventh hour, we had no choice but to keep to the script and hope our luck would turn.

The talisman in my back pocket felt cold and heavy. If there was any Hungarian magic in that odd medallion, I hoped it would do its thing around midnight. I'd grabbed the large flashlight from under the sink, and I hefted it in my hand. It could do double-duty as a weapon, if warranted. I was as prepared as I could be.

As I approached the car, my phone rang. It was Berni.

"Hey Nathan," she said. "Are you all set?"

"Yes!" I tried to put some positive energy into my response, but I wasn't feeling all that upbeat. "I'm walking to my car now. Everything all right on your end?"

A long silence on the line; I thought we might have been disconnected.

"Yeah, it's … it's okay. Uh, we've had to make some minor alterations to our plans. One or two little changes."

I'm as flexible as the next guy, but last-minute deviations are not my cup of tea. "What do you mean, one or two little changes?"

Berni was trying to minimize it; I could hear it in her voice. "Well, first, you can see how foggy it is," she said. "I had to move my truck closer or I'd never get a clear image of your guy. I'm parked on 4th Street instead of Atlantic … closer to the Life Saving Station."

My instant reaction was negative. "Won't your truck be visible to the Puzzler? I don't know if he'll recognize that it's yours, but still …"

"Relax, Nathan. And give me some credit for making the right decision."

That put me in my place.

"I'm a little ways down from the Station, parked under one of the sidewalk trees on 4th Street. I think I'm inconspicuous enough."

Yes, Berni probably knew what she was doing. Try to be positive, I reasoned.

"Oh, and one more thing," Berni said.

Any budding positivity I'd gained wilted with her

words. "Go on," I said.

"Bob had a minor incident."

I let out a long breath. Better to bite my tongue and let her explain. She must have sensed the frustration in my silence.

"It's okay. Don't get upset," she said. "I'll conference Bob in and he'll tell you about it."

I heard a couple of beeps, and Bob got on the line.

"You there, Nathan?"

"I'm here. What happened?"

"It's this damn fog. I couldn't see what was in the road." He paused for a moment. "You there?"

"I'm here. Go on."

"I must've run over something. I got a flat tire and ditched the bike. I'll get it later."

Little by little, our plans were falling apart, a combination of poor visibility, debris in the road, and plain old bad luck. "Where are you? What are you going to do now without the bike? We need you mobile."

If Berni was defensive, it was nothing compared to Bob. My tone of voice might not have been that understanding.

"Look, it'll be okay," Bob said. "I'm on foot in the alley. A few houses down from the Life Saving Station. Can't do anything about it right now. Let's move on. Okay?"

What choice did we have? My stomach growled—more from nerves than hunger. "Alright," I said. "I'm about to drive over. Wait! What about Mrs. Murphy and Mrs. G? Are they in position?"

"Yes, Nathan," Berni responded. "Mrs. Murphy is

parked on Atlantic, just as we'd told her."

"And Mrs. Gyul … Mrs. G is further down the alley from me," Bob said. "She's not parked by Corinthian Avenue, but she's in a good spot."

"Okay. Okay. Put your phones on mute. Let's see how much of our plans we can salvage."

Berni tried one more time to calm my fears. "It will all work out, Nathan," she said. "Don't worry."

Right. Don't worry. The best laid plans of mice and men and former English teachers …

Chapter Forty-One
Midnight Meeting

Still too early to arrive at the scene, I circled around the streets on the North End, then drove up Corinthian Avenue and eventually turned onto 4th Street. I didn't see Mrs. G's car in the alley; I assumed she was nearer to the Life Saving Station. It was just like her to want to be closer to the action.

All the street signs were hidden by the hanging mist. If you didn't know the area, it would be easy to get lost. I eased up to the curb in front of the Station, put the gearshift into Park, and shut the engine … only to realize that I might be blocking Berni's view. I cranked the starter again—so nice to have a new battery—selected Drive and eased forward about a dozen feet to give her a more direct line of sight. My watch told me it was two minutes to midnight. Time to meet my nemesis.

As I got out of my car, I scanned the area for the Poe Puzzler, but resisted the urge to look over my shoulder at Berni's truck. If he was watching, there was no reason to give him a clue to our plans.

I walked along the white fence to an opening into the

yard—there was no gate—and once more stopped to check out the Station and all the likely hiding places. The streetlights on Atlantic Avenue did little to illuminate the property. Their normally bright glare now only deepened the shadows on the wide porch. I froze when I saw the shape of someone crouching by the door. But my flashlight beam revealed a simple wooden bench. I could hear my heartbeat in my ears.

The wet gravel in the Station's yard made a soft crunching noise, and the smell of damp earth rose up with my passage. Sounds of traffic from Somers Point were muted by the veil of fog, as if the whole world was holding its breath.

The old rudder from the S.S. Sindia stood out in front of the Station. It seemed the perfect place to take in the Puzzler's approach, no matter from which direction he arrived. Another glance at my watch—a minute past midnight. And around the corner of the porch he came.

The same gray hoodie cast his face in shadows. The same black-rimmed glasses, barely visible under the hood. But there was something odd across his mouth, some kind of shiny black mask. He stopped a good ten feet away and slowly turned his head from side to side, no doubt looking for an ambush, looking for my friends.

"You're late!" His voice was strange. Unnaturally loud and alien. That face mask must have hidden some sort of electronic device.

I shone the flashlight on my watch. It was only a bit past midnight. "I'm on time," I said. My words came out weak and trembling, not at all how I wanted to sound.

He tilted his head back and laughed, a garbled,

electronic cackle that sent chills down my spine. His laugh trailed off, and he pointed a finger at me. "Can't you follow simple instructions? I told you to meet me at 11:59. Not 12:01 or 12:02. 'Simple instructions.' That's what you said to me, that's what you said in front of the entire class. 'Can't you follow simple instructions?' You made me feel like a fool. Did you think for one minute how your off-hand comment affected me? No? Well, who's the fool now?"

Frantically searching my memory, I still couldn't make the connection. He'd been one of my students, but which one? I raised the light to his face.

"Get that out of my eyes!"

As instructed, I lowered the light. No reason to anger him more. "Why are you hiding behind that mask … and altering your voice?"

Again, that maniacal laugh. "That's the point. You don't know who I am! That's so rich. And I'm not going to help you. You, Mr. Poe, the detective. We were all just faceless kids to you, weren't we?"

He'd put me on the defensive, and I couldn't resist countering him. I was fair to all my students. At least I felt I was. "I'm sorry if my comment upset you," I said. "But is that what's making you harass me like this? Tell me who you are so we can talk about it."

His hands curled into fists. "That's just it, Mr. Poe. That's what rubs salt in the wound. It's not just what you said, but how you belittled me. And you don't remember me at all."

My mind searched for some clue from his appearance, something about his stature or his glasses that might help me remember. I couldn't admit he was right. "I'm getting closer," I said. "You're slowly giving yourself away."

"Ha!" Again, that horribly twisted voice. "Even with the help of your lesbo girlfriend, you can't figure it out, can you?"

That got my dander up. How dare he insult Berni! I swung the light up into his face again, my arm trembling as I spoke. "You leave her out of it. This is just between you and me."

"Too late, you miserable excuse for a teacher. Oh yeah. Way too late for that!"

Despite my better intentions, I lurched toward him, raising the flashlight over my shoulder like a cudgel. He backed away as he saw me approach, then turned on his heels and ran toward the alley. Before being swallowed by a wall of fog, he saluted me, shouting in that strange, unnatural voice. "Be seeing you!" The echo of his words hung in the misty air.

And that's when it all fell apart.

I glanced behind me and saw Berni jumping out of her truck, running toward me. The squeal of tires reached my ears, and I glimpsed Mrs. Murphy's green Buick careening down the alley. The noise of her car was soon met by another, and I heard a loud, hollow bang followed by a moment of pure silence ... which was broken by a litany of obscenities from Patrolman Bob.

It was a testament to how deserted Ocean City is in

the off-season—no lights came on in neighboring houses, no sleepy eyes peered out bedroom windows to see what was going on. I was the last to arrive at the scene of the crash—with my bad leg, the best I could do was fast-walk—and what a scene it was.

Mrs. Murphy's Buick and Mrs. G's Mercedes were stopped nose to nose. They were both out of their cars, Mrs. Murphy crossing herself, and Mrs. G bent over the front bumper, examining it with the help of a light from her phone. Bob stood on the side, his head down and slowly shaking. Berni was next to him, glancing back and forth between the older women.

"Is anyone hurt?" I asked.

"Nah, I doubt it," Bob replied. "They both got out of their cars after the crash. They seem mobile enough to me." He yanked off his police cap and threw it on the ground. "What am I going to tell them at the station?"

It took me a moment to realize he meant the police station, not the Life Saving Station that was so central to our plans. And that's when I started to snicker. I couldn't help it. Bob glared at me, but Berni caught the giggles, too. Soon, I was holding onto her shoulder to keep from falling down laughing. What an unmitigated farce!

Chapter Forty-Two
Picking Up the Pieces

Neither car seemed damaged—no broken headlights or crumpled sheet metal. Mrs. G insisted her bumper was scratched, but I couldn't make out any marks on it. Mrs. Murphy's Buick was liberally "pre-dented." There was no way to tell if the impact had resulted in any new blemishes.

The greater damage was to their friendship. Who was at fault? That was the question they bandied back and forth, with Mrs. Murphy taking a conciliatory tone at first, only to be pushed too far by Mrs. G, who insisted that somehow she had had the right of way. Neither one had turned on their headlights. The fog was so thick, the alley so narrow, it's astounding they hadn't run over Bob.

After much debate, it was decided that Mrs. Murphy should back up—there was no way Mrs. G was going to, and to be fair, she had already driven most of the length of the alley. When Mrs. Murphy still hesitated, Bob offered to drive the car for her. We hadn't considered how difficult it was going to be backing out of the misty alley in the dark.

Mrs. Murphy got into the passenger seat. Bob picked up his cap and trudged to the driver's side of the Buick. It took him a while to adjust the seat so he wouldn't be scrunched up against the steering wheel. With a few muttered Hungarian words, Mrs. G settled into her Mercedes, turned on the headlights—finally—and eased forward. She reluctantly agreed to deal with any remaining issues in the morning.

That left Berni and me to pick up the pieces of our shattered plans.

We made our way back to our vehicles, my steps slow and heavy. I couldn't stop thinking that the night had been a complete disaster. Berni must've read my mood.

"Well," she said, "we've learned a few more things about your Poe Puzzler, haven't we?"

"Not much," I said. "We still don't know what he looks like, or what his voice sounds like ... or his name. He's obviously a former student. Just as we suspected."

She was quiet for a moment, but I knew her rosy outlook would bubble to the surface. I only wish I could be so optimistic. "Maybe some of the photos I took will help," she said.

"Do you think so?"

"Yeah ... Maybe. It was awfully misty, and that hood covered most of his face. I don't know. When I upload the images to my laptop and enlarge them, we might see something ... some new clue."

I'd hoped my meeting with the Puzzler would jog my

memory, help me remember who he was and why he was so bitter. Replaying his harangue in my mind revealed very little about him, however, other than his overwhelming bile. I ground my teeth, thinking about what he'd called Berni. "Aren't you upset about, you know, what he said about you?" I stopped walking and looked hard at Berni. "Doesn't that bother you?"

"I've heard worse." She chuckled as she turned to me. "He's not wrong, you know. I am your girlfriend … in a platonic way. And as for the other part, well, that's true, too."

"Still. He was pretty crude."

"As I said. I've heard worse."

We continued our slow walk toward the Station, each lost in our own thoughts. "Something else is bothering me, though," she said. "What did he mean by it's too late? Did that have something to do with me, or was it just part of his rant?"

What had I said right before he'd made that nasty comment? Was it something like, "Leave Berni out of it"? Putting those thoughts together rattled me even more.

"I'm worried about you, Berni," I told her. "You're helping me sort out this … this crazy situation. I can't have you in any danger. That wouldn't be right."

She reached out and put both arms on my shoulders as we arrived at the Station. "Nathan. You are and will always be my friend. We look out for each other. That's what good friends do."

I had to hold back tears. I've had plenty of close relationships over the years, but somehow the bond between the two of us seemed deeper than anything I'd known since my marriage to Anna.

Our moment of tenderness was interrupted by Bob jogging over to join us. "I guess Mrs. Murphy has a hard time turning around in her seat to back up," he said. "And that old Buick doesn't have a rearview camera." Realization dawned on his face as he took in the two of us standing close together. "Hey, am I interrupting something here?"

Berni and I both said "no" at the same time, and then we both laughed.

Bob turned red. I don't know why he should have been embarrassed. He coughed before speaking. "Look," he said. "I gotta get some shut-eye tonight. I'm helping marshal that car parade tomorrow. And I need to get my patrol bike back."

"No problem, Bob," Berni assured him. "I'm going to be in that parade, too, in Kathy's classic Chevy. Hop into my truck and we'll gather up your bike and get you back home, pronto."

As much as I didn't want to continue to lean on my friends, all this seemed a letdown. "Is that it for the night?" I directed my question at both of them.

Bob blew out his breath. "What more damage can we do? It's definitely 'it' for me."

Berni stifled a yawn. "Sorry. Way past my bedtime, too. I'll sort out the photos tomorrow afternoon—after the parade. I can bring over my laptop and we'll look at them together. That work?"

"Sure," I said. "I guess there's no rush."

Unless my Puzzler does something else in the meantime.

Chapter Forty-Three
French Stole from Magyar

I drove home with so many thoughts bouncing around in my head. When we all ran into the alley chasing the Poe Puzzler, where had he gone? He could have doubled back, hidden behind the shed next to the Station, or slipped between the houses that backed onto the alley. The fog gave him plenty of cover. Just one more thing we hadn't planned for.

How did he get to the Station, and where did he park his car? Of course, he could have come on a bike, but a lone rider on the streets of Ocean City around midnight would have attracted more police attention than a car. He was more wily than that. And I couldn't believe he lived in this relatively well-to-do neighborhood. He must have driven here. Bob didn't mention seeing any out-of-place vehicles, though … at least not when he had air in his bike's tires.

And, again, what was the point of our midnight meeting? If he was ratcheting up his harassment, what could come next?

More than that, how did he do everything he'd done

to me so far and go undetected? Was he some kind of mastermind? I had so little to go on, so few clues about his identity and his actual grievances. I blew out a breath that turned into a yawn. Just as Bob and Berni had mentioned, it was past my bedtime, too.

When I unlocked the front door and walked into the kitchen, all my negative thoughts melted away. Lenore trotted out from the hallway, stretched her whole body, even her toes, then flopped onto her back, looking at me upside down with her adorable green eyes.

"Oh, Nori Girl, it's so nice to see you acting like yourself again!" I crouched down and rubbed her belly, and she rewarded me with soft purrs. "You seem better. I still think we should visit the v-e-t tomorrow, though. That blood on your mouth was not a good sign."

She flipped right-side up and pushed her head against my hand, begging for more affection. Who could resist this cute little kitty?

I opened a can of cat food and scooped out two teaspoons—not too much, in case she'd have a hard time eating it. She looked up at me with eyes wide, impatient for her late-night snack. When I set it down on the kitchen floor, she gobbled it without hesitation. Her injured mouth was another mystery for me. But this seemed like it might have a happy ending.

It was past one by the time I got into bed. As tired as I was, I couldn't settle down. Why was it so hard for me to remember a former student, someone I'd inadvertently slighted or treated differently than the others? Even with his disguise, I should have had enough clues. Some crucial piece of the puzzle seemed just beyond my grasp. It was like riding a boardwalk merry-go-round, the shiny brass ring so tantalizingly close with each revolution, but always out of reach.

How much time passed before I dropped off to sleep—minutes or hours—I couldn't tell.

A ringing phone jarred me awake. I glanced at the clock—eight-thirty. How had I slept so long?

The garbled hello that came out of my mouth was unintelligible, even to me.

"Is this Mr. Poe?"

I cleared my throat and tried again. "Yes. Yes, this is Nathan Poe."

"It's Kayley from South Shore Animal Care. You left a message with our answering service … about your cat?"

My head began to clear. Of course, Lenore. And there she was at the foot of the bed, wide eyes staring at me. Rather than give Kayley a succinct reason for my call, I relayed the entire story, leaving no detail out. I rambled on and on about how Lenore first stopped eating, then hid in my closet, and then I found blood on her mouth, but late last night she seemed fine and finally ate some canned cat food.

The poor woman must have said, "yes, yes, okay," more than a few times before I trailed off, giving her a chance to speak. "Well, Doctor Goldstein has an opening at ten-forty," she said. "Could you bring Lenore in then?"

I only hesitated a moment, searching my foggy brain for any reason that would prevent me from going. "That's good. Yes, I'll be there. With Lenore, of course."

After I hung up, I looked at my furry little friend, now sitting up and eyeing me suspiciously. "Yes, Nori Girl, we'll be going to the v-e-t." Don't tell me cats don't understand what we say.

I showered and put on an old long-sleeve shirt that wouldn't show white cat hair too much. Next on my agenda was breakfast, first for Lenore and then for me. It was easier for her—another couple of spoons of cat food, which she ate with abandon.

Not so easy for me. I opened the refrigerator to see what I could scrounge together from my meager provisions. It didn't look promising. With my head in the fridge, I heard a thump by the front porch that sent a shiver down my spine. Oh, don't start the day like this, I thought. But no, it was Mrs. G, holding a Corningware dish, banging her elbow against the door. What a relief … in more ways than one!

She started talking the moment she stepped inside. And in typical fashion, she used as few words as possible to get her thoughts across. "Last night not good. I polish front bumper. Okay now. Woke up early, so I make palacsinta."

I had no idea what that was, but the thin, rolled-up pancakes in her dish looked appetizing. "Ah, French crepes! How delightful."

"Not French!" She stamped a foot on the floor. "French stole from Magyar! Palacsinta. Hungarian dish. Good for late breakfast."

When it came to the provenance of anything Hungarian, there was no arguing with Mrs. G. Not only that, but I was hungry. "Tell me how to pronounce it, please."

"Easy," she said. "Palacsinta."

"Slowly, please."

She puffed out a breath. Patience is definitely not one of her virtues. "Pah. La. Chin. Tuh."

Using her phonetics, I gave it a try and was rewarded with a Mona Lisa smile. "Okay for English boy," she said.

Satisfied with this left-handed compliment, I put the kettle on to boil. Mrs. G's Hungarian delicacy called for a simple, plain tea, devoid of the ubiquitous orange pekoe or other citrus spices. And since I wasn't one-hundred percent awake yet, something strong. Good old reliable PG Tips would do the trick.

Yes, it's often derided in some circles as being too bitter or lacking in "character," whatever that is. I tend to think the tea elites who criticize it can't stomach the idea of this inexpensive tea being any good. Well, that's not me.

The trick to PG Tips, as with any black tea, is to limit the time it steeps. Two or three minutes is the maximum. The whistling kettle brought my ruminations to an end, so I poured the steaming water into two small mugs and dunked the tea bags. A bit of sugar and milk for me, and none for Mrs. G. I almost mentioned that Russians also drank tea with no milk or cream, but it was probably not a good time to mention other nationalities. And I didn't dare offer her coffee.

With the tea served and the two of us sitting at my small kitchen table, it was finally time to dig into Mrs. G's homemade breakfast. The glass lid to the dish held small bubbles of condensation from the crepes—dare I call them that?—so they were still warm. I lifted the lid and caught a warm, buttery aroma with a hint of something both sweet and tangy.

"What's inside?" I asked.

"How you say? Cheese from cottage and raisins, yellow ones. Others have jam, apricot. You take one of each."

I didn't have to be told twice. The cottage cheese filling was not as milky as the usual stuff I buy at the grocery store, and she must have added sugar and maybe lemon zest. Golden raisins added a fruity flavor. It was a delicate and comforting invitation to my palate. Most impressive of all were the Hungarian pancakes themselves. Thicker than French crepes, they somehow managed to be lighter and more lacy as well. Oh my, what a treat!

Needless to say, I ate more than I probably should have. The apricot-filled palacsinta—there I'm learning to say it—were good, but the cottage cheese and raisin-filled ones were my new favorite.

I mentioned before that Mrs. G doesn't have much patience. Well, she did at least wait until I'd finished eating to bring up issues from the previous night.

"Okay," she said. "We talk now."

Here it comes, I thought.

"Fiona. She drive too fast."

Somehow, I thought it was the other way around. "Maybe," I said.

"No 'maybe'! She at fault."

The last thing I wanted was to open up a rift between the two of them … or reopen an old wound. "Please don't blame Mrs. Murphy. If anyone was at fault, it was me, not her. I should've been clearer in my instructions to both of you."

"Hmph!"

Oh boy, I'd have to work on this. Who holds a grudge longer, Hungarians or the Irish? In my experience, it was hard to say.

"Look, I've got to take Lenore to the vet this morning. Maybe we could talk about this later today?"

She frowned, but slowly nodded her head. That was probably as close to an affirmative as I was going to get.

Chapter Forty-Four
Attic Finds

I need to go through an elaborate process when I take Lenore to the vet. Each step must be performed in order. Failure to do so can doom the entire operation and result in an embarrassing call to the vet to cancel the appointment.

First, give Lenore some cat treats, and when she's distracted by the food, scoop her up in my arms. Hold her firmly to my chest, but not too firmly. Think of it as a decisive hug.

Lenore is a gentle kitty, so this doesn't result in hissing or scratching; more like pitiful meows and squirming. She'll know what's up, though—she's smarter than the average cat.

Next, carry her into the bathroom and gently set her down. She'll more than likely scurry to hide behind the toilet. Then, quickly shut the door. This part can be tricky—she may try to run between my feet to escape.

Only after she's ensconced in the bathroom can I retrieve the cat carrier from the attic. If she sees it any sooner, she'll be spooked and crawl under the bed where

I can't reach her. If all goes well, however, I'll bring the carrier into the bathroom, extricate her from behind the toilet, and get her into the black canvas carrier without too much fuss. By that point, she'll be resigned to her fate. As I said, she's a smarty, my Lenore.

My attic space is very limited. Because of the slope of the roof, I can't stand up in it. Not only that, but the plywood flooring is only secured to floor joists around the stairway opening. If I'd venture too far beyond that perimeter, I could put a foot through the floor.

On that fateful day—was it just yesterday?—I'd successfully sequestered my furry little friend in the bathroom and went into the bedroom to change my pants, which I should have done earlier. My good jeans were freshly laundered and would show dust from the attic, not to mention white cat hair, all too clearly. I grabbed a pair of pants from the laundry basket and felt a strange lump in the back pocket. What the heck? To my chagrin, it was Mrs. G's Hungarian medallion, the one I was supposed to keep with me at all times. I must have worn those pants to the Life Saving Station the previous night.

I reached in and hefted the strange talisman. Mrs. G's warning echoed in my mind: "Protect you from bad man!" I was just driving Lenore to the vet, but why not listen to her advice? The only downside would be some discomfort in my hindquarters while driving.

Suitably dressed for the occasion, so to speak, all I

had to do was get the cat carrier from the attic.

The age of my North End bungalow was nowhere more apparent than when I pulled the rope in the hallway ceiling to release the fold-down stairs. It was like a gateway to another time.

A fine shower of dust floated to the floor, and the creak of the springs and rusty hinges as I extended the device was like fingernails on a blackboard. The wooden treads are narrow, more like a ladder than a staircase, and every time I go up there, which isn't often, I remind myself to look into installing a more modern and safer contraption.

Halfway up, I grabbed the pull chain to a lone 100-watt bulb, which cast deep shadows on the cobwebs between roof beams, many of which were darkened and water-stained from some long-ago leak in the roof. A panorama of cardboard boxes was arrayed around the opening, and wedged between two of them sat the cat carrier.

I was almost at the top of the stairs when I reached for it ... and my foot slipped. Either the tread swiveled on its mount, or there was something slippery on it. I only slid two steps before I caught my fall, but I came down hard on my right foot, the one attached to my weak right leg ... the one that was damaged in the accident five years ago.

Lenore probably heard me swear. Heck, Mrs. G next door may have heard it, too. I eased down the steps and went in search of some Advil. Like most people, I keep painkillers in the bathroom cabinet. But trying to maneuver into and out of that room without Lenore escaping was out of the question. No painkillers for me.

There was nothing to do but bite my lip, steel myself, and try the stairs again. I climbed up gingerly, putting as little pressure on my right foot as possible. With a few more grunts and cuss words, I made it to the top and snatched Lenore's carrier.

But I had another surprise in the harsh light of the bare lightbulb. As I glanced at a box to my right, I saw the label, "School Stuff." And sitting on top of the box was a dusty bronze trophy. A kaleidoscope of memories came flooding through my mind.

You've no doubt heard about the seven-year itch with some marriages. For teachers, there's a similar ennui that sets in after the same number of years. You've been teaching the identical curriculum, and you wonder if you're getting stale. You want to try something new, but you're afraid it won't work as well as the tried-and-true approach you've been using. And you start to wonder what seven more years of the same thing will feel like.

It was around my seventh-year when I had the best group of students in my last-period English lit class. Yes, they were bright, but they also seemed more mature than usual and more eager to learn. They were sponges for knowledge … and they encouraged me to give them everything I had. I don't know how other teachers reacted to this group, but for me, it reinvigorated my love of teaching. And it made me look forward to every new day.

A couple of days before these seniors graduated, one of them, a perky young woman named Sarika, came up to my desk and asked if she could make an announcement. I had no idea what was coming. Instead of addressing her classmates, she spoke directly to me.

"Mr. Poe, you've meant a lot to us this year, and not only did we learn about literature, but I think we also learned some things about life. So … well, we put our heads together and decided that maybe you deserve a special award from our graduating class. Here it is."

She motioned to a student in the first row, who pulled a small gift-wrapped package from her backpack. When I opened it, I had to hold back tears … tears of happiness, of joy.

Now, so many years later, I grabbed this Oscar-like trophy from my attic and brought it down to the kitchen table to dust it off. Again, I felt my eyes water. Inscribed on the base of the trophy, it read, "World's Best Teacher."

It was like a weight had been lifted from my shoulders; a weight I hadn't even realized had been there. I've certainly made mistakes in my 20 years of teaching, and the biggest one was probably how I treated the young man who held so much resentment against me—the young man who became my Poe Puzzler.

But I'd also done some things right. I'd also made a difference to that group of high school seniors; a difference that I hoped followed them into their adult lives.

Chapter Forty-Five
Pet Names

With Lenore settled inside her carrier on the back seat—secured with a seatbelt, of course—and I in the driver's seat, gently pressing on the gas pedal with my sore right foot, we headed off to the vet, across the bay in Somers Point. My slow driving probably annoyed the few drivers behind me, but it simply hurt too much to extend the sole of my foot. They would just have to be patient.

When I got only as far as Bay Avenue, however, my phone rang. Since I hadn't taken the time to plug in my Bluetooth cable, I pulled over by the Ocean City Sailing Foundation to answer. It was Mrs. Murphy.

"Nathan? Nathan, are you there?"

"Yes, Mrs. Murphy," I said. "I'm heading to …" She was so riled up, I couldn't finish the sentence.

"You know I was waiting for your call, don't you? I'm sorry if I sound too blunt, Nathan, but I think you're being a bit inconsiderate for not calling me earlier. It's about last night. You know—the little altercation. I think you'll agree that Klara was going much too fast. Yes, of course, everything worked out alright in the end, and I shouldn't be concerned about who's at fault, but still. She was driving too fast."

With that pause in her tirade, I could finally get a word in edgewise. "Mrs. Murphy. I'm in the car. I was just heading over to Somers Point."

"Well, I certainly hope you're being careful, talking on the phone while you're driving. You know that's against the law, don't you? Do you have one of those blue cables? I wouldn't want you to get into trouble, Nathan. Especially not with everything you're going through."

That made me laugh. She was looking out for me, which was very sweet of her. "I'm fine, Mrs. Murphy. I've pulled over so I could talk to you. I'm taking Lenore to the vet in Somers Point."

There was a moment of silence on the line, a rarity with her.

"To the vet? Is she ill, Nathan? I hope it's nothing serious. That poor dear!"

"Thanks for asking. I'm not exactly sure what's wrong with Nori, but she had some blood on her mouth. Maybe there's something going on with her teeth or gums."

All her agitation subsided. "Well, you take care of her then. Don't you worry about me. We can talk later." And with that, she hung up.

The waiting area at the South Shore Animal Care Center is a pleasant enough place, with wide, padded benches, and a clear separation between the cat side and the dog side. I have no idea what they do for parrots or other species. Lenore's ears perked up, and I saw her little nose twitch in reaction to the strange smells. I lifted the flap on top of the carrier and reached in, hoping my touch would comfort her.

I'd arrived on time, and Kayley said Dr. Goldstein would see us shortly. With any doctor's visit, however, whether for people or pets, there's always a wait. I usually amuse myself by reading the names on the "welcome" board. Dog and cat names are intermixed, so it's also fun to guess, simply by the name, whether it's one or the other. I went down the list.

Luna. A very nice name—the moon. Depending on the phase of the moon, the cat could be white or black. Somehow, I don't see Luna as a dog.

Raven. Now there's a name close to my heart. It had to be a cat and it had to be black, no two ways about it.

Apollo … that's pretty highfalutin. Naming your pet after a Greek god? It was probably a dog, and one I'd hope was very bright!

Then there was Diesel. Really? Who would name their pet after a petroleum product?

Casey—an interesting one. Casey used to be a boy's name, as in "Mighty Casey at the Bat." These days, almost all names are gender-neutral, and I suppose the spelling can vary as well ... probably a dozen or more variations. A dog or a cat? Hard to tell.

Lost in my mental musings, I almost missed Dr. Goldstein asking me to come into the examining room.

"Nathan! Let's see what's going on with your Lenore."

I've known Julie Goldstein for a number of years, and she's monitored Lenore's health since kittenhood. It's important to trust your doctors, and that goes for veterinarians, too.

While we extricated Lenore from the carrier—the same carrier that she'd been so eager to avoid—Dr. Goldstein asked me a series of questions. Had she gone outside? Had she been in a fight with another animal? Had I noticed any odd behavior other than not eating? Did her gait seem abnormal? Did I detect any bad breath?

The answer to every question was, "No," and all I got after my response was a slow nodding of her head. I suppose she was ruling out one thing or another, trying to connect the dots. After a cursory physical examination of Lenore, including squeezing her abdomen and lifting her tail to check for who knows what?—all of which my well-mannered kitty didn't seem to mind—Dr. Goldstein grabbed a long cotton swab and a small penlight from the table behind her. "Now let's take a look inside her mouth."

She directed me to hold Lenore's head from behind, using both hands, my forearms cradling her body. Prior experience must have taught her how to avoid getting bitten. She was doing a very thorough job, gently lifting Lenore's lips, then getting in closer and using the flashlight and cotton swab to rub against her gums. Everything was fine until she must have touched a sore spot.

Lenore growled, hissed, and pushed back against my grip. I'd never known her to be so aggressive. I guess even the most mild-mannered kitties have their limits. You could say the same for us.

"Okay." Dr. Goldstein stood up, threw the swab in a bin, and set down her penlight. "I don't see a fractured tooth or any obvious signs of trauma. But her gums on the right side are slightly inflamed."

She paused, and I resisted the urge to ask an obvious question. I couldn't resist for too long. "So, does that rule out anything really bad?" I asked.

That brought a smile to her face. "I like the way you put that, Nathan." She leaned closer to Lenore and whispered. "Hey, we still friends?" Nori was having none of it; she squirmed and did all she could to put some distance between the two of them. "We could do a dental x-ray, but that may be premature."

And costly, I thought.

"Since her teeth appear to be intact, I think she might have damaged her gums by chewing on something hard ... difficult to say what." She frowned, as if in thought. "By all means, if you find whatever it is, throw it out."

"Okay. Where do we go from here?"

"The simplest course of action may be to monitor her condition for a week or two. Let me give her an injection of antibiotics, and then we'll send you home," she said. "You probably know the routine—put her on a soft-food diet and keep an eye out for any unusual behavior. And if you see more blood in her mouth, call."

With any doctor's visit, for humans or pets, we hope to get a definitive answer. You know, here's the cause of the symptoms and here's how to treat it. Far too often, that doesn't happen. Lenore's bleeding gums were still a mystery, for both the vet and me.

I had to wait my turn before checking out, so Lenore and I were back on the bench in the waiting room. She curled up in a tight ball as far inside the carrier as possible. If she had the power to make herself disappear, she'd definitely use it.

An older woman cradling a small white terrier was paying her bill, and I couldn't help eavesdropping.

"Do you have any questions about the medication?" Kayley asked.

"No," the woman answered. "Casey and I have been through this before."

Aha! So this was the Casey I'd noticed on the welcome board—definitely a dog. Male or female? I couldn't tell by looking at the pup, but found out quickly.

"I hope he's feeling better soon," Kayley said.

It was a simple enough puzzle, and now at least it was solved. That made me smile.

After a few minutes, Kayley told me my bill was ready. The vet has my credit card on file, so the process didn't take long. While my receipt was printing out, I decided to share the source of my amusement. "I like to play a mental guessing game with the names on the welcome board," I told Kayley. "I couldn't figure out if Casey was a dog or a cat, female or male. Now I know!"

She indulged me with a smile. "We have several Caseys in our files, and I guess they're pretty evenly split between dogs and cats." She hesitated, a slight blush on her cheeks. "Funny. Casey was actually my nickname in college."

That was confusing. "How did Kayley become Casey?"

She shook her head, and her light auburn bangs danced back and forth. "My last name is Collins. So … Kayley Collins became K-C. But here's the best part." She was warming to the subject. "I was K-C One, and my college roommate was K-C Two."

"Let me guess," I said. "Her name was … Kathy … Carlson?"

"No! You're way off. Her name was Kimberly Lyone."

She must have noticed my puzzled look and saved me from asking. "Her middle name was 'Celeste'—kind of pretty, isn't it? So, she was Kimberly Celeste Lyone, and that became K-C Two. At least I was Number One!"

On the ride home from the vet, I should have been thinking about Lenore and her sore gums. Something else was bothering me, though. It was like an itch at the back of my mind that I couldn't reach. I knew there was no point straining to figure it out. The answer would come to me when I least expected.

Still driving slowly because of my aching foot, I watched a stream of brightly colored muscle cars zip past me on the Somers Point bridge. Lemon yellow, strawberry red, green apple green—like a bunch of big jelly beans. They were all in a hurry to get to the boardwalk parade … the same parade Berni and her new friend, Kathy, were so eager to attend. The parade that Bob was patrolling to maintain order. All my close friends were there. And that thought irritated my mental itch some more.

As I came to the left-turn light at Bay Avenue, a purple Dodge Charger cut me off to turn left before the light changed to red. I slammed on the brakes, and an electric jolt of pain shot up my right leg. A hollow clunk in the back made me think someone had tapped my bumper; a glance in the rearview mirror disproved that. I have so much stuff in the trunk, the noise could have been from anything rolling around in there.

Then I thought of Lenore and turned in my seat to make sure she was okay. Her face was pushed up against the netting of the carrier, her eyes wide. I was glad it was belted in. "Sorry, Nori. I had to stop to avoid hitting that guy." Her distress made me angry. Mess with me all you want, but don't upset my cat!

"We're almost home, Lenoreo. Try to stay calm." When I got the green light, I eased onto Bay Avenue, heading north. I couldn't escape the swarm of classic cars until they all turned right on 5th Street, no doubt heading to the ramp onto the boardwalk. According to my Saab's less-than-trusty clock, it was a few minutes past noon—that's when the parade was supposed to begin. If so, they were getting a late and unorganized start.

Once I reached 2nd Street, I zig-zagged my way toward my North End neighborhood, where I'd hoped life would move at a slower pace. At the stop sign for

Atlantic Avenue, my eyes were drawn to a hand-lettered sign outside the Catholic church: "K of C Meeting Tonight, 8 PM."

Life is full of coincidences. The more you look for them, the more you'll find. Still, I got the distinct feeling the universe was trying to tell me something. And it was spelled with a K and a C.

Chapter Forty-Six
Ask a Librarian

I parked at the curb in front of my house, unclipped Lenore's carrier, and limped up the porch to my door. As I was fumbling with the house key, my phone vibrated in my pocket. Probably Mrs. Murphy again, I thought. She'd just have to wait.

Once inside, I set the carrier on the floor and unzipped the front. Lenore leapt out, ran around the kitchen table, and then shook like a dog who'd just had a bath. Her relief at being back home was palpable. Who could blame her? A visit to the vet plus a panic stop in a car would unnerve any pet. Lenore wasn't used to such disruptions in her routine.

Figuring she still must be hungry, I grabbed a cat-food can from the pantry. As I placed it on the kitchen counter to open it, she reached up her paw to tap me on the calf, eager to be fed. And the moment I put the dish down on the floor, she lapped it up. Now I felt relief as well.

My phone buzzed again. With a sigh, I reached down to see what Mrs. Murphy wanted. To my surprise, it wasn't her or Mrs. G. It was a text message from an unknown caller, someone in the 540 area code. My friend, Ed, lives in Virginia and has the same area code, but it couldn't be him. I've got his contact information in my phone, and it didn't come up with the message. Who else did I know in Virginia? A mystery …

The text read, "Solve the puzzle yet?" It could've been from any of my former clients or even old friends who'd moved south. But …

Virginia … mystery … friends.

The text had to be from the Poe Puzzler. But how had he gotten my number?

Virginia … mystery … friends.

I paced the floor, straining to put all the pieces in place. After a moment of sheer frustration, the answers flooded into my mind like a tsunami, gaining strength as it approached the shore. The realization hit me so hard, I almost fell over.

K and C. My call to Berni last night, the call that someone had picked up but didn't say anything. K and C—Casey. Wasn't that the name of Kathy's troubled brother? And the text from Virginia. Berni said that's where he'd gone after high school. But maybe his name wasn't Casey. Maybe K and C were his initials, like Kayley's story at the vet.

So … his first name probably began with the letter K. His last, or middle name, started with C. I didn't know Kathy's last name. It might not even be the same as her brother's. Casey, or whatever his name was, had to be my Poe Puzzler. It was starting to add up.

I texted Berni and got a "notifications turned off"

reply. Of course. She was in the parade with Kathy and probably didn't want to be disturbed.

The letter K swirled around in my mind. A boy named ... Kevin or Karl or Keith...? I had to go through the high school yearbooks again—another trip to the library.

I was halfway to the door when I noticed the cat carrier on the kitchen floor. No point in upsetting Nori by leaving it there, and I wasn't about to climb the attic stairs again. Best to throw it in the back seat, at least temporarily. I grabbed it and half-ran, half-limped out the front door.

There was an open space by the library entrance, so I pulled in, checked to make sure it wasn't reserved or a handicap spot, then hurried up the ramp to the entrance, gritting my teeth against the pain in my foot.

I smiled at Nickie, sitting at the circulation desk, but got a frosty look in return—there was still some work to do to patch up our relationship. By contrast, Dawn, the reference librarian, gave me a friendly wave, which I returned in kind. There was no time to pause for a chat, however. I made a beeline for the high school yearbooks in the back corner.

The books were out of chronological order. Someone must have been leafing through them earlier, or a library assistant or intern wasn't doing a very good job. After a moment's panic when I thought the book I was looking for was missing, I found it on a lower shelf—a record of my students in my last year teaching, five years ago.

My heart raced; I had to make a concerted effort to slow down. The sprint to the end of a mystery is always so exciting. I knew I was close. An empty carrel nearby, with autumn sunlight streaming through a tall window, offered a perfect spot to go page-by-page through the yearbook.

After zipping past the sports team and school club images, I slowed to examine the individual senior class photos more carefully. The kids all looked alike—dark sports jackets and white shirts for the guys, mostly without ties; dark dresses for the girls. Plastered smiles on some, serious looks on others. Very few appeared happy to be sitting for their yearbook pictures. Ah, the angst of high school!

Of course, the kids were listed in alphabetical order by last name. Finding a boy ... a young man ... whose name began with K was laborious. I couldn't recall how many graduating students were in that year's class, but it was surely a couple of hundred.

Nothing in the A's, B's, and C's. So many last names beginning with D and F. This was frustrating. Thankfully, there weren't many I and J names. K ... and then L: Lambert, Lee, Lippincott, Lorenzo. I stopped and stared at the photo of a young man from my last semester English class.

If this were a Hollywood movie, the camera would zoom in on that photo, vignetting the borders, making the image jump out at you. Flitting bits of memory came back to me. The kid who always sat in the back, dressed in black. The one who never volunteered an answer, never did his assignments. Had I failed him that semester? Likely.

Kenneth C. Loughman. The other kids used to call him Low Man. He was probably bullied; probably didn't have many friends. I read the caption under his photo: "Catch Kenny, if you can, behind the wheel of his modified Subaru. A certain Amy ranks high. D&D and techno rock rule!"

Kenneth C. Loughman—KC. That's what his sister, Kathy, called him—Casey.

My phone vibrated. Another text. "Doing your homework?"

I spun around, scanning the library floor for a kid in a gray hoodie. Was he here, watching me? No, that couldn't be. Just my paranoia again.

Stop and think—that's what I repeated in my head. I had to engage him, text him back. I thought I knew the answer to this question, but I asked it anyhow: "How did you get my number?"

His reply came quickly: "Your too dumb to figure it out." Once an English teacher, always an English teacher. It took an effort not to correct his text—it's "you're"! Best to ignore that. What now? I knew who he was. I knew some of his background—his fight with his sister, Kathy, his time with his aunt in Virginia. His mother's recent passing. He was here in Ocean City now. And hellbent on making my life miserable.

My fingers pecked at the keypad; I can't use my thumbs like kids do. "Isn't it time we end this nonsense?" I wrote back to him.

A long pause with no reply. Would he continue our

stunted conversation, or wait for another opportunity to harass me?

A screaming gull flew past the library window, startling me. Clouds were moving in from the shore, the day darkening. But it wasn't even one o'clock. I'd laid my phone on the desktop of the carrel, and the vibration of an incoming text made it jitter across the surface. I picked it up.

"Meet me at shirk.deride.flukes." A moment later: "NOW come alone."

Was this some kind of code? Did his phone's auto-correct jumble the words? I looked around, trying to find some kind of reference book that would help me decipher the Puzzler's text … if it warranted deciphering, that is. I was at a standstill.

Sometimes, when you need help the most, the universe provides it. Dawn walked over to say hello. Perfect timing, and a reference librarian was exactly what I needed. "You look perplexed, Nathan," she said.

"I am! I got this strange text … long story. Um, someone wants me to meet somewhere, and he gave me a jumble of three words as the location."

Dawn scrunched her eyebrows together. She was giving this some serious thought. "Could I see the words?"

That gave me pause. I didn't want her to see my back-and-forth text with the Puzzler, but I had no choice. I raised the phone to her eyes. After reading the text, she smiled. "Of course," she said. "It sounds like a geo-locator. Some birders were asking me about that last week. Follow me to my desk."

I wasn't sure what a geo-locator was, but Dawn seemed confident. She woke up her computer as I stood in front of her desk. After clicking away at the keyboard, she met my eyes. "Yes, that's it," she said. "What three words."

Was I not being clear? "I've already shown you: shirk, deride, flukes, with a period between them."

She laughed. "So, you're Abbott and I'm Costello? Or is it the other way around?"

"I still don't get it." She was having fun with my request, while all I wanted to do was figure it out and rush to meet my Puzzler.

"That's what it's called, this geo-locating system— What3Words.com."

"Okay, so what does that mean?"

"Oh, I don't know all the ins and outs of the system, but it's a way to precisely designate a location, a location without a street address, with three seemingly random words."

"And where … where is shirk, deride, flukes?"

She clicked away at her computer again, then gestured for me to come around and look at the screen. "It's on the other side of Corson's Inlet State Park, on the beach."

"Why couldn't he just tell me that?" I mumbled. I had to be sure about this, so I asked her to confirm. "That's the park just before the Strathmere bridge, right?"

"Exactly. But it looks like you'll have to park your car at the boat ramp and then walk down a trail to get to this location. See the dotted line on the map?"

I couldn't rely on my memory to get it straight, so I asked Dawn if I could take a cell-phone picture of the screen. I knew how to get to the state park, and from there I'd walk along the trail to the spot. Meeting my Puzzler on a deserted section of the beach—was I out of my mind?

Chapter Forty-Seven
Calling for Backup

My nemesis—was he really that bad or just a very frustrated young man?—wanted to meet "NOW" and "alone." I hadn't agreed to either.

As for the former, there was no point in keeping him waiting. The longer I delayed, the more agitated he'd likely become. And I still believed, naively as it turned out, that I could apologize profusely for his perceived insults and try to help him work through his problems. Since he was a former student of mine, I owed him that much.

As to his directive to come alone, I would … but … I also wanted backup, just in case. I found a quiet corner in the lobby and dialed Berni—it went straight to voicemail. In retrospect, my message to her may have been incoherent. I couldn't clearly explain the geo-locator system, but I'd hoped she'd understand that I was meeting the Poe Puzzler at Corson's Inlet. "Come as quickly as you can," I said. "And bring Bob if he's available." I didn't mention my assumption that the Puzzler was Kathy's brother. That could wait.

My call to Bob rang and rang. When I tried to leave a message, I was informed that his mailbox was full. Two strikes against me so far.

That left my not-too-old neighbors as lifelines. Speaking frankly, although I love them dearly, one would want to know far more details than I had time to explain, and the other would ask pointed questions that would imply the situation was all my fault.

On the other hand, I could reassure Mrs. G that I had the Hungarian talisman in my back pocket—that I took her warnings seriously. The weighty object was pulling down one side of my pants. In fact, I was surprised Dr. Goldstein hadn't mentioned my cockeyed trousers. It was out of character for her to be so polite.

When I walked out of the lobby and shuffled down the ramp toward my car, I was stopped cold by what I saw. A woman in a black rain slicker—at least it looked like a short woman—was peering into my Saab's windows and trying to open the passenger door. This simply does not happen in Ocean City! We supposedly live in one of the state's safest towns. And it was broad daylight … or maybe not so "broad," since dark clouds were rolling in from the ocean.

I contemplated how to deal with this would-be car thief as I approached her from behind, as silently as I could with my limp. Once I was directly behind her, I yelled. "Hey! What do you think you're doing?"

She spun around so quickly that she fell into my arms, sputtering in shock. I grabbed her by the shoulders and raised her face to mine. Only then did I realize she was probably a decade or two older than my senior neighbors, and weighed about as much as a Costco bag of kitty litter.

"You …, you…" She stammered to get the words out.

My red haze of anger slowly dissipated, but I was still outraged by her actions. "What were you doing with my car?"

Her eyes widened, then narrowed as she stared at me. "That's your car? How dare you lock your pet in there! That's inhumane. You could be arrested for animal cruelty."

My held-back laughter appeared to infuriate her even more. With all my energy directed toward my upcoming meeting with the Poe Puzzler, I couldn't help but find her actions absurd. I finally got the words out. "There's no pet in there," I said. "It's empty. The cat carrier is empty. My Lenore is safe at home."

While realization eventually dawned on her reddened face, she still managed to rustle up some indignation. "Hmph!" She turned from me and mumbled as she walked away. "What kind of fool keeps an empty cat carrier in his car?"

I was speechless. She was well-meaning enough and obviously an animal lover. Her assumptions, however, crossed the line. Did she walk through parking lots looking for careless pet owners? Most people mind their own business. Others seem intent on minding ours.

I closed my eyes and blew out a held breath I hadn't realized I'd been holding. Now that I was so close to confronting my Puzzler, I had no time for this kind of diversion.

It takes less than fifteen minutes to drive from the library to the Strathmere bridge and the entrance to the state park; hardly any cars are on the South End in the off season. That gave me enough time to make two calls. With Mrs. G top of mind, I reached out to her first.

Instead of saying hello, she answered the phone by saying, "You call me about bad man." It didn't sound like a question. I'd never thought she was clairvoyant. That sent my mind on a mental detour that left me tongue-tied.

"Well, yes," I finally responded. "I guess I am."

I told her about driving to meet the Poe Puzzler at Corson's Inlet. She asked plenty of questions; I responded as best I could. While I certainly don't have any psychic ability, I knew what her final question would be.

"You have Magyar medallion?"

"Of course," I said, even though I hadn't been very diligent about keeping it with me up until then.

"Good. You good then."

I wished I had her confidence.

Next, I called Mrs. Murphy. It rang so many times, I was sure it would go to voicemail. She finally picked up, sounding out of breath.

"Nathan? Is that you?"

"Yes, Mrs. Murphy. I need to ask a favor. I'm meeting ..." She didn't give me time to finish.

"Well, I must say you're being inconsiderate. I

expected to hear back from you sooner. Then, again, you were taking Lenore to the vet, weren't you? Is she alright? Please tell me she's not seriously ill."

As I'd expected, this wasn't going to be easy. "She's okay. She'll probably be okay, but I've got an urgent request right now."

"Urgent? What's so urgent, Nathan?"

I explained about my meeting on the beach, and asked her to try to reach Berni and Patrolman Bob so they could join me there.

"Isn't it going to be dangerous to meet this fellow by yourself? I'd be very careful if I were you, Nathan."

I reassured her as best I could, then cut off another one of her long diatribes as I approached the left turn off Bay Avenue. No doubt she thought me rude—again—but it couldn't be helped. It was time to meet my Poe Puzzler, Kenny C. Loughman, man to man.

Chapter Forty-Eight
Mano a Mano

The pavement takes a sharp dip as you enter the park, and the parking lot is a patchwork of filled-in potholes. I took the turn too quickly, and the same resounding clunk I'd heard earlier echoed in the back of my Saab. Even though I was in a rush, I had to find out what was making that clamorous noise.

I pulled to a stop near the boat ramp, got out, and popped open the trunk. All the usual detritus I keep back there, including my trusty P.I. kit, was commingled with the engine cover I'd never reinstalled after I'd put in the new battery, the unsecured jack and tools from changing the flat tire, and the two-foot "Archimedes" water pipe I'd used for leverage on the lug nuts. It was amazing I hadn't heard a regular cacophony of sounds with every bump in the road.

My eyes zeroed in on the pipe—one-inch steel and long enough to be a weapon. Although I didn't want to appear ready for a fight, it was better to be prepared. I grabbed it, shut the trunk lid, and locked my car. Then I unlocked it. My mind was doing somersaults, visualizing different scenarios.

I moved the empty cat carrier to the front passenger seat and turned on my car's emergency flashers. If things really went south with the Puzzler, this would act as a signal to Berni, Bob, and nosy old ladies who roam parking lots. To be sure I was in the right spot, I pulled out my phone and examined the fuzzy image I'd taken of Dawn's computer screen. Satisfied that this was the place, I scanned the lot to see what I could deduce from the vehicles parked there—just two pickup trucks and a Jeep.

It didn't take the mind of C. Auguste Dupin to determine that the pickups, complete with small trailers, belonged to boat owners. After all, the ramp at the park is an ideal launching point into the inlet. The dark gray Jeep, on the other hand, could belong to anyone. It looked beat up and rusty, and I noticed one of its front tires was almost bald. If my Poe Puzzler had arrived in one of these three vehicles, it was probably the Jeep.

I looked around to make sure no one was watching. It was easy to imagine a burly fisherman getting as upset with my inspection of his car as I was with the woman in the library lot. No one was around, so I took a quick photo of the Jeep's license plate. If my deductions were accurate, that image could come in handy.

The trailhead was about a hundred feet from the boat ramp. The entrance was so narrow and overgrown, I might have missed it if not for a weathered wooden signboard nearby. Since my cellphone image gave only the vaguest notion of where to go, I looked for a map indicating the path to the ocean.

A faded print-out under yellow plastic informed me that the Ocean Trail wound its way to the Atlantic shore for three-tenths of a mile—manageable, I thought, even with my limp. As soon as I'd entered the trail, however, I realized my assumption was wrong. Except for a few short sections with wooden boards over brackish marsh, most of the path was loose sand. My progress was slow and awkward. The hefty water pipe I'd taken with me was too short to use as a cane, so I rested it on my shoulder like a rifle.

There were enough hand-painted warning signs along the way to make me feel like Dorothy traveling to Oz through the haunted forest. "Caution: poison ivy." "Stay on marked trail." "Watch for wildlife." The only things missing were two red-eyed vultures leering down at me and a sign that said, "I'd Turn Back If I Were You!"

No Cowardly Lion here, I thought, as I continued to trudge ahead.

At first, the trail was bordered by short, scrubby bushes, and I had a clear view of the inlet to my right. The air held the scent of waterlogged cattails and the sharp tang of the sea. Eventually, I entered a section canopied by taller trees and vines, a tunnel of foliage with only a patch of daylight in the distance. The threatening clouds I'd seen earlier shadowed the path in twilight, and the wind gusted through the treetops.

After what seemed an eternity, the sound of gulls and seabirds was drowned by the pounding surf; I was nearing the beach. Then my ears caught a series of sharp, rhythmic susurrations. Ssh…ing! Ssh…ing! A piercing sound, like a blade being sharpened on a whetstone. I emerged from the trail and saw the back of my Puzzler, shovel in hand, digging a shallow pit.

He plunged the spade into the sand … and there was that sound again, sharp and angry. The blustery wind whipped at his hoodie, but he didn't seem to notice. He worked tirelessly, rhythmically, pulling heaping shovels from the beach and piling the sand first on one side, then on the other of the long, narrow trench.

I lifted the pipe from my shoulder and called out to him. "Kenny! Kenneth C. Loughman!"

He froze for an instant, then turned to face me, the shovel held out in front of him like a spear. There were only a dozen feet between us.

"You're late, Mr. Poe." His voice rose above the howling wind, his face a mask of anger. Then he laughed, a tight, abrupt noise like a bark. "No, I'm not going to call you 'mister.' You don't deserve that. How about Nate? Should I call you Nate? Or maybe just 'old man.'"

My pulse pounded in my ears, adrenaline kicking in. I had to get him off guard, to trip him up. "Does your sister know you're here?"

His face reddened, and he poked the shovel blade at me, forcing me to backpedal. I almost fell over. "You leave her out of this!" he yelled.

My initial approach had failed; that was obvious. I had to de-escalate, to calm him down. Although he still had the sharp end of the shovel pointed at my midsection, I lowered the steel pipe to my side, an act of submission.

"I'm sorry, Kenny." It was time for an apology.

Wasn't that what I'd originally planned? "I'm sorry for so many things … that I treated you poorly in school … that I failed you as a teacher." Wrong choice of words, again.

"You failed me, alright." He waved the shovel blade in agitated circles, his eyes glaring into mine. "That F in English. I almost didn't graduate because of you. You screwed up my life. It all started with you. I couldn't get a job. Then my Subaru blew a head gasket and I couldn't afford to fix it. It started with you!"

A thought sprang into my mind and out of my mouth before I could filter it. "That was after you raced Eli on the Parkway … wasn't it?"

"Eli. God, poor Eli." His arms went limp, the shovel now held loose in one hand. "We were neck and neck. He started to pull ahead. I don't know what happened. Maybe he blew a tire or something broke. He lost it … lost control of his car. Went into the woods. The flames, my God, the flames. I knew it was over. There was nothing I could do."

Here was an opening, I thought. He had regrets, too. "You should have told someone."

"Who? The police? Not with my record. I'd lose my license for sure."

"What about Eli's mother? Maybe it would've given her some closure. About losing her son. She seems so … so bitter about the way things turned out."

"Yeah, there's enough 'bitter' to go around, isn't there? And you. You're still at the heart of all this. What was that book we were supposed to read? 'Heart of Darkness'? That's you. You're the heart of darkness. And it's time to bury that telltale heart."

It's ridiculous, the way my mind works. All I could think was he was mixing up Joseph Conrad and Edgar Allan Poe. I didn't have time to dwell on this literary mistake because he'd lifted the shovel again and raised it over his shoulder like a battle axe, lunging at me, his face purple with rage.

I swung my pipe in self-defense. It hit against the shovel's handle as he brought it down at me. The impact sent a shockwave through my wrists. I tightened my sweaty grip on the pipe. He pushed back, and I tried to slip to the side to make him stumble. We went at it like two medieval warriors locked in battle, circling the pit. He was stronger than I was, but his anger made him clumsy. I kept backing up, trying to sidestep without twisting my ankle in the sand.

The rain came down on the wind, and I saw his glasses fog up. That only made his advances more brutal, swinging the shovel from side to side, trying to connect with me. I didn't have time to look down, to check my footing when we locked weapons like swordsmen, my short metal pipe pushing against his longer wooden shovel.

A sound came out of my throat, an animal sound, something I'd never heard before. I had no rational control over what happened next. It was all red rage and adrenaline. I released one hand's grip and raised the pipe to hit him as he lurched toward me.

It all happened in slow motion. He fell onto the sand in front of me. As he looked up an odd smile grew at the corners of his mouth. Still holding onto the shovel, he knocked it against my legs and I toppled backward … and kept falling … arms flailing to keep my balance … metal pipe slipping from my grasp … legs kicking out to gain a foothold as the pipe slid beneath me. I landed flat on my back into the would-be grave he'd dug, my breath knocked out of me. I heard a snap before I felt the pain. My trusty pipe, my makeshift weapon now lodged between my legs, had done far more harm to me than it ever did to him.

The next moments are lost to me. I must have blacked out. When I came to, I looked up from the sandy grave and saw him sneering down as he threw shovel upon shovel of sand on top of me. My leg felt like it had snapped in two, pain like I've never experienced before. I reached up to pull myself out of the hole. Whatever small handfuls of sand I could grab fell on top of me. The rain was coming down harder, turning the beach sand to sludge.

"This is crazy, Kenny," I yelled up to him. "Don't do this. Please. Tell me what I can do to help you. Kenny! What do you want?"

With a final grunt, he tossed the shovel on top of me. I winced as it landed on my chest, but the weight of the sand had softened the blow. He laughed, that short, brutal sound he'd made earlier. There was no mirth in it. "What do I want? You, more than anyone, should know that … from all those Poe stories. Revenge, that's what I want. And that's what I got."

He stared at me, hands on hips. I tried to think of something more to say, some way out. My mind was paralyzed by pain. It may seem overly dramatic now, but

I thought this was the end of me. Poe's deathbed words escaped my lips in a whisper. "Lord, help my poor soul."

Then he just walked away. I lost sight of him almost instantly. All I could see were the walls of my sandy grave and rain clouds rolling across the sky. The screams of seagulls on the wind seemed to laugh down at me as they soared overhead.

I felt my phone buzz in my back pocket, impossible to reach, impossible to answer. My arms were free, but my body was buried in sand, and the pain in my leg sapped all my strength. Maybe help was coming, I reasoned. Maybe my messages had gotten through. My breath was ragged. I tried to control it, to slow my racing pulse.

A wave crashed nearby, and I felt panic overtake me. I had to get out of that hole. I feverishly grasped at the sides of my sandy grave, my head almost reaching the surface of the beach.

The sound of the wind seemed louder; rain coming down in buckets. I flashed back to something Mrs. G had told me about Houdini, how he'd expand his muscles while being shackled, then relax them to help wriggle out of his chains.

When I expanded my chest, I was able to free my shoulders, inch by inch, but it was progress. I reached up again and leveraged my body higher, slowly pulling upward. Repeating this process, taking a few moments to catch my breath in between, I finally slid my head up to the surface. My legs, however, were still buried in sand.

My joy in making it that far was doused by a splash of seawater in my face. I turned to the left and saw the tide coming in on waves. I had no time to lose. It was a race between what little strength I still possessed and the Atlantic Ocean.

I grabbed at the edges of the pit, trying to slide the rest of my body out, but muddy sand oozed through my fingers. Was this how I would die? Realizing I'd never get out on my own, I yelled for help.

Chapter Forty-Nine
My Saviors

My neighbors, my dear sweet neighbors, they were the ones who found me. They were the ones who freed me from the sandy grave that Kenny had dug. And here's a strange twist—they used empty casserole dishes Mrs. G had in her car.

Once they'd uncovered the shovel Kenny threw on top of me, they bickered about whether using that implement would inflict more pain on my broken leg. Exactly how they extricated me is lost in my foggy memory. All I know for sure is that it was slow work by dedicated friends.

Whether Kenny, my Poe Puzzler, had planned things this way or not, the incoming tide never reached farther than the waves that had splashed against my face. I wouldn't have drowned, even if I were still buried in the sand.

By the time Berni and Bob finally showed up, and then a park ranger, I was mostly free—soaking wet, coated with sand, shivering as much from pain as cold, but free. The Beach Patrol drove up in a military-looking

ATV with a small pickup bed in back. They were well prepared. After a cursory exam, they secured a splint to my right leg and strapped me into a litter that they loaded onto the back of the vehicle.

We drove along the coast to 59th Street, where an ambulance was waiting for me. You know the rest.

So that's what happened. And I've told you far more than you'll ever write about in your feature story or blog or wherever you want to print this.

It's funny, isn't it? How crazy life is! The guilt, the regrets. Fear that creeps up your neck. Relief that makes you feel like you're floating in the air. And when the sun breaks through the clouds and rises above the shore, it's all so beautiful.

I need to rest now. Everyone has been so supportive. All my friends, my dear, dear friends. What would I ever do without them?

Chapter Fifty
Back Home

The journalist who'd interviewed me was kind enough to email a transcript. I needed that text to continue my investigation. Yes, I knew that Kenneth C. Loughman was my Poe Puzzler, and he'd certainly told me why he did what he did. What I didn't know, and had a powerful need to find out, was how. I needed to fill in the blanks and write a sort of epilogue for my files.

So, this is it.

After three days in the hospital, it was good to be back home. I spent a lot of time on the green chair, in a fog of painkillers, with Lenore on my lap. She was a comfort, as glad to be with me as I was with her. Of course, Berni was a constant visitor. She started me on my initial at-home exercises before I had the strength to go to physical therapy.

Mrs. Murphy and Mrs. G fussed over me and plied me with food. One positive thing that came out of my encounter with Kenny was getting them back together as friends. I owed them more than I could ever repay. The food, as always, was delicious. And I could never look at casserole dishes in the same way again.

I returned the Hungarian talisman to Mrs. G, letting her know in as nice a way as possible that it had done little good. She disagreed, saying, "That why you only break a leg." Now, that's looking at the bright side of life!

Detective Rietti interviewed me while I was in the hospital and again back home. When I showed him the photo I'd taken of the Jeep's license plate number, he shook his head. You wouldn't think it possible to take an out-of-focus image with a smartphone, but somehow I'd managed. He gave me a "and you call yourself a private investigator" look. I couldn't blame him.

I didn't exactly tell him the whole truth about my encounter on the beach. I refused to blame Kenny for my broken leg. "I fell into the hole he'd dug," I told the detective. He didn't believe me, and I didn't care. Kenny had been through so much in the years since high school; I couldn't bring myself to add to his pain. His anger, his hatred of me, was misguided, I believe, but there's no doubt he thought I was the catalyst for his ongoing misfortunes.

According to the Ocean City police, Kenny Loughman was still "at large." He was probably back in Virginia with his aunt. Whether they'll pursue an interstate warrant remains to be seen. I hoped not.

But back to my continuing investigations.

Recuperating at home, with my leg in a cast and one of those four-footed canes to assist me, severely restricted my mobility. I still had plenty of resources to help answer my unanswered questions, chief among them, how did Kenny do all this to me? I don't mean my physical injuries, which, as I told the police, are partly my fault. Kenny didn't make me fall on top of my two-foot water pipe.

He had the chance to enact a fatal revenge when I fell into the hole … the grave. He could have finished the job and truly buried me alive. He could have bashed my head in with the shovel. He didn't. He walked away. Maybe his better angels got through to him. I'd like to think so. Or maybe he was just tired of fighting against his fate.

My innate curiosity, a blessing and a burden, continued to gnaw at me. What puzzled me most was how he'd placed all those notes and taunts, and what started him on his delayed desire for revenge?

Start at the beginning, I told myself, with the first notes.

If you want to hide, do it in plain sight. That was the key to Poe's "The Purloined Letter." While I don't have absolute confirmation, I'm quite certain Kenny was one of the hoodie-wearing youths in the offshore windmill protests that had paraded up and down my street. Maybe it's my age, but young men in gray hoodies all look alike.

I really needed to go back earlier than that, however, to discover his motivation. Kenny had left New Jersey and lived with his aunt in Virginia for several years. He'd returned, according to what his sister, Kathy, told Berni, due to the death of his mother. So what triggered his need for revenge against me?

My answer to that puzzle came while I was hobbling around the house with my cane, pacing back and forth in my small living room. I kept glancing out the window at my neighbor's place across the street. A white commercial pickup was parked in front, with workers going back and forth to get lumber and tools.

Like many Ocean City houses, it has a sign on the porch with a real estate agency's name and number—an advertisement for potential summer tenants.

Had Kenny been working right across from me, and I'd never even noticed? I called the real estate agent, and after quite a bit of cajoling and a reference to Detective Rietti, I found out that Kenny had been hired as a part-time caretaker. He was tasked with looking in on the house every day and doing some minor clean-up and repair.

All I can assume is that seeing me again after so many years set him off … set him on his plans to harass me. He was probably in plain sight any number of times, and I just didn't see him. I think there's a Sherlock Holmes story along the same lines, where everyday people around you—vendors, taxi drivers, garbage collection and sanitation workers—blend into the scenery.

And that thought led me to another. I got Patrolman Bob to look into the records of temporary helpers the city had hired. Sure enough, Kenny Loughman had gotten day jobs at the public works department. He could have easily disguised himself as a Bin Buster, too. Or maybe Jacob Weiszman, Mrs. Murphy's neighbor, really was senile! Any one of those explanations could explain the trash can mystery.

With a few logical deductions, the rest of the puzzle pieces fell into place. His eventual discovery of my phone number was happenstance. He must have picked up my call to Berni when her phone was sitting on a table or kitchen counter at Kathy's house.

Berni and Kathy. I'm sorry to say the case of the Poe Puzzler put an end to their budding relationship. Berni gave the police her somewhat fuzzy photos of Kenny at the Life Saving Station. Kathy was questioned by the police. It's easy to imagine how the wayward brother and Berni's loyalty to me were at the center of their disaffection. I hope she can find love again.

There is a coda to the Poe Puzzler story. A final communication.

About a week after I was home from the hospital, I received a note in the mail. There was no return address, the postmark was smudged, and the note was not signed. It was pretty obvious who the sender was, however. It read: "In my mind, you grew to be a monster. But you're no monster. You're just a pathetic old man with your books and your limp and your dead wife. I didn't want to kill you. Not really. But I wanted you to think I would. I'm done with you now."

He was no monster, either. He was just a young man who'd gotten off to a bad start in life—always the victim, always with someone else to blame. I hope he can turn himself around. But for me, well, I'm done with him, too.

I'd closed the file on Kenneth C. Loughman, and was relaxing in the green chair with Lenore on my lap when my cell phone rang.

"Nathan Poe? It's Detective Rietti."

More questions? I wanted to be done with the police as well. I tried to put a smile in my voice. "How can I help you, detective?"

"Well, I have a strange situation here. It's not something the Ocean City police would normally get involved with."

He paused. He'd certainly piqued my curiosity. Before I could ask for more details, he said, "I was wondering if you'd like to take it on … you know, as one of your little investigations?"

I no longer had to fake a smile. "Yes, I would. In fact, I'd be delighted."

Thank you for reading!

If you've enjoyed *The Poe Puzzler*, please write a brief review on Amazon or Goodreads. Your comments are very important—they help establish a book's worth to other readers. Please make my next book possible by leaving a review today!

Acknowledgements

It takes a receptive group of friends to create a novel like The Poe Puzzler. For biweekly reviews of each chapter, the **Schooley's Mountain Writers' Group** was invaluable. Reyna Favis, Mark Christmas, Lauri Berg, Emily Thompson, and David Chubb each provided a unique perspective. Especially appreciated was Reyna's help with the intricacies of independent publishing. The **Middle Valley Wordsmiths**—Renny Hodgskin, Mark Kitchin, Charles Levin, D.J. Murphy, Starr Diethorn, and Dave Watts—also helped shape the narrative. I'm in debt to Charlie Levin for his marketing tips and ongoing encouragement. When doubts or everyday roadblocks stymied my progress, both groups of indie authors inspired me to continue working. **My beta readers**, Mandy Szigethy, Eric and Kathleen Berg, Mark Christmas, and Marcy Wieseman, helped me avoid last-minute pitfalls. When all is said and done, however, any remaining errors are mine alone. Special thanks to the **Ocean City Police** for showing me the Triage Room and explaining how it's used. The volunteers at the **Ocean City Historical Museum** were also helpful, especially regarding the wreck of the S.S. Sindia. Finally and most sincerely, I thank **my wife, Martha**, for being a willing listener and my Number One supporter.

My Ocean City

I came into this world across the bay from Ocean City, in Shore Memorial Hospital, Somers Point, NJ. According to my mom, I was almost born on the car ride to the hospital. That may explain my love of automobiles! Growing up, "going to the shore" meant Ocean City. Once I had my driver's license, I spent many summer days with friends there.

After moving away, getting married, and living in Pennsylvania, Indiana, California, and then back in New Jersey, however, Ocean City was mostly a fond memory. I owe an enormous debt of gratitude to our friend, Marcy Wieseman, who reintroduced the town to my wife and me. Some caveats are in order, however—my Ocean City, the Ocean City in this novel, does not necessarily reflect the actual town.

For instance, Ward's Pastry still exists in Nathan Poe's storyline (my tastebuds still remember biting into a chopped suey); Gillian's Fun Pier does as well. Most of the other establishments mentioned in the book, from Positively 4th Street to Yianni's, are doing a fine business, and I highly recommend them. (And I still say "Mack & Manco" instead of "Manco & Manco"—old habits die hard.)

Over the two-plus years that I took to write this novel, my wife and I visited Ocean City many times in all four seasons. That helped me visualize locales for Nathan Poe's adventures. Yes, I've tweaked a few things for the story. I hope my readers will forgive these variations.

E.A. Poe & Me

From my early teens to well into college, I was an avid reader of all things Poe—poems, short stories, and his letters. I even convinced my family to visit The Poe Museum in Richmond, Virginia, and more recently, my wife and I spent time at the Edgar Allan Poe National Historic Site in Philadelphia. Boston, Baltimore, and New York City also claim Poe as one of their own. For those who want to find out more about this troubled genius, I recommend a visit to these museums and Poe-related locales. You may also enjoy Peter Ackroyd's Poe: A Life Cut Short, which helps dispel so many of the myths about his life and death.

Teachers & Students

Of all the teachers I've had, Bob Wigglesworth in 7th and 8th grade had the most positive influence on me. He made learning fun, and he set the stage for much of my career. I graduated from college with a New Jersey Teaching Certificate, and taught for two years in the most disparate schools imaginable—a 2,500-student regional high school, and a rural middle school in my hometown. While I enjoyed the kids, seeing the lights in their eyes when they "got it," frustration with school administration and with a one-size-fits-all approach to curriculum led me to enroll in graduate school and leave teaching behind.

After a long and winding career path, however, I can look back on those two years of teaching with some fondness. I encountered students who were amazingly eager to learn, as well as those who were aggressively averse to it. At the time, I was not mature enough to realize the impact I would have on their lives ... and appreciate how difficult it is for teachers to treat all of them equally.

I can only hope that I left more of my students feeling like Sarita, who gave Nathan Poe the "World's Best Teacher" award, rather than like Kenny Loughman!

AP vs. CMS

Mild-mannered writers can come to blows over this topic! After journalism grad school, I was a strict adherent to Associated Press style, even for magazine articles. It made sense to me. But the Chicago Manual of Style has become the standard for books. So, here we are. I refuse, however, to spell out numbered streets (such as 4th Street or 59th Street). And there's no way I'll put an extra period on an ellipsis at the end of a sentence. It's not just that old habits die hard (even though they do). Some things just make more sense in AP style.

Automotive Realism

Besides being an avid reader, I'm also an automotive enthusiast. As a result, when I come across an obvious car-related error in a novel, it rankles. One well-crafted novel I read had the main character driving a Ford Mustang in 1962 ... two years before it was introduced. Another best-selling author featured a four-door Mercedes-Benz SL in his novel, a vehicle configuration that does not exist. To avoid these errors in The Poe Puzzler, I researched many picayune details about Nathan Poe's Saab convertible, from the location of the spare tire and jack to how to change the car's battery. I hope I have avoided any automotive faux pas.

Questions for Book Club Readers

The Poe Puzzler is a cozy mystery—no gore, no swear words, and a generally happy ending. However, the novel does deal with some ethical and moral issues. Here are some questions for book-club readers to discuss.

1. Before reading this novel, how familiar were you with the works of Edgar Allan Poe? How did that affect your enjoyment of the story?

2. Nathan and Berni are close friends who support each other in times of need. While Nathan is attracted to Berni, he knows they will never become lovers. Do you think their friendship will develop into something more? Why or why not?

3. Both Nathan and Berni are dealing with grief over the loss of a loved one, but they do so in very different ways. Nathan's memories of his wife's death are vivid, almost visceral. Berni handles her demons in more subtle and pragmatic ways. How does this difference affect their interactions and their relationship?

4. Nicole, the assistant librarian, bent the rules to help Nathan find out if the Poe Puzzler had used the library for his research. While she was a former student of Nathan's, Nickie is now in her thirties and has a casual friendship with Nathan. Do you think Nathan took advantage of that friendship? If you were in Nickie's place, what would you have done?

5. Nathan comes to realize that his last semester of teaching had a negative impact on at least one student, if not more. Have any of your teachers had a particularly positive or negative impact on you? Please elaborate.

6. At the end of the novel, Nathan decides to forgive Kenny, even though Kenny had caused him harm, both physical and emotional. Why do you think Nathan made that decision? What would you have done in Nathan's place?

About the Author

Neil MacNeill is the pen name of Neil M. Szigethy, an award-winning copywriter of advertising, marketing, and sales training content. Neil grew up in a small town close to the Jersey Shore. The 59th Street beach in Ocean City was his favorite destination. He currently lives in New Jersey with his wife, Martha. *The Poe Puzzler* is his third novel.

You can reach the author at:
NeilMacNeill.books@gmail.com.